Be My Friend

MERLE NYGATE

For Tika Cope

prologue

'Pull over! You're not fit to bloody drive,' Tony says.

But the VW Golf picks up speed.

'Are you deaf or just stupid? What do you think you're playing at?'

The Golf swerves as a Mini slices across its path. In the passenger seat, Tony wriggles and his breath rasps.

'Pull over, you crazy bitch!'

The stench of sweat rises off the middle-aged man and his panting makes him sound like a distressed dog. The Golf picks up speed and shimmies off the roundabout. Ahead, two cars screech to a halt to let the Golf pass and it bounces up the small hill into the narrow tree-lined streets of Hinchley Wood.

Tony grips the overhead grab handle as the car swerves in and out of the parked cars.

'I said, stop the fucking car!' He's yelling now; spittle sprays the air.

Just then the car whacks a speed bump and two tons of metal crunch down and swerve into a skid.

Time seems to stammer as the red brick wall of the corner house fills the windscreen followed by the thud and crash of metal on brick, then a boom and a cloud of white dust from the airbag.

But Tony's airbag doesn't engage. Neither does his seatbelt. Like a dummy in a car safety demonstration film, he swings up and smashes through the windscreen.

one

The message on my voicemail was garbled. I'd played it three times and all I'd managed to grab from Greg's hoarse voice was 'crash', 'hospital' and 'dying'. I froze and when I did move, a wave of stress-dizziness made me sway.

Emms was dying.

On automatic I stood up and allowed the towel to drop so I could drag yesterday's clothes onto my shower-damp body. I struggled to dress, my hands trembling as I hauled a tee shirt over my head. It seemed as if there was a weight in my guts, a dead load pressing, pushing, trying to stop me breathing.

'Get a grip,' I said aloud.

Somehow I got to my car and after twenty minutes of dangerous driving through the early morning traffic, I parked on the kerb in the overcrowded hospital car park. I didn't bother with a pay and display ticket. I also ignored the couple that were easing their shiny new convertible in and out of the single available spot as if it mattered. As if anything mattered when my best friend was dying.

What about the twins? I was supposed to be their godmother. Robbie and Tessa were what? Four this year. If Greg fell apart - as no doubt he would – how would I cope?

As I sprinted towards the main hospital entrance, I slammed down the shutter on that particular thought. This was definitely not the time to think ahead. For now it was far more important to concentrate on the immediate problems, like finding the ward for starters.

My leather jacket was too hot for running and my shoulder bag thwacked the side of my thigh with each pace. But I needed to keep going, hope that I wouldn't trip myself up and that I'd get there in time. The other nagging, nudging, pinching thought, was whether I'd be capable of doing what had to be done: see Emms die.

I like to think that these days I have a little more control over my emotions, and I'm not bouncing around like a rubber ball. But it's one thing saying that over a glass of chilled white whilst mouthing off something the Dalai Lama might say; it's quite another when you're gearing up to watch your best friend sign off. Who was I kidding, who was I ever kidding? Never mind Greg falling apart, it's me, because, I don't know what I'd do without Emms in my life.

I burst through the main reception and then stood there, panting, looking around like a lost child, trying to work out which way to go. Needless to say, there was a snake-like queue of stressed-out people trying to get attention from the overworked staff at the reception desk. Since I might already be too late, there was no way that I was going to stand in line and lose another ten minutes. I saw a sign for A&E wards and took off, down a corridor, past another sign that said Hospital Crèche.

As I ran, I glanced down a side corridor and scoped a woman holding the hands of two small children. One was flame-haired, like Tessa, the other mouse blond, like Robbie. Surely not? That couldn't possibly be Emms with the twins. I lurched to a halt.

'Emms?' I called out.

Nothing.

The woman knelt down to listen to something the red-haired kid was saying and once again, I felt dizzy. Of course, it wasn't Emms; it wasn't anything remotely like her. This woman was small and blonde, not tall and dark. It was a complete stranger.

'Get a grip,' I heard myself say as I pounded off down the corridor, dodging oncoming people, past the patient wheeling a drip, between the criss-crossing wheelchairs and self-important white coats. Somehow I had to ready myself to stand by Emms' side and hold her hand, as I said I would. As I said I would when we talked about dying.

At last I'd reached the nurses' station in the A&E Ward.

'Emma Harens,' I said.

'Family?' the nurse said looking up from her computer. I nodded the lie.

'Room two, please don't stay long.'

I crossed the floor to Room Two and nudged it open. Greg was shielding Emms and he seemed to be rearranging her pillows. At the sound of my sneakers squeaking on the polished floor he turned round and smiled. Smiled? When he stood back, I saw Emms, arm in a sling, head bandaged, hair sticking out in mad clumps, her other arm wired up to a monitor.

'I'm okay,' she croaked. She waved the wired-up arm around. 'This is all just in case. Concussion and all that. My arm's broken in two places, but it's the left one, so nothing to worry about. Could have been an awful lot worse.'

'But Greg, he phoned... I thought...' I trailed off. 'Jesus Christ, Emms, I thought you were dead. Or, at the very least, dying. I've been shitting myself all the way between home and here.' I pretended to laugh, but I was angry with her for frightening me. 'I ought to kill you for scaring me like this.'

'It's Tony,' Greg said. 'Tony's dead.'

two

For the second time in an hour my safe little world tilted off its axis and I felt unbalanced. Emms was alive, Tony was dead and it wasn't even eight-thirty in the morning. No wonder I felt giddy. What's more, besides the shock that Tony was dead, I felt not one iota of sorrow, regret or remorse that he'd shifted off the planet. Not one.

You see Tony was an arse. Truly. I'm not exaggerating. He was worse than an arse, he was a total shit, and of all the employers, trainers, teachers and people in authority I've come across during my entire thirty-eight years, Tony was the biggest bullying bastard I'd ever met.

Does that sound harsh? I promise you it isn't, and if you had any idea of the number of times Emms and I had to talk Sue, our office receptionist, out of her tears, her self-doubt, not to mention the toilet cubicle in which she'd locked herself, you'd feel the same way.

'He didn't mean it,' Emms would say.

'He thinks he's being funny,' I would add.

And we'd insist that when Tony said Sue was a half-wit, the statement was not only rude but it was also untrue.

Besides "half-wit", "stupid little girl" was another of Tony's favourite expressions. And he'd go on and on and on, like a dog worrying at a bone, nibbling, tugging and gnawing, until he hit the sweet marrow of her self-esteem. And the best bit was that it was all supposed to be humorous and he was being witty when he spotted a spelling mistake and bellowed the correction, letter by letter, across the open-plan office.

That was all over with now, thanks to Emms' accident. What's more, there was no way that I was going to pretend there was a gaping hole in my life.

'You're sure you're okay?' I approached the bed and took Emms' hand. It was dry and hot. There were scratch marks all along her forearm and, near her eyebrow, spidery black stitches. Her skin, usually clear and creamy, was blotchy, and there was dried blood under her ear lobe.

'I'm fine, how bad do I look?' Emms said.

I glanced at Greg.

'You look beautiful,' he said, and he meant it.

'Sure, I bet I look like a regular movie star,' Emms said. 'Liz? Is it bad? Tell me the truth.'

I didn't turn round, 'Greg's right. You look fine. A couple of weeks and you'll be back to normal – whatever that is. Thank God for seatbelts.'

'In that case, Greg would you please go and find out when they're going to take this catheter out so I can go home. It's really uncomfortable.'

Greg disappeared and I went back to the bedside. Whatever Greg had said, she looked like shit and the only recognisable part of her swollen, bruised face were her eyes. Her dark, almost, but not quite, black eyes. Gypsy eyes, Emms likes to say, inherited from some exotic relative.

'Sorry I scared you, Liz.'

'I forgive you. It's hardly your fault, is it?'

'It is my fault,' Emms said.

'Don't be daft, it was an accident, these things happen, and it could have happened to anyone. I promise you, it's not your fault.'

'No, you don't understand. I was driving - it's my fault.' And now her eyes became shiny, filling up with tears.

'For goodness' sake, don't waste your time wondering if only you'd done this or that Tony might still be alive. It won't help anyone, and it certainly won't help Tony. Don't do the guilts, Emms. Trust me, it's a one-way ticket to post-traumatic stress disorder.'

Before Emms had the chance to respond, the door opened and a hollow-eyed doctor, plus two nurses, crowded into the room with Greg bringing up the rear. The white coat muttered something incomprehensible and left it to one of the nurses to say, 'Would you mind waiting outside?'

Half an hour later, we were back in Emms' hospital room, Greg, once again, fuss fuss fussing around her pillows and whispering words of love while I hovered by the door. Just as I was wondering if I should leave them to it and disappear off home, I became aware of movement and sensed a shadow in the doorframe. There was a small blonde woman clutching the hands of Tessa and Robbie.

It was them, I thought. It was the twins I'd seen by the crèche when I was rushing to be by Emms' imaginary deathbed.

'We desperately wanted to see how Mummy is getting on, didn't we?' the woman said. 'And how could I resist these two angels?'

Now my godchildren are a lot of things but "angels"? No. That's way too much of a stretch. I looked at Emms, Emms looked at me. It seemed that we shared the same thought: 'Who the hell is this woman and what's she going on about?'

At that, the woman tiptoed further into the room. Yes, tiptoed. I looked down and she was wearing those elasticised pumps. Tight jeans clasped pert buttocks and a peasant blouse slipped off one shoulder, showing a rose pink bra strap. She tiptoed past me, leaving an overpowering contrail of patchouli. 'I'm Mairi Sondergaard,' she said. 'From the crèche.'

Her voice had a singsong quality that was also authoritative, no doubt used with great effect to say: 'Put the toy back in the box and sit down'. In conversations with adults, it sounded fake.

She led the children into the middle of the room. Tessa tripped towards Emms' side but Mairi Sondergaard held on to Robbie, who gazed up at her with an expression of slavish love.

Then, with a ceremonial gesture, Mairi gave Robbie's hand to Greg, as if it was a sacred gift, as if she was a priestess. When she passed the son's hand to his father, she clasped their hands together between her own. Afterwards, she turned and still tiptoeing, fairy-stepped towards me, stood too close and made locking eye contact.

'You must be Mummy's best friend,' she said. She can't have been more than five feet tall and she was standing too close to me. I tried to take a step back and felt the wall hard against my shoulders.

'Yes. I'm Emms' best friend And I'm also Tessa and Robbie's godmother.'

'Like a fairy godmother, I'm sure. How lucky you are, to be the godmother of two such wonderful children.'

'Exactly how I'd describe them,' I said.

The woman could only have been thirty but her speech patterns made her sound like she was auditioning for a 1950s TV show. Her voice rose at the end of every sentence. It was as if she'd rehearsed and knew exactly what was going to happen next.

three

Later that night I was back home, standing on my balcony, looking over the road to the river beyond, trying to process the events of the day. In other words, trying to dilute the drama. The shock of losing Emms, then finding her alive, the news about Tony, and to top it all, that somewhat bizarre nursery nurse who had seasoned the day with an almost surreal quality. Each of the elements circled my head like flies around a light. Shivering from the damp night air, I stepped back inside the flat and shut the doors, locking out the dark, troubling thoughts, securing my safe place, my home, from fear. Believe me, I know better than anyone the danger of uncontrolled emotion. It needs to be contained.

I tugged at the full-length curtains, and heard the rattle on the metal pole. I switched on sidelights and illuminated the corners of the sitting room and finally, I pressed the remote and music flooded out of the speakers. As the music filled the room, the night, the river and the balcony were safely shrouded, out of sight, out of mind. At last I was able to take a deep, if slightly ragged, breath.

Above my head I heard faint footsteps on a wooden floor and the low hum of a TV stopped. There are forty flats in the block and I had no idea who this particular neighbour was, because I try not to get involved with any of them.

Without turning on the light, I padded across the wooden floor towards the open-plan kitchen and switched on the kettle. I knew what was bothering me: it was the drama of the day.

Tony's business - Francis, Day and Hunter - ran role-playing programmes to develop leadership, sales and negotiating skills. My job was to give the events a quasi-psychological spin; Emms did the numbers and Tony performed, delivering the training programmes I wrote with all of the passion you'd expect from a former actor.

Aside from Tony's lousy man-management skills, the outfit worked well, so it's not hard to understand why he was cashing in his chips. But it was the way he did it that was so crap. In one of the best examples of an actor who needed his lines written for him in order to say anything remotely memorable, Tony actually said, 'They gave me an offer I couldn't refuse'.

He'd told us at the last staff meeting, only two weeks ago. When I caught Emms' expression I almost dropped my coffee into my lap. It was such a pathetic line; it was funny. Of course, Sue didn't understand but everybody else knew what was coming next.

'There will be a period of transition,' Tony paced the room in his thespian way. 'It can't be avoided. And if during the period of transition any of you don't want to move to Brooklands, that's understood.'

Even Sue knew what 'period of transition' meant in corporate-speak: voluntary redundancy and no pay-off; or at best one week's pay and a cardboard box of stationery. But now that Tony was dead, maybe we'd all be out of a job giving Emms yet another reason to say it was her fault.

The next day, I went back to the hospital at teatime to cover for Greg, who was looking after the kids. While Emms dozed in bed, I skimmed through the paper. By five o'clock, assured that Emms was definitely on the mend, I had more than half a mind to slope off home. I was just wondering whether I should wake up Emms to tell her I was going, when two uniformed policemen appeared in the private room.

'I'm P.C. Cole and this is P.C. Patel. We're accident officers from Surrey Police,' the older one said. He was grey haired and had a soft Scots accent. His colleague was younger, Asian and at least six foot four. No wonder the room felt small. Emms stirred in bed and opened one swollen red eye. Her bruises were starting to come out so she looked, if anything, even worse than she had the day before.

'Can't this possibly wait?' I nodded in Emms' direction. 'My friend's not going anywhere and she can barely speak.'

'Initial response interviews need to be carried out with witnesses within twenty-four hours of an incident. We've spoken to the medical staff and they agree that Mrs Harens is well enough to be interviewed.'

'Be reasonable,' I said. 'She's got an armful of painkillers and if you start giving her a hard time, the chances are you'll make her even worse than she already is. Do you really want to do that? She has been in a fatal car crash, you know.'

'It's procedure.' P.C. Cole's expression said that they were not budging. Slowly, I stood up and reached for my jacket and bag. From the bed, Emms croaked, 'Can my friend stay, please?'

'Yes she can. But I need to caution you. There has been a fatality, which is why we're here. The statement you make may be used in evidence against you.'

'In that case, wouldn't it be better to wait till Mrs Harens is out of hospital and she can come and see you with a solicitor?' I said.

'Get it over and done with,' Emms said. 'Ask away, but first, if Liz could please pour me some water?'

I got the water and Emms took a few sips. I could see that it hurt her to swallow. Meanwhile, the police beetled around the room, setting up and testing their recording equipment.

Once the tape machine was set up, time and date were recorded. Emms' identity was established, it was noted who else was present and the time and location of the accident were detailed. In a few questions, Cole and Patel learnt that Emms was driving Tony because his car was being serviced and they were on their way to the new offices to see what needed to be done before the move.

'We examined the vehicle and it's been noted that the airbag was disabled,' Cole said. 'Why was that?'

'The airbag has always been disabled,' Emms said. 'I've got two very young children. When they were babies, they were on the front seat. Tessa, that's my daughter, well I've only just managed to move her to the back seat – with a lot of complaints, I might add.'

Emms pressed her lips together. 'The airbag would have saved his life, wouldn't it? It never occurred to me. You see Tony usually drove. And if I'm with my husband, we always use his car. Does it mean it's my fault?'

Neither policeman commented. I watched the cops, willing them to say something comforting, to say it was an accident. They were silent. Maybe P.C. Patel was being trained up by Cole which might explain their visible lack of sympathy but after all, Emms was the one wired up in the hospital bed with a bandage round her head looking like Frankenstein's sister. It was patently obvious that she'd very nearly copped it herself.

Airbag discussion over, they moved on to the seatbelts.

'Were you aware that Mr Day was not wearing a seatbelt at the time of impact?' asked Cole.

Emms didn't answer. She was probably still thinking about the airbag. Outside the room, I heard a trolley and the rattle of cups as it trundled past. Eventually, Emms spoke slowly. She sounded resigned. 'Tony was not wearing a seatbelt. At least, he was when we set off, but then he undid it. He was complaining about the car, nothing was right that morning. He said it was too hot, then he said the seatbelt was uncomfortable. Finally, he undid the seatbelt because he was trying to take his coat off.'

'Did you tell him to do it up, or that it was illegal not to wear a seatbelt?'

'He was always unclipping his belt, if he wanted to make a phone call and couldn't reach his phone. Even when he was driving his own car. But you didn't tell Tony anything, because Tony knew everything and he didn't take to being told. Isn't that right, Liz?'

I nodded in agreement. 'That does rather sum him up.'

P.C. Cole asked me, 'Are you saying Mr Day was likely to refuse to wear a seatbelt, even when cautioned?'

'Yes,' I said.

Whether or not Tony had unclipped his seatbelt didn't seem important. Neither did it seem important that I'd confirmed Emms' account of the events to the police.

Emms and I met two days later at Five on the Bridge, a café near Hampton Court. She was back home and making a fast recovery, no doubt aided by Greg's cooking and caring. Even if she was one-handed, she was certainly well enough to use laptop and phone, judging by the bundle of emails she was copying me on.

Besides being one of my favourite places, Hampton Court is equidistant between Emms and Greg's cottage and my flat, so we often meet there. If you sit outside at the metal tables you can just about see the Palace across the river.

Late September, and it was still warm enough to sit outside if you were wearing a jacket. Emms had bagged an outside table, her head was down and even though her arm was still in a sling, she was tapping resolutely at her mobile phone.

'What's up?' I said, when I reached her. I was standing over her. Her bruises had changed colour, yellowing and she looked much less the victim of a murderous attack as she nodded to a chair and smiled.

'All good,' she said. 'If we can work it, all bloody brilliant.'

Emms doesn't really swear, or hasn't since the twins were born, so her 'bloody' was significant. A waitress approached and we smiled and ordered. Emms did her soup thing – she only eats soup during the day, she's only ever eaten soup during the day apart from at weekends because she is rigorous about calorie control. I ordered my usual bacon baguette. As soon as the waitress had gone, I settled myself down in the metal seat.

'So the Canadians aren't going to close us down?' I said. Emms shook her head, 'Nope, and get this. They want you and me to be joint managing directors for a care-taking period of a year with – wait for it – a fifteen per cent raise.'

Emms leaned back in her chair, and brushed her hair off her forehead. Just then my baguette arrived with her soup and for once, I ignored it.

'Look, fifteen per cent is a really nice whack, but – Emms, can we actually do this?' I really meant, do we want to do this? Or to be precise, 'whatever made you think in a million fucking years that I would want to do this?'

'No idea,' she said. 'But if you don't try ... There's another carrot and stick we have to consider. If we don't keep the company going, Tony's widow won't get paid off. So if Sheila's going to have the slightest chance of getting her well-deserved whack, we have to step up and deliver.'

I could feel the weight on my shoulders, like wet sandbags. This level of business responsibility was far more than I wanted, but I didn't say anything, perhaps because Emms had nearly died only days ago. Perhaps because she looked so happy. I don't know. So I just sat there and watched Emms' careful manoeuvre as she spooned in a mouthful of soup, making sure she didn't drop any down her perfectly white, perfectly ironed shirt.

Soup safely swallowed, Emms said, 'There's something else I need your help with. I've got to go back and review my police statement this afternoon.'

'I thought they'd got everything they needed and we'd established that the airbags and seatbelts were simply bad luck,' I said.

'I want to try to anticipate what they're going to ask. You can give me some of your psycho-smarts about body language. You know the sort of thing. It's so easy to give the wrong impression.'

four

During the next week, the phrase 'wrong impression' kept popping up like molehills on a pristine lawn. I heard it on the radio, read it in the paper, it even cropped up in a training programme. 'Wrong impression.' Each time, I twitched like a cartoon rabbit caught in headlights, but it was nothing more than stress causing a little neural pattern-seeking: in other words, an irritating but insignificant nuisance. And I was stressed. The amount of work had ratcheted up and I was spinning in a whirlwind of meetings, targets and lists, close to being overwhelmed. By contrast, Emms was on a roll and you really have to see Emms on a roll to appreciate the passion she has for a balanced spreadsheet. Across the desk, I'd see her sit for hours, hunched over the screen, clicking, dragging and smiling.

I managed to hold my own by dealing with the clients, reassuring them that all contracts would be fulfilled and, even though Tony wasn't around, it was business as usual. I also had to reassure the staff that in spite of Tony's death, everyone would still get paid. What's more, I had to reassure Tony's widow, Sheila, that ... well, here I struggled. How could I possibly reassure her that everything was going to be tickety-bloody-boo when she was grappling with the reality of early widowhood? For heaven's sake, the woman was only fifty-five.

And whatever her relationship had been with Tony, however unpleasant living with him must have been, this particular life change hadn't been her choice. The best I could do was to try to reassure her that she would be financially secure. And since Sheila's economic future depended on Emms and me making a success of the business, this particular reassurance wasn't grounded in certainty.

So, there was a whole lot of reassuring going on and, at times - usually about 2.30 in the morning - I wondered who was reassuring me. It wasn't that I was anxious; I know anxiety and I can almost recognise the sensation of cortisol being released into my central nervous system. And I certainly know how long it takes to process through my metabolism. I just felt uneasy.

Even though I had consciously decided not to analyse Emms' elaborate preparations to review her police statement, even though I had dismissed each and every 'wrong impression' echo as simple psychoneurosis, I was still bothered. I suppose I should have phoned Emms and simply asked but I stopped myself because, like most neuroses, there wasn't an ounce of logic in my thought process. I finally concluded that Emms felt the need to be prepped because of her background.

Emms' father was some sort of builder who'd pissed off to France with a friend of the family and, for all I know, is still there getting drunk on cheap red wine, and boring to death any British tourists he can latch on to. I met him for the first time at Emms' mother's funeral and if ever there was a real life Jack the Lad, it was Emms' father. He probably had a wardrobe of kipper ties and sideburns when he met her mother. 'Just call me Kenny,' was about as far as could be from Greg and his chummy, school-fee-paying, Sunday-lunch-eating family. Maybe, that's what this was about - a residual cultural distrust of authority as a result of having a father who was perhaps no stranger to crime. But I still felt uneasy. Was Emms' police paranoia solely because of her shifty father?

'I told you,' she said. 'I don't want to get bogged down in any more interviews. That's all there is to it.'

We were in the office; boxes were stacked up around us like a mini fort. They were arranged according to their coloured labels and we were sitting on the floor among the fluorescent pink stickers that read "Stationery Current".

It was Thursday night and the following day we were moving to the new Brooklands offices. Everybody else had gone home, as exhausted as we were. But it was done and we were ready for the movers. Emms' bottle of Baileys was the only thing that wasn't packed. Back in the day, Emms and I used to consider Bailey's on ice the height of sophistication and decadence. It was like an alcoholic chocolate milk shake. I didn't realise that she still had the taste for it.

'We've got a chance here,' she held out her plastic cup for a refill. 'We've got a chance to set ourselves up for the future. And it wouldn't have happened if Tony hadn't died in the crash. Does that worry you? Dead men's shoes and all that?'

'Since you ask - no, it doesn't worry me. But I'll tell you what does - I don't understand why you had to get all prepped up to review your police statement. I don't understand why you said that they might get the wrong impression.'

Emms rolled her eyes and brushed her hair back with her good arm.

'Because, my dear friend, this particular part of Surrey has the lowest crime rate in the entire country. This means that if the cops don't find a reason to justify their hours, then their hours get cut. Simple. I do not want to be a reason for them to justify their continued employment when we're going to need every minute of every day to make this business fly.'

Emms rolled onto her knees and holding on to a desk stood up, still clutching the plastic cup. It was quite a feat with her left arm still in a sling.

'Liz, we've got to do this. We've got to make the business work. We'll kill ourselves if we don't and you know why? Shall I tell you why? Because we'll be like our mothers.'

I thought about what Emms said when I was driving home. To tell the truth, I wouldn't mind being like my mother who lives with my dad in a nice little house in Manley and seems to spend a vast amount of time either on holiday, or planning the next one, but I got what Emms was driving at. For her, the business was a shiny opportunity that we ought to grab with both hands. For me, it was a lot of hard work, extra responsibility and tons of stress. Unnecessary stress. What did I need it for?

A few days later, I pulled up outside Emms and Greg's Victorian cottage on Summerbrook Road. It's the kind of house I would have wanted to live in before I got married. It's quaint and romantic, a gingerbread house with draughty windows, a dark hall and a downstairs bathroom but, like I said, it's quaint. It's positively picturesque. Because it overlooks the Green, all year round, you see people coming down to take photographs of the pond, the swans, the ducks, the cricketers and all the other little houses.

It's beautiful, a clichéd English idyll, a scene that's so jigsaw-picture perfect that it's almost fake. The first time I saw the house and looked out of the bay window I told Emms that it's country without the smell of cow shit.

Before I accepted the invitation for a kitchen table supper on Saturday night, I made sure that it was only going to be the three of us. I had something to say and I didn't want chitchat, about schools, supermarkets and the conservation society, stopping me. It had been a busy week; apart from the business, Emms had successfully reviewed her police statement, no doubt giving the right impression, and the cops had signed it off. Next week we had Tony's funeral but, more importantly, the business contracts were to be signed. That night was my last chance to make a stand against being legally committed and I was going to snatch it. Emms may have verbally agreed to the pair of us taking over the care-taking period, but nothing was signed.

I had various arguments carefully prepared and as I hit the brass knocker on the blue front door, and saw the shadows bobbing towards me through the glass, I had one over-riding thought: get out of this deal.

If Emms really wanted to go down the path of corporate slavery, fine, that was her choice, but I was not going to be dragged along in the undertow.

With her good arm, Emms hauled the door open and hugged me. She smelt of warm home, soap and something sweet and smoky.

'Come in you,' she said, 'Ooooh, what's that?'

I offered her the wrapped up bottle of wine.

'Not Bailey's?' she said.

'As if I would,' I said. 'Unless it was a secret.'

She turned and I followed down the dark narrow passage to the kitchen at the back of the house.

'The problem is that Greg and I don't have secrets,' she said. 'Do we, Greg?' she yelled ahead. 'Isn't that the deal?'

Greg was hunched over the stainless steel hob, stirring a pot, tea towel tucked into jeans pocket. I could see his brow crinkled in concentration, he looked worried, but then he often does.

'What deal?'

'No secrets,' Emms said.

Greg frowned up at the big old clock that hung over the oak refectory table, 'Hi Liz, I hope the secret is that you've already eaten, because I think we've got a disaster here. I put in too much redcurrant jelly and now it's gone all runny.'

Emms slipped her arm around his waist for a second. 'I'm sure it'll be great.'

'You're a genius, Greg. You should have your own show.' I came over and pecked his hot cheek. 'And I'm starved.'

On the tiled floor, by the floor-to-ceiling windows, Robbie and Tessa sat pink-cheeked in pyjamas. They scrambled up as I came in and I got a hug from Tessa and a shy smile from Rob.

'OK you lot,' Emms said. 'I told you; you could wait up to see Liz. So now I want you to take a jolly good look. Don't miss a thing. Nice hair, smart specs, we like the blue shirt, don't we, kids? So now you've seen her. What happens next? You. Go. To. Bed.'

There are times when I've been at Emms' and feel as if I'm in the middle of an advertising agency dream. Little cottage on the village green, devoted husband at the hob, two adorable children. Redheaded, creamy-skinned Tessa with her sparkling eyes and Robbie, dreamy, sweeter, with only a stubborn little chin to hint at his less malleable side.

Fortunately, my sense of unreality never lasts more than ten minutes, mostly much less. Today, Tessa attempted to negotiate extra time downstairs by showing me Mou Mou, her doll, who wanted to ask me a question. After I had admired and communicated with the shapeless doll and Tessa had exhausted this particular attempt to delay bedtime, she asked for an oatcake. Emms agreed to the oatcake but then said, 'That was last orders. Bed now and story. Bed in ten minutes and no story.'

Tessa hesitated, weighed up the threat, visibly considered the likely outcome of the negotiation. And then she and Robbie trundled off with Emms for story time. Forty-five minutes later we were round the table. Greg was right. The meat was sweet and the sauce was runny but what do I know about venison? Isn't it supposed to be like that?

I cleared my plate, pushed it away and launched in with a lot less subtlety than Tessa: 'I'm worried about signing the agreement next week. What if I had to go see my folks in Australia for a few months? Dad's mid-seventies, he's had a stent and he's not getting any younger.'

'What are you talking about?' Emms said. 'If anything happened of course you'd be on the first flight to Oz. I'd drive you to the airport myself.' Her venison was piled on a corner of the plate. 'You mustn't even think that, of course family comes first, that's why we're doing this, Liz.'

'I just have this feeling that the business could take over our lives. My life, I suppose.' It sounded lame but I pushed on. 'I just think that I don't really want to be as committed as you and if it's a choice between share options and freedom...'

Greg leaned over and filled our glasses with red wine that glinted in the candlelight.

'Shall I leave you two and check the kids?' he said.

'No. You're part of all this,' Emms said. 'Liz, I know being a managing director isn't your life's ambition but it's been handed to us on a platter. Tony's not throwing his weight around and it would be... it would be wrong to let it slip away.'

Emms' face looked dreamy in the soft light, 'You know there's a house out on the Shere Road, near Newlands Corner,' she said. 'There's a long drive up from the road and a massive oak tree out the front. That tree has got to be three hundred years old. Greg and I have been driving past that house and that oak tree ever since we moved this way. We see it flowering, in leaf, in fruit before the acorns drop, we've even talked about being buried under the oak tree, haven't we Greg?' Greg nodded, I saw his Adam's apple bob.

The sentimental moment passed and Emms went on, 'Of course, I realise you don't need this, Liz, but besides our fantasies about being able to buy the dream house, Greg and I've got two kids to put through university, never mind the big fat wedding that I am certain Tessa will demand.'

'Then you do it, I'm fine with that, I'll be the working grunt, I'll even doff my cap if it makes you happy. I don't have to be the joint MD.'

'You do,' Emms replied. She picked up her plate from the table and carried it over the sink; I could only see her slim black back. 'I need you,' she said to the wall. 'Tell her Greg. It's not just about continuity, it's about -'

'What if you have to be at home with the kids? What about the holidays? If there's a board meeting with the parent company, you won't be able to dash back to pick up Tessa or Robbie. There'd be a lot less flexibility and a lot more travel away from home.'

This was my last resort. I know it was dirty bringing up the kids and childcare. I know full well that the cost of live-in help of any sort is staggering.

'Greg and I have talked about that.'

Greg put his glass down. 'I could quite happily and quite easily set up my business at home. It's not the first time Emms and I have talked about this; Rob hasn't settled into nursery particularly well and we hate dumping him at breakfast club at 7am. And there's another thing, I'd really love to have the chance to be a real part of the kids' early years.'

I had the unpleasant sense of being cornered. Greg went on: 'I'd easily be able to take some of my clients with me, and that would mean I could cover childcare, school run and after-school activities. And if I do have to go to town for a meeting or an audit we could bring in extra care. Remember that crèche nurse at the hospital?'

'The sugar plum fairy? What was her name?' I said.

'Mairi,' Emms said. 'Mairi with an 'I'. Mairi Sondergaard.'

'Anyway,' Greg said. 'She's local, West Molesey. She's mobile and she's up for it.'

'Up for what?' I hadn't forgotten how Mairi had clasped Greg's hand at the hospital.

'I bumped into her in Waitrose,' Greg said. 'She'd been to the town hall picking up info about setting up a nursery school business, so I think I may even have found another client.'

Emms had sat down and both their faces were looking at me expectantly. Greg with his full lips, fleshy nose and sticky up Tintin hair and Emms, sharp cut, dark eyes and black polo neck. I pushed my specs up on top of my head. Their faces became softer and gently blurred.

'OK,' I said. 'I'm in as joint MD but only for a year and I'm going away at Christmas.'

'Two years,' Emms said grimacing in a pleading way. 'A year will go so fast.'

'Two years? Oh come on, Emms - that's forever.'

'No it isn't. And how about if your Christmas holiday is part of your bonus?'

'I still don't want to do it, Emms. Listen, ever since I got out of my marriage I promised myself to keep it simple and not over-commit, and being MD -

joint or otherwise - is everything I don't want in one package. It will do my head in.'

Greg tried to refill my glass. I stopped him but I did take another sip. Greg filled up his own glass, 'As an admittedly interested outsider, the way I see it is that you two would really work well together. Liz, why don't you sign up for two years but after a year see how you feel. By then, if you want out, the new owners will have got to know Emms and won't care if she wants to go it alone. How about it?'

'Well -'

'And you still get the Christmas holiday bonus,' Emms said.

I looked from one to the other and back again. I'd been poleaxed.

'Oh, alright then.'

Greg raised his glass and took a large glug. 'To the business.'

On the way home, I threw the car around the corners. My BMW1-series skittered up the hill as I accelerated towards the High Street. I was deeply pissed off with myself because I'm an adult, I've got bankable, marketable skills and I'm supposed to have some control over my life, but evidently I don't. How had Emms and Greg persuaded me so easily?

By the time I'd pulled up in the car park outside the flat, I was calmer and managed an affable fifteen-second conversation with one of my neighbours about bin collections. The woman seemed to know me and was irate because, believe it or not, there are degenerate people who put rubbish in other people's bins if their own is full.

Once inside the flat, I closed the door and leaned my back against it. For a couple of sweet seconds, I stood in the quiet dark, pleased to leave the outside world beyond the door. I'd have a cup of tea, check my email and perhaps make some notes for the To Do list. It would be better doing it at 10pm than waking up at 2.30 in the morning fretting about not having already done it.

I sat at the dining room table that's never used for dining and booted up my laptop. Whilst I waited, I sipped my tea and looked at the darkness across the street and the river beyond. The tea was hot and it hit the back of my throat clearing the cloying sweetness of the meat I'd eaten. What made it so difficult for me to plan ahead and commit? Of course, I knew. And equally, I wasn't going to examine the shiny new skin over the old scar.

'Not tonight, Lizzy,' I said aloud.

There was an email from Emms:

Hey Liz

Couple of things. First and most importantly I feel bad for twisting your arm about the business. I appreciate you doing it. I'm not going to go on. You know what I mean and how I feel.

Meanwhile, yet ANOTHER favour. Is there the slightest chance that you can take me to the hospital on Monday? Greg can't take me because he's in town and Mairi will be picking up the twins from nursery and taking them home for tea. I want to leave them with Mairi for as short a time as possible.

Let me know.

xEmms

I typed back an answer:

Of course I'll take you.

xL

I remembered how Mairi had clasped Greg's hand in the hospital and those oh so tight jeans and the peasant blouse that slipped off the shoulder.

Then again, just because Mairi looked like she'd strayed out of a sexy nursery rhyme, it would be irrational to label her as dangerous.

five

After my dash around the hospital following Emms' accident, to find myself so soon in another medical facility might have given me the heebie-jeebies but it didn't. That's because the New Victoria Hospital doesn't look, sound or smell like a hospital. With its leafy trees framing the car park, low-level buildings and discrete signage, it could be a suburban hotel, the kind of place a weary sales rep might rest up overnight after a hard day round the M25.

The weather had turned and there was a bite in the damp air on my face. Not cold enough for thermals, fleece and puffa but certainly sharp enough to make me wish that I'd pulled out my quilted parka from the back of the cupboard and wasn't hanging on to my leather jacket as a pathetic attempt to cling on to summer.

Her arm still in the sling, poor Emms looked like Nelson with the limb pinned to her waist under her black military coat. Because she was strapped up, she was also unstable, so I held on to her as we marched, like comrades in the dusk, towards outpatients' reception.

Once we'd checked in, I was able to look around my surroundings. Private hospitals.

For all Tony's faults, he had put us all on top whack medical insurance as part of our package. I have no doubt it was for corporate tax benefits and not pastoral care for the team, but what the hell. I've never used mine, but Emms is punctilious about keeping all the twins' jabs, development and anything else you happen to think of up to date, stamped, sealed and filed. It's her way. 'No slippage,' she says. 'Not with the kids, not with Greg.' And she gets that tight expression around her lips that makes her look the way she will in twenty years' time.

I've long suspected that she has some residual guilt about not picking up on her mother's cancer and this is what's made her so "health aware". Or maybe having kids makes her scared of losing them. Maybe when you've got it all - got the great husband, gorgeous kids and perfect life - you hang on to it with every last ounce of your strength.

'Has Greg called to say what time he'll be here to pick you up?' I asked when we were settled on the blue wall benches eyeing up the other rich or insured sick.

Emms put her good right hand on my arm, 'Why don't you stick around? We thought we might have a drink and a curry since we're here, and don't forget, for once, we've got childcare.'

'I thought you didn't want to leave the twins with Mairi.'

Emms smiled. 'I haven't. It's half-term which means that Sally, the vicar's daughter, is back from uni. Anyway what do you think about coming out with us? Our treat. There's someone Greg and I want you to meet. He's a doctor –'

'What? Emms ... no.'

'Emma Harens ... Emma Harens." A blue-uniformed, desiccated blonde with a clipboard and smoker's skin scanned the rich sick for recognition.

Emms stood up and before I could say another word we were bustled down the passage towards the consulting rooms. On the way, Emms shot me a pained "please" look, but I didn't respond. I don't know how many times I've told her not to set me up with anybody, surprise or otherwise. I'm 100% not interested. I do not want to share my life with someone. Been there, done that, got the broken and reconstructed nose. How hard is that to understand?

To be fair, Emms and Greg don't know about the broken and reconstructed nose. But that's hardly the point. As a friend, Emms should know better than to manoeuvre me into a situation where I'm paraded as a likely partner for some oddball. For one thing, it's disrespectful, and for another - well, it really pisses me off. I could see from Emms' expression that she was regretting the notion and I wasn't going to let her off the hook.

When we went into the anodyne room, the orthopaedic surgeon shook both our hands. Bad lighting made his pale skin look waxy, but he was tall, dark and long-limbed. He looked buttoned-up (and it wasn't just the unimaginative white shirt and charcoal suit). I noticed he had fine blue eyes - they were like a ski slope at dusk. Cold. Clear. Rather beautiful.

Hands were shaken, seats were taken, and notes were read. Despite what I guessed to be the formal courtesy of a public school education, the surgeon was detached. I helped Emms off with her coat, and undid the Velcro on the sling, then watched while he tenderly examined her arm. He didn't talk much. Just studied her arm and hand as if there was nobody attached to the end of it. Finally, he put her arm on her lap and sat back in his seat, still not making eye contact. It was clear that as far as this doctor was concerned, Emms was '6.30pm Arm Trauma.' I was intrigued by his total detachment.

He didn't engage. Didn't meet her gaze. He just made a steeple with his hands. 'All the evidence points to a hundred per cent return on functionality of the limb. But any further trauma could rupture tendons that are still healing and that would require surgery.'

'Just as well it's my left arm, not my right, drinking, punching arm.' Emms said as she stood up.

He smiled faintly, as if she was a halfwit. It was polite but dismissive and my irritation about her matchmaking helped me to relish her discomfort. Not nice of me, but hey, I'm only human, I'm allowed to have a moment or two.

On the way out Emms had a minor strop, 'Talk about charm by-pass! Well, at least if I keep my arm safe I won't have to wake up in a recovery room and see that face. What a bad-tempered, thoroughly unpleasant, totally unattractive git.'

'Bad-tempered, certainly. But unattractive? Do you really think so? I thought he was okay,' I said, if anything to contradict Emms and wind her up a little. But I'd underestimated her good nature and single-mindedness. You see, Emms wants me to be happy and believes that "happy" is a domestic set-up just like hers: kind and caring husband, adorable but spunky kids. And because it works for her and it's the bedrock of her existence, Emms believes that it's what the rest of humanity needs. So she stopped in the middle of the car park, swung round to face me, eyes and face wide open and said, 'You really did? You mean, you thought he was okay, in an, "I-could-shag-you kind of way?" That's great news. It means you're in the right frame of mind to meet Mike.'

'Mike? You mean Greg's friend? Don't be ridiculous. I'm going to drop you at the Slug and Lettuce, and then I'm going home to watch a documentary about the Everglades and eat beans on toast.'

'Oh come on, come in for five minutes. Mike's just come back from Australia so you're bound to have something in common, you might even know the same people. Greg was at school with him. They were pals and Mike used to stay at Greg's over half term because his parents were splitting up. Greg wouldn't have brought him home if he hadn't been a good guy.'

'That's total bollocks, and you know it. Greg would have brought him home because he felt sorry for a kid who was having a bad time, so that's not a recommendation, and I don't bloody care if Greg and this bloke were twins separated at birth. I am not having a curry with a set-up.'

'Why not?'

'Because I don't want to. Because I don't do blind dates and because I don't want you meddling in how I live my life.'

Emms paused, 'I knew you'd say that. I told Greg it was a complete waste of time and that you'd be really pissed off with the both of us and Greg said that Mike is a neurologist, as if that would make the slightest bit of difference. I'm sorry Liz.' Her capitulation made me feel mean and even a little foolish. After all, what would it actually cost me to have a drink with them?

'A neurologist,' I said. 'Gosh. Well I never. Wow. You see that changes everything. Why didn't you say so? I've always, always been desperate to meet one. I'm sure we'll have heaps to talk about.'

'Will you?' Emms said. 'Will you really come and meet him?'

'Yes. Five minutes. And I mean it.'

Five minutes was too long. Mike Durbin was a pleasant enough human being but, besides the lack of common ground with our careers, he was a dedicated gym jock. Now, I'm not totally averse to the treadmill, I even have a fondness for free weights, but I'm not obsessed. Mike was. So, this meant a fantastically boring conversation about how often he went to the gym, what he did there, and how he'd gone from ten-ton lardass to toned triathlete. It left me with a desperate desire to drain alcohol that was impossible to give in to, as I had to drive home. Across the table, I could see Emms squirming and even Greg was going glassy-eyed as Mike detailed, and I do mean detailed, the need for regular rehydration and painstaking monitoring of calorie intake. He did not let up. Not for a moment.

They were in for a fun night and it served them right. I was going home. I'd stood up to make my excuses, when a blast of cold air came in from the open door. Mike leapt to his feet.

'Look who's here! If it isn't my gym buddy and triathlon rival,' he said. 'Come on in, Richard. Meet my old school friend, Greg and my new friends, Emma and Liz.'

I cringed. I really cringed. Mike's gym buddy was none other than Emms' orthopaedic surgeon who, I'm happy to say, looked deeply uncomfortable about being clapped on the back by Mike.

'What a coincidence,' Emms said.

'Come and sit down.' Mike was tugging at Richard's arm. 'Let me buy you a drink.'

'I've ... I've ... just need to ...' Richard said, looking at me.

I took the opportunity to go. 'See you, guys. Nice to meet you, Mike. Speak later, Emms.' I gave her a look and slid out of the open door where I stood for a moment in the cold air, fishing in my bag for my car keys. Behind me I heard the door open and Richard was by my side.

'You didn't finish your drink,' he said. 'I'd very much like to talk to you in a different social setting - if that's acceptable? Do you have a card?'

'A card?'

'Yes, a card.' He reached into his pocket and then handed me a business card. 'Like this one, but with your contact details.'

I took it. We were both outside in the cold; he was standing in the shadows to the side of the door. Even in the dark, I could see he looked composed and the moment of panic I'd seen in his face had passed. The bar doors opened and Emms burst through. She didn't see him.

'Sorry, Liz. Really sorry. I didn't realise Mike would be such an arse. I promise never, ever to set you up again. It was completely thoughtless and stupid of me to agree that someone Greg hadn't seen since school should join us on a blind date.'

'Please accept my apologies as well,' he said. 'Not all the medical profession are arses – I hope.' He turned and walked back inside. Even in the dark, I could see Emms' face was a white disc of discomfort.

'What have I done? Liz, I've just made it even worse, I'm so sorry, how stupid of me and my big mouth. How can you ever forgive me?'

I have to admit, I was steaming with embarrassment but there was no point rounding on

Emms - after all, it was a mistake, hardly life-threatening and why spread the pain? 'Forget about it,' I said. 'If looking like a loser whose best friend sets her up with a dork is the worst thing that ever happens between you and me, then we'll be lucky.'

six

Later that night, I lay in bed as the rain spattered against my bedroom window punctuated by gusts of wind. The storm seemed fierce, angry, trying to reach me through the cracks in the pointing, cracks in my psyche.

I was awake, the digital clock on the floor read 2.30am. Had I been woken by the rain or by the events of the evening? I stretched out in bed; my pillowcase was damp to my cheek. Sweat, dribble, fever? I threw back the duvet cover and let the air in the room cool my skin. My stomach was strapped with cords of anxiety. I took a deep breath and heard the rough exhale.

'What the fuck?' I said aloud.

Without switching on the light, I padded to the kitchen and felt around for the light above the hob. Blinking like a mole, I rooted around the back of the cupboard and found a box of herbal teabags. Boiled water sloshed on the bag and I studied the changing colour of the water through one eye before hooking out the bag with my fingertips.

After all that palaver, the drink still tasted like old socks. No wonder I hadn't used those tea bags.

Finding my way to the dining room table, I sat in the dark in front of my laptop. Out of habit, I woke it up. Out of obsession, I opened my search engine and typed in my ex-husband's name. I got as far as 'John'. Then my finger hesitated over the keyboard. What if he was dead? What if someone had succeeded where I'd failed?

It had been six months since I'd last looked for him. Back then, I'd found a Companies House set of accounts and a Facebook page. Did I really want to know what he was doing? Probably not. I rubbed the bridge of my nose and stroked the ridge where it had been broken and mended in a couple of extremely painful operations.

I bloody hated doctors, particularly surgeons. Maybe I should have explained to Emms why, but having never told her in the early days of our friendship, it was a little hard to open up now.

Richard, of the apparently arrested emotional development, must think I'm a complete loser. But do I care? No. Not really. Since I had no plan to see him again, it made absolutely no difference what he thought of me.

I swallowed another mouthful of the old-sock tea. The red mug left a wet circle on the table. Was I kidding myself? What if my anguish was less about Emms and Greg's misguided matchmaking attempts and more about looking like a prat in front of a coolly interesting, possibly interested, man?

How long had it been since I'd had sex? Nearly a year. I remembered the event, even if I didn't immediately recall the name of the American I'd met on my weekend break in Milan. After meeting him in a bookshop near the Duomo (in the English language section), I had lied about my name so determined was I to keep the fling exactly that – a fling. Because that's all I'd had in the ten years since my divorce. Flings.

My hand stroked the mouse pad. I watched the cursor move around the desktop. Then I started typing. Instead of googling my ex-husband, I googled Richard. He'd completed his training at St Mary's and then done a stint in Chicago; he'd also written a couple of papers on indecipherable elements of orthopaedic surgery. There was a picture of him looking saturnine and slightly cranky.

Maybe it was time to move on. Maybe I would even call him. That would make Emms and Greg get off my case.

I smiled at the thought and padded back to bed. I still remember the moment, even now. The rain seemed to have stopped and I knew I would sleep because I recognised that I was ready to move on.

For the good of my psyche, not to mention the good of my sex life, I decided to make a conscious effort to be more open about the possibility of a relationship. To this end, I bought a new outfit to wear at Tony's funeral and while it wasn't exactly hot pants and body art, it was a break from Planet Functionality and an outward indication that I cared. I also figured that the navy military style coat would double up for board meetings with the parent company. As well as the coat, I also bought a skirt. And – this was huge stuff for me – a pair of tights and shoes with heels.

On the morning of the funeral, I looked out of the open balcony window to see decent weather after days of heavy rain. There were still puddles but the trade-off was the freshly washed scent.

As I sat on the sofa, struggling to pull on the tights without sticking my finger through the nylon mesh, I decided that my mission for the day would be to respect Tony and not say that the world was a better place without him. Even though it was. The office had become a happy hive of industry, where people put in the hours because they cared about what they were doing and they liked being there.

Half-term was over which meant that Sally, the vicar's daughter wasn't available so Mairi was the babysitter of choice. When I arrived at the cottage, to take Emms to the funeral, Mairi answered the door. Her cheeks were flushed - though that might have been makeup. Her dewy lips definitely came out of a tube and her artfully dishevelled hair was exactly that – artful. To compound Mairi's retro maiden-in-distress look, she was wearing one of her peasant blouses, this time with black jeans. There was no denying it; she had a pert little bum.

'Come in,' Mairi said, waving her arms in welcome. With the raised armpit, I caught her signature whiff of sweat and patchouli. I stepped into the hall and she didn't back away, 'How lovely to see you again, Liz. You look amazing.' She pirouetted and called up the stairs. 'Emma, Liz is here in the most fabulous outfit.'

Why did her comment make me want to check to see if I had spinach in my teeth? Odd. I needed to think about that. 'I'll go up,' I said stepping past Mairi's grin. I climbed the narrow stairs to the first floor of the cottage. At the top of the landing, I turned, and walked past the kids' room and into Emms and Greg's. Emms was standing in front of her wardrobes frowning. 'How cold is it?' she said. 'Scarf or coat?' She turned. 'Wow. Look at you.' She walked round me and stroked the fabric on my arm. 'Nice outfit.'

'It's the new me. Come on, we can't be late.'

Emms turned back to the open wardrobe. 'I'm not sure what to wear.'

'Don't tell me the system has failed.'

I caught a glimpse of Emms' wardrobe and saw the rack upon rack, shelf upon shelf, hanger upon hanger of black and white and neutral tones arranged by colour. At the beginning of each week, Emms selects five different outfits and they're always clean and mended and dry-cleaned if necessary. Even bloody ironed.

However, at that moment she was paralysed, holding up two scarves to wear over her long jacket. One was rust, grey and black paisley. The other was plain grey cashmere.

She selected the colourful paisley and swiftly folded the other scarf and replaced it on the shelf, in the right place – with the other grey scarves,

'Everything back in its place,' Emms said. 'I do like a system to rely on.'

'Unless there's a funeral, when it goes into meltdown.'

'Granted,' she said.

'Me, I like to live closer to the edge. You know, what will it be, the only clean shirt, the Spanish mantilla or the off-the-shoulder number?' We were outside on the landing about to descend the stairs. I lowered my voice and tilted my head in the direction of the ground floor. 'Speaking of which.'

Emms rolled her eyes and put her finger to her lips.

When we were in the car, Emms spoke. 'She is fantastically irritating but her CRB checked out, the twins love her and they wouldn't have had her at the hospital crèche if she wasn't any good. Still I'm with you. The thing is, I don't know if she really is creepy or if my guilt that I can't be the perfect mother and she's in my home looking after my children is kicking in and making me think she's creepy. I mean, it's not as if we haven't had other people babysitting, so maybe it is her.'

'I wouldn't say she's exactly creepy, just a little odd. Probably too much time sitting round the toadstool singing I'm a teapot or whatever it is they sing at nursery. If the vicar's daughter can't babysit because she's back at uni, maybe find someone else?' I swung the car off the roundabout and onto the A3. I put my foot down.

'I would, but it's really difficult with Greg,' Emms said. 'He's helping her set up some sort of nursery business and he says I'm being mean-spirited.'

'You? You're the least mean-spirited person I've ever met. That's ridiculous.'

'I'm not going to argue with Greg, particularly not about Mairi. And not at the moment. Getting his business going is slower than Greg expected. He's been meeting all his old contacts to try to drum up some work, so he's hardly ever at home. And Mairi's always available to pick up the kids, give them their tea. So, for the moment, we're stuck with her.'

I slowed down as we moved through the Victorian gates of the crematorium. I could see people parking up ahead and getting out. They were sombrely dressed and looked prepared for the service.

'Is there anything we should be doing now that we're here?' Emms said.

'My mission today is to try not to badmouth Tony.'

Emms didn't respond to the quip. When I glanced over she looked tight-lipped. Okay, given the circumstances, what I said wasn't in the best of taste, but Emms wasn't usually so disapproving.

The funeral was in one of the bigger chapels, and we sat near the back. There was quite a turn out for someone who had been – as far as I could see it – consistently unpleasant. But maybe it was his age; maybe the middle-aged mourners were Tony's anxious peers peeking at their own encroaching mortality. He must have been one of the first of their number not to make old bones.

Aware that a blister was developing on my heel from my new shoes, I shifted around on the seat, anxious for the service to start and finish. Of course, it wasn't just the physical discomfort of new shoes rubbing; I did feel hypocritical taking part in a service to celebrate Tony's life when I was more inclined to celebrate his death.

Emms leaned over and whispered, 'Do you really think we need to go back to the house? Would it be cowardly if we skipped it? After all, we're at the formal part of the proceedings and Sheila must have seen us.'

'Nothing would give me greater pleasure than to go to the office, where I can take these bloody shoes off, but we have to go to the house, even if it's only for half an hour. The rest of the staff will be there, and whatever we feel, we need to show respect to Tony for Sheila's sake.'

Tony lived in Burwood Park, one of the local private estates where you have to drive through barriers and over bumps to enter the hallowed precinct. Typical Tony - he must have loved the fake exclusivity of the barrier going up and down, shutting out the riff-raffy rest of us. It wasn't quite as posh as St George's Hill where a lot of the big showbiz money lives, or Black Pond where the footballers' mansions loomed, but Burwood's detached houses, set among leafy, lush lanes, would have offered our boss a fat slice of the good life in his mock Tudor mini-mansion.

From time to time, I'd picked up Tony at the house, but I'd never been inside. When we walked through the dark wooden door, I thought it was surprisingly homely. I could see fat sofas and soft throws in warm golden colours in a side room. For the occasion, there was a marquee attached to the back of the house with long tables laid with sandwiches and drinks, and by the time we arrived, there was a cheery buzz suggesting the relief among the living gathered to talk about the dead, or in this case "celebrate Tony's life". This seemed to take the form of knocking back a lot of wine and scoffing the canapés that were brought round by black-clad waiting staff.

I handed Emms a diet coke. 'You know what? I'm starting to think that Tony had a whole other side to him. I just heard some bloke saying how much he'll be missed. And he really meant it.'

'Shut up,' Emms said. 'Someone will hear.'

Emms wandered off to the other side of the marquee to join Brendan and Sue. Before I could follow, I spotted Sheila. I wouldn't say she looked joyful, but at a distance she was certainly in control. Usually I thought she looked a little overweight and over-blonde, but today she looked slighter. Greyer. And despite the air of composure there was a brittle stiffness in her bearing.

I went over to her. 'It was a nice service,' I said.

'Thanks for coming,' Sheila said. 'I can imagine how busy you must be now.'

The comment was typical Sheila. Good manners – no matter what storm was pounding and buffeting her soul. Up close, the makeup creased round her eyes and the dark shadows under her eyes gave her face a hollow, empty look. She went on with a cool smile, 'It's so nice to see you. Half the people here are Tony's golf club friends. I've absolutely no idea who they are. For all I know, they could have walked in off the street.'

The slightest slur to her speech indicated that she'd probably had more than a single glass of wine, and who would blame her? I opened and closed my mouth a couple of times struggling to find something sincere to say about Tony, and failed. 'He was obviously highly respected,' I said. 'I just overheard someone saying how much they'll miss him ...' I trailed off. It was crap. Really, really crap. But Sheila didn't notice.

'You know, I'm surprised how much I do miss him, for all his ways,' Sheila said. 'Anyway, that's life. Nothing much I can do about it, is there?'

I took Sheila's hand; it was red and worn. Dry with sunspots on the back that looked odd next to the diamond eternity ring and the jangling gold bracelet.

'I'm sure it's not going to be easy,' I said. 'But I want you to know that Emma and I will do everything we can to help. That's a promise.'

Sheila regained her hand. 'I think Emma's done quite enough.'

On behalf of Emms, heat rose up from my neck to my ears. The comment was a little harsh even if it was understandable. I opened my mouth to say something, but I couldn't respond.

Sheila took pity on my vacant expression, 'Don't worry, Liz. I'm not going to fall apart. My mother became a young widow when my father was killed in the war. She used to say to me, "We Paulstons are made of stern stuff".'

'I can see that,' I said.

There was a pause, and I was aware of a question in her eyes. 'But there's one thing that's really bothering me.' Sheila massaged a swollen knuckle that heralded arthritis 'Tony was absolutely obsessed with seatbelts. He had a cousin who got killed in a crash and it affected him deeply. He was always nagging me about buckling up, he was a complete tyrant about it and he refused to start the car if I wasn't strapped in. So I simply can't understand why he wasn't wearing a seatbelt.'

seven

I woke up with a start. My brain seemed to have shrunk inside my skull; I was dehydrated. After the funeral, I'd driven home and - in the safety of my flat - made myself a gin and tonic. I'd sipped it whilst filling the bath; the mingling scents of juniper in the drink and bergamot in the bath were heady, to say the least. Now, five hours later, I was experiencing the hangover from the second gin and tonic, the one that tipped the balance.

I didn't blame Sheila for her comment "Emma's done quite enough". But since it was an accident, I couldn't help wondering if there was anything else behind it. My mind flipped around between various ideas, from Emms driving badly to the airbag being switched off, but it still seemed unreasonable of Sheila. Maybe there was something else, maybe Sheila was suggesting that something was going on between Emms and Tony? Maybe she thought Tony had unclipped his seatbelt for an early morning vehicular fumble. And maybe pigs might fly.

I stretched out in the dark for the bedside lamp and the ceramic base was cool to my fingertips. A click and I was blinking away the light overload, trying to see clearly. More like trying to think clearly.

My bedroom is my hideout. One entire side of the room is devoted to wardrobes which contain not only clothes, but the life trophies I'm not yet ready to throw away. Among them is a pale blue dressing gown with singe marks. At one time I was considering framing it like a Japanese kimono, but why expose myself like that? It's nobody's business and not for sharing.

I scrabbled around in the bedside cabinet for a couple of paracetamol and knocked the tabs to the back of my throat with a gulp of water.

Of course, it was patently obvious, even to a corporate psychologist such as myself: Sheila was working through the Kubler Ross stages of grief and had reached anger. She was angry about being widowed, angry about the forced change in her life, and my guess is that there would have been a good slab of anger about the relationship with Tony itself. Who could blame her? She should have been celebrating a wedding anniversary, not mourning at a funeral.

From anger to blame was barely a breath. It was clear - Sheila was searching for a whole host of explanations to try to make sense of her new life, and the risible notion that Emms was Tony's bit on the side might well seem logical in her current fragile mental state.

I swallowed some more cold water and let the liquid momentarily rinse the clagginess from my mouth. I empathised and I sympathised. For all

Tony's faults, Sheila would be facing long, lonely nights in an empty bed.

Just like mine.

I turned off the light and snuggled down into the duvet, satisfied with my interpretation of Sheila's comment. It meant nothing. She was grieving. It would pass. I closed my eyes and shifted around, trying to get comfortable and switch off my brain, but I was still wide awake. The fastest way for me to get to sleep would be to masturbate, and I even had the coolly stuffy doctor as a fresh fantasy.

I settled into a rhythm, my pulse and heart rate rose, saliva flow increased. Why not call him? Why not call him to warm my own cold bed? What have I got to lose? The worst that could happen would be that he'd tell me to fuck off in an interesting and patrician way. He certainly wasn't going to kill me.

The next day I had to run an all-day training course for a customer service team in Kingston. At 6.30am, before my shower and - more importantly - before I lost my nerve, I tapped out a text and pressed send.

'Your gym buddy Mike went to school with my friend Greg. Do you remember?'

No name, no explanation.

I barely had time to place the phone on the kitchen work surface and reach for my coffee cup before the phone vibrated and chimed a response.

'Of course. Plsd you found my card and used it. May I invite you for a libation tonight at 6.30?'

Libation? Who does he think he is? Noel Coward? But there was no denying it; I had a little heart rush. A flush of warmth spread like an ink spill all the way up to my ears and neck.

However, by the time I strode into the meeting room, I'd locked down any potential girly blush. It was neatly parked right at the far end of the emotional car park. I had a job that required a level of competence and I had to deliver.

Today, we were in the Rose Room at Warren House, a fine mansion built in the 1890s and used for small conferences and afternoon teas. Throughout the morning, I stayed on track and I whizzed through the morning session without incident. During the lunch break, Brendan and Susan looked after the participants in the dining room while I scanned their morning submissions in solitude. I'd almost finished when Emms turned up to see how it was going. As soon as we were alone in the meeting room, she shut the wooden double door and with some ceremony took a purple and white paper bag from her workbag.

'I thought you might fancy some sushi instead of the sandwich lunch.'

'You are kind. You know I hate fighting with the participants over the smoked salmon sandwiches - it looks so bad.' I reached for the single box. 'What about you?'

'I'll eat later,' she said. 'I've got to get back and do a conference call at 2.30. Finish the spreadsheets and then get home and see if I've still got a family.'

Between mouthfuls of rice and fish I told Emms about my date.

'This is absolutely brilliant. And it's fate.' She wagged her finger at me and fished once more in her leather workbag. This time she withdrew a gift-wrapped box.

'What's that? What's fate? What are you talking about, Emms?' I dipped my sushi in soy sauce and shovelled it into my mouth. I had about ten minutes before the afternoon session and I needed to prepare the next exercise.

'I bought this for you this morning. I couldn't resist it.'

I wiped my fingers on the paper napkin and ripped open the packaging. Inside was a box containing a chunky silver ring, with an uncut rose quartz stone.

'That's really lovely.' I slipped it on to the middle finger of my left hand and admired the smooth silver lines and candy pink crystal.

'Do you really like it?'

'Of course I do. I just don't know why you started thinking of me in the middle of the morning and buying me jewellery. You're not getting weird on me, are you?'

Emms pushed her hair off her forehead. 'Can't I give my BF a present? Anyway, besides the fate aspect of this gift, I wanted to thank you for all the help you've given me since the accident. And, I suppose ... saying yes to the business. I know you didn't want to do it and I feel bad.'

'A bribe. I can live with that,' I held out my hand and admired the ring on my hand.

Emms glanced at her watch and started packing up her bag. 'There's something else about the ring. Rose quartz is the love stone. It opens up the heart chakra to all sorts of love - including self-love.'

'And your point is?' I said.

'That you're meeting this guy tonight, and you might be open to a relationship, which you haven't been ever since I've known you. And –'

I stood up. 'When did you start getting into this superstitious tosh? This is something new, isn't it?'

'I've just been thinking about a few things lately. What harm can it do?'

'A lot of harm. Emms - you know as well as I do that it's a load of old rubbish developed by people who want to feed off the vulnerable, anxiety-ridden, sad sack members of society.'

'How can you be so sure? Anyway, don't knock it if you don't understand it, Liz. Just because we can't see something, it doesn't mean it's not real. There are many things in heaven and earth that we don't see or understand, but they're there.'

'That's ridiculous. You *know* it's ridiculous.' I glanced at her throat; and at the base of her open-necked shirt there was a new silver pendant that had small leaves entwined with swirling branches. I pointed back at her. 'Is that from the same shop? Did you buy an angel or a dream-catcher or some other load of magic bollocks while you were in there?' Emms looked away and I felt like a shit for putting her down so brutally.

'The ring is lovely and I'm an ungracious cow,' I said. 'I'll wear it tonight and if he falls under my spell and swears total love over the first beer and packet of crisps I will tell him the source of my power.'

'You can take the piss all you want, I just think it would be nice to have an open mind and for you to have someone in your life. That's all. Just don't shag him.'

'Why on earth not - if I feel like it? Haven't we just agreed that my new positive energy love-quartz is going to open up my chakra along with everything else?' I waved my hands about, fingers splayed.

'Two reasons,' Emms said. 'Two very logical reasons - neither of which are based on what you call superstitious bollocks and I call keeping an open mind.'

'Go on, then.' I crumpled up the paper bag and handed it to Emms. Outside the room, I could hear the hum of the participants. It was already 2pm -

time for the session to begin - and I wasn't prepared which is never a pleasant sensation.

'First reason,' Emms said. 'You might just want to have a relationship with this bloke, and if he thinks you're a sex-starved trollop, he might find you less alluring as a future partner.'

I groaned. I really groaned. But I didn't interrupt, because I just wanted to let her finish and shunt her out of the room. Emms wagged her finger at me. 'And second, you don't know the man from a bar of soap beyond the fact that he has a medical qualification and is private insurance approved.'

I shook my head. 'He's a bloody doctor.'

'So was Dr Crippen. And then there was that nice Dr Shipman —'

I heard a tap at the door, it opened and a middle-aged woman with unrealistically black hair popped her head in. She was one of the participants.

'Come in,' I said. 'We're just about ready for the afternoon session.' I briefly made the introductions and shuffled Emms out of the meeting room.

'I mean it, don't shag him,' Emms whispered, just before I closed the door behind her. She had to have the last word: 'You're much too trusting and you're a lousy judge of character.'

eight

During the rest of the afternoon, whilst the participants had their heads down and were scribbling their responses to my ten-minute exercises, my eyes were drawn back to the ring. The coconut-ice pink of the rose quartz and silver looked good. Was this truly a gift, or was it sub-textual hush money? Maybe there had been something going on between Emms and Tony. I remembered Emms' "wrong impression" explanation for her obsessive police interview preparation. The idea of an affair with Tony seemed ridiculous, but she was fretting about something. I'd have felt a whole lot better if I'd known what it was, but with a roomful of participants - to be followed by my first hot date in a long time - I had no choice but to park my concerns about Emms and try to wrap up the afternoon promptly.

As soon as the last participant was out of the door, I was stuffing work papers, laptop and whiteboard markers into my messenger bag while checking my phone for messages. Maybe Richard was going to be late and I might have an extra thirty minutes or even an hour. No such luck. There was only an email from Emms.

Liz,

Please remember to pick up the feedback forms from reception on your way out.

Hope the date with Crippen goes okay. If you use his loo, check to see if there are acid stains in the bath!

Bad news here. Greg's just told me he's raising finance for Mairi's nursery project. I can see the financial logic of it but...

Anyway, don't forget the feedback forms and DON'T SHAG HIM!

xxEmms

The pub was Hart's Boatyard on Kingston Road. It was uncomfortably close to my flat, but it was the first and only place I'd been able to think of when Richard had suggested meeting. It's half boathouse and half wine bar, with stone-tiled floors, leather sofas and discreet softly lit corners. On the tables are tea lights and laminated menus with plates of nibbles to share. In other words, it's a dating venue.

I saw Richard before I pushed through the glass double doors. He was on one of the leather chairs in the main bar, positioned so that he could eye the entrance. Through the glass I watched him, legs crossed, suited, with a worry dent etched between his eyebrows. I pushed open the door and he uncoiled and came towards me. His expression was uncertain. Maybe I wasn't the only one who was uneasy about this dating lark.

'Thank you for coming.' He stood a good arm's-length away from me and made no attempt to kiss cheeks, grab hands or make any other inappropriate physical contact. I liked that.

'I reserved a table overlooking the river,' he said.

I didn't like the table reservation. Don't ask me why, but at that innocuous comment, a shrivelled ball of panic rose from the base of my stomach all the way up to my throat and lodged there.

The table he'd booked was in a little nook near the open steel staircase, well away from the main action at the bar. Beyond the glass, river and sky met in the dark, and the twinkling of the houses on the opposite bank lit up the water.

It was choppy out there.

As soon as the white wine arrived, I took a gulp. The cold liquid anaesthetised my jittering mind.

'Why did you choose medicine?' I asked, just for something to say and hating myself for sounding like an HR manager.

'I suppose it chose me. My father was a doctor. And my grandfather.' He leaned back and the shift allowed the tea light on the table to shadow his features. His voice was a pitch above deep brown, and for someone who sounded so stuffy, with his "libations", he was hot.

He'd barely drunk any of the wine in his glass and I wasn't sure that he even liked it or whether he had ordered the bottle because I asked for a glass. His hands held the base of the glass down to the table as if it might slip away. Long fingers, long smooth fingers. How would they feel on me?

The plate of nibbles to share did nothing to slow the rush of alcohol into my bloodstream, but at least they drowned the butterflies in my stomach. I took off my specs and polished the lenses with one of the napkins. Emms' ring glinted on my finger, picking up the candlelight on the rustic wooden table.

What the hell did I have to lose?

'You know, I live just across the road. Why don't you come back to mine and I'll make you my signature dish. Beans on toast? How's that for an offer?'

The sex had been clumsy and tender. It was shy sex, exploratory sex, first-time sex, and I was pleased that he wasn't some slick trickster showing his skill as if it was just another contact sport. I felt a little safer.   Afterwards, Richard held on to me as if I was a life raft in choppy seas. He was hot and his sleeping breath on my neck tickled. I grasped his arm and lifted it from across my body. He grunted something incomprehensible.

'Gotta pee.' I slipped out of bed and tiptoed into the sitting room. The chill air hit my naked skin. Stupid of me. I needed my dressing gown.

I sat on the sofa and dragged the throw around me. Sitting in the dark, I felt the unaccustomed post-sex aches. It had been a while. The throw was soft, fake, furry fabric bought by Emma on my birthday.

A mock comic fur. Her ring was still on my finger pulling me away from my after-sex mellowness.

Was there something going on with her? The spontaneous present-giving, coupled with her superstition jag, was out of character. And Tony ... Somehow I'd get to the bottom of it next time I got to see her for more than five minutes. Meanwhile, wouldn't she have some fun with her Dr Crippen theories when I told her that I'd shagged Richard?

'Liz? Liz ... are you by the window?'

'Shall I put the light on?' I said. 'Or do you want to fall over the furniture?'

'This will be a challenge in spatial awareness,' Richard said, his voice husky from sleep. 'Very well, set the timer ... ouch – that hurt.'

I got up from the sofa with the throw over my shoulders and wrapped it and myself around him. His body was smooth and I could smell a residual lemon and leathery scent mingled with his own, true smell. It was good.

On the floor, under Emms' throw, it was even better.

'What time do you think it is?' I said afterwards. 'I hope you're not operating on somebody's hip tomorrow. Or more likely today. It might be a good idea to get some sleep.'

'Unfortunately in this instance, you're right. I'd better get back and change,' he said, holding on to me, making no effort to get up.

'I don't even know where 'back' is.'

'For the past six weeks 'back' has been The Tollhouse Lodge in Cobham,' he said.

I felt his muscles tighten. Or was it mine? I pulled away from him and sat with my back to the sofa. I could see his shadowy figure in the dark.

'Why are you staying there?' I said.

His voice was lower, graver. And he cleared his throat before speaking. 'I have recently separated from my wife,' he said with all the pomposity of a cabinet minister giving an explanation about dirty deeds to the press. 'On the advice of my solicitor, I am staying at the Lodge pending an equitable conclusion to our divorce negotiations.'

Don't ask me why but I felt like a first-time hooker. Being naked with this total stranger made me feel not only vulnerable but also shamed. I stood up and hurried to the bedroom where I grabbed my dressing gown, specs and his clothes. When I got back to the sitting room the sidelight was on, and he was sitting on the sofa with the throw over his shoulders, hunched, his dark eyes cast down, avoiding my gaze. I dropped his clothes on the sofa next to him and they pooled in a tangled heap.

'I think you'd better go,' I said. 'I don't do married men at any stage in the process.'

'But it's over,' he said. 'Bar the inevitable fall-out and negotiation.'

'I've been divorced. Your inevitable fall-out is not going to be my problem. What's more, I have to ask myself why your wife chucked you out of the family home.' He opened his mouth to speak - no doubt to excuse, to mollify, to wriggle and to cajole. I held up my hand.

'Just go.'

After he'd gone, I had a hot shower and exfoliated till my skin was pink and shiny. The bed had to be stripped and remade too. I was not going to lie in sheets that still held sex sweat, thank you very much. It was 2am, and as I loaded the washing machine, I found a black sock. It went into the bin.

Job done. My stomach was still churning and I was wired. Neurons pinging at each other, muscles stretched. I'd never get to sleep. The only thing I could do was make myself a hot milky drink. How could he not tell me that he was still married? How stupid was I not to ask? That was the nub of it; my stupidity and associated shame.

I made a cup of hot chocolate and wrote to Emma:

Dear Emms

Total cock-up on the Crippen front. He's an arse and a married arse to boot. Separated and living at that hotel on the Portsmouth Road where they have those vintage car fairs. I shouldn't have trusted him. And I certainly shouldn't have shagged him.

You was right. I done wrong.

Love

Liz

There was something cathartic about admitting one's mistakes. Especially so soon after the event. If I hadn't shagged him, I wouldn't have felt so angry with myself. Yes. There was some logic there. If I hadn't shagged him, I would have politely sympathised with his situation and gone home. Alone. If I hadn't shagged him, I wouldn't have cared. I wouldn't feel like a loser, I wouldn't be sitting up dallying on the edge of the self-loathing pond, considering jumping in for total immersion.

What the fuck.

I was almost at the end of my hot chocolate and starting to think that I might be able to sleep when an email pinged back from Emma. I glanced at the clock on the desktop. It was nearly 3am. What was she doing up so late?

Dear Liz

Surely if he's separated that means he's preparing to be single. Are you, possibly, maybe, perhaps, looking for a reason to back off? Why don't you give him a chance? You were divorced and you aren't a complete loser.

Can't sleep. Mairi was over for supper – again. It's the THIRD time this week. It reminds me of my Aunty Jane, and we all know how that ended up.

XE

During the course of the week, there was no time to have a proper catch-up with Emms nor was there the opportunity to self-flagellate about Richard. Workwise, we were swimming against the tide: running the business was a lot more complicated than delivering training courses, and I thought about little else. This was good.

However, I did take on board Emms' advice about Richard. After half a dozen emails, texts and unanswered calls from him, I relented and set out the terms of any future contact. It started with him not contacting me until he was at least in rental accommodation. And I said 'No promises'. And ended, 'This does not mean we are in a relationship'.

The 'get a flat' proviso gave me a breather to try to get the work done. By Thursday the presentation to the new owners was structurally sound, but there were gaping holes. So Emms and I decided to get together on Saturday morning and blitz it, somewhere quiet, away from the office, away from phones, clients and staff. Emms suggested her place, saying Greg had promised to take the twins so we could spread everything out on the kitchen table.

As I drove along Hampton Court Way, past the Palace, I glimpsed a group of deer through the gates of the home farm. I pulled up and got out of the car to watch them through the gate as they strolled and gambolled - elegant, stately animals, fat from the summer grass. Beyond the group of deer, I could see that the trees were turning; green to gold.

I'm always torn during the autumn. I love how it looks, I love the prospect of open fires, and the transition, but when it's over, when the nights close in and it's dark, I feel trapped. As I watched the deer on that Saturday morning, I knew that winter was coming, but I didn't know just how dark it would be.

nine

As soon as I arrived at Emms we went into action mode. We had just about got the coffee in the cafetière, spread the files out on the kitchen table, opened both laptops and fired them up, when the doorbell chimed.

'That'll be Steve,' Emms said glancing at the big old clock.

'Steve?'

'Postman,' she called back from the hallway, already on her way to the front door.

I poured my coffee. The plopping of liquid in cup and the aroma prepped me for the hit. Not for the first time in my life, I wondered why I lazily splashed boiling water over instant freeze dried – this was so much better. I added milk, watched shiny black turn to mud brown and swallowed a mouthful.

Emma was a few moments longer than I expected and I heard her companion before I saw her. Oh, for God's sake.

'This is so kind of you,' Mairi said. 'I'd love a cup of coffee.' She tiptoed into the kitchen. This morning she was in pink. A rose-coloured parka trimmed with fake fur. Of course, it was oversized - anything would be. Think Little Pink Riding Hood and you get the picture. In her arms she cradled a pile of brown A4 envelopes. From the way she squeezed them to her breasts, they were obviously some precious treasure, not to be given up without a struggle. The Big Bad Wolf would have a tough old time getting hold of those envelopes.

Behind Mairi, Emms towered in her trainers. Our eyes met. Emms shrugged and shook her head with a 'this is completely out of my control' look.

'Oh God!' Mairi said at the sight of the cafetière. 'Real coffee. That is so delicious. There's nothing I like more than real coffee. Apart from chocolate.' She gave me a conspiratorial twinkle that actually made me clench my teeth. What was it with this woman?

'Hi Mairi,' I said. 'Were you in the area this morning?'

'Well,' Mairi said in her once-upon-a-time voice, 'I've been gathering all the brochures from all the other nursery schools in the area, just as Greg said I should, and I wanted to give them to him. Have you heard? Greg and I are business partners. I'm so excited.'

'Yes, I have heard,' I said. 'Why don't you leave the brochures with us, we'll make sure that Greg gets them when he gets back, won't we Emma?'

Emms was at the cupboard, finding a mug for Mairi. She had her back to us.

'I've already told Mairi that she can totally trust us to pass them on to Greg,' Emms said. 'I also told her that we were working.'

'I'm so sorry to be a nuisance, but I really, really have to see Greg, just to ask him one little question,' Mairi said. 'You did say he wouldn't be long and I promise I'll be quiet. You won't even know I'm here. Or I could go and sit in the front room?'

Emms came over with Mairi's cup and sat down. 'Why don't we have our coffee? Greg has to bring the food back from Waitrose before he takes the twins to Horton Farm. So when he gets back, you can ask him your question. Problem solved.'

Emms was tapping her pendant as she spoke. If it kept her calm in the face of this provocative woman then way to go. I'd get one. How could Mairi be so unaware that her visit was inconvenient and we were busy?

But Mairi got her way and the morning's work was halted. She sat on the oak bench with her knees pulled up under her, no doubt to emphasise what an itsy-bitsy morsel of humanity she was. She took a sip of her coffee, licked red lips with red tongue and for a moment, but only a moment, Mairi appeared content.

'Delish!' she said and placed her cup on the rubber coaster.

'Would you like some more coffee?' Emms said, reaching for the cafetière to top her up. But Mairi had now covered her face with her hands and her shoulders were shaking. Could she be crying? The sound of a mewing sob confirmed it.

'What... what's the matter?' I said, looking at Emma who was shaking her head again in disbelief.

'Are you okay?' Emms said.

'No!' Mairi wailed.

'What's the matter?' I repeated and feebly patted Mairi on the shoulder. I suspected she wanted a hug, but there was no way I was going to be manipulated into some girly clutching.

'I've just been for a walk by the river ... on my own,' Mairi said.

'Oh no. Did something happen?' Emms said. 'Where exactly were you? I know sometimes there can be some odd people about and there was that incident down by –'

Mairi interrupted, 'It's my birthday today.'

I stopped patting her shoulders. So that's what this was all about. Her birthday.

'Well, that's good, isn't it? Happy Birthday,' I said.

'It's not good, it's terrible. Absolutely terrible. I'm another year older and I didn't get any birthday cards and my ex won't talk to me at all. And my life is completely awful. I've got no family, my parents are dead, I'm all alone and I realised this morning that nobody would care if I died. I could die tomorrow and no one would even look for me.'

'Oh come on, Mairi, surely that's a bit of an exaggeration?' Emms said. 'I mean, my mother died four years ago, my dad pissed off to France with another woman when I was sixteen. And I'm an only child.'

At that, Mairi stood up and threw herself into Emms' arms, nearly knocking her over. I almost laughed. Almost.

'You do understand, don't you?' Mairi said. 'I feel so utterly alone and so miserable.'

Mairi withdrew from Emms and held both of us in her tear-wet gaze. For a single, chilling moment, I saw emptiness in Mairi's eyes. Raw despair. Maybe this wasn't all hysterical, attention-seeking bullshit. Perhaps she really did feel isolated, worthless and alone. Emms saw it too. I watched her shudder as she put her hand on Mairi's shoulder and gently guided her back to the table.

'Mairi, you sit back down, Liz will put the kettle on and we'll make some fresh coffee, I'll find some chocolate and we'll talk about birthdays and life and everything. But first... first... I've got to go to the loo.'

As instructed, I put the kettle on while Mairi dabbed at her eyes with kitchen towel. She seemed to be recovering, which was encouraging. 'I'm so sorry,' Mairi said. 'That outburst was quite stupid. I think I'd better go. I'll catch up with Greg by email.'

However, before Mairi had the chance to wrap herself up in her pink parka and take herself away, Emms was back in the kitchen. Her voice was warm and kind, 'Why don't you enjoy your coffee and stay awhile,' Emms said 'Come on. It's your birthday. I've just texted Greg, he'll be back soon and I know the twins will be thrilled to see you.'

A smile relaxed Mairi's face, 'I really love them so much. There's a sweetness about Robbie that's spiritual, as if he's an old soul. Do you know what I mean?'

No matter how sorry I felt for Mairi because of her lonely birthday - and I genuinely did pity her - this cloying description of Robbie was stomach-churning. I had to walk to the window to compose my features. If this is what Emms was dealing with three times a week, no wonder she was getting stressed. Mairi seemed to have taken Emma's silence as encouragement to go on. 'And Tessa is the girl I wish I'd been when I was little. Were you like her, Emma? She's so brave and funny and confident. And beautiful. Like you.'

I turned back from staring into the garden and saw that Mairi looked as if she was going to start crying again. Fortunately there was a sound from the front door and the children pounded through the hall, into the kitchen.

'HAPPY BIRTHDAY!' they yelled and threw themselves on top of Mairi, climbing all over her.

Greg brought up the rear, holding aloft a huge bunch of lilies: Emms' favourite flower. Bad choice, Greg.

He also had a boxed bottle of champagne. Talk about overkill. Mairi was now weeping again, this time with joy.

'Thank you... thank you so much.' Mairi disentangled herself from the children with hugs and kisses, then she uncurled herself from the chair, tiptoed to Greg and threw herself into his arms and hugged him. The children laughed, delighted at her obvious pleasure.

In her own time, Mairi let go and turned to Emms.

'That's so you... you told Greg. I feel terrible. I didn't mean for you to do that but thank you so much. This is the best birthday I have ever had. I don't know what to say... you've changed my life. Thank you so much.'

Emms walked me to the front door. All thought of a Saturday morning outing for the children and a working session for us was sabotaged.

'Come over to mine later?' I said.

'I'll try,' Emms said. 'Otherwise we'll just have to do it over the phone and by email.' She pulled me towards her in an unaccustomed hug. 'The business is getting out of hand isn't it? Thanks for not saying, "I told you so".' She squeezed me to her and I smelt soap and Eau Dynamisante.

In my peripheral vision I caught a flash of orange and the sound of brakes on a bicycle.

'Steve,' Emms said over my shoulder. 'We've been expecting you.'

'Busy morning.' A grizzly bearded man climbed off his bike. 'Not much for you today.' He handed Emms a few envelopes.

'Thanks, Steve.'

Emms scanned the envelopes and ripped one open. It was brown. Official. From the house I could hear whoops and squeals. Emms' hand trembled as she read the letter. When she looked up, her face was drawn.

'What is it?' I said.

'It's the date for the inquest; I'm being called as a witness.' She looked at me, took a deep breath. 'You've got to help me get through all this, Liz. I really can't do it on my own.

ten

The entire way home, I bounced round the events of the morning.

What did Emma mean by "help her get through all this? Was it the business that was already crashing in on us? Or Mairi, who seemed to be sucking up her energy. Or perhaps it was the kicker: the inquest. Why was Emma so razzed about the inquest? Of course she was going to be called as witness. Unpleasant, no doubt, but it was only a formality. After all, the body had been released for the funeral. You don't have to be an expert on TV crime series to know that there is a lot of box-ticking and form-filling between death and burial, and if there were any problem at all, there'd have been no funeral.

Maybe Emma was losing it? Worrying about things that weren't real. Imagining a dark box of blame that would be opened at the inquest, evil black thought-bats flying out at her. Oh yes, I know all about that. I'd been in a world where every corner yielded a new danger and even the most prosaic items could be pits of imaginable disaster. The cough that's lung cancer, the flight that's doomed, the wrong number that's a stalker. Once you're in that world, there's no neon exit sign to lead you out of the dark, no wooden door in a red brick wall, no way to safety. All you've got is the slithery spiral into a pit of black shit.

Emms had the additional pressures of children, husband and poor, mad, encroaching Mairi. I knew that I had to help Emms any way I could, because that's what friends do. It's what women have always done. It's probably why we've survived this long. Men killing animals and each other and women sitting round the cave fire, sharing, cooperating, looking after each other's children. And protecting each other.

I had to protect Emma.

Well, the only way I could do that would be by dealing with one thing at a time.

If the business was on track, then we could deal with the rest. It wasn't much of a plan but it was better than nothing.

Later that day, I was still worrying about Emms and I was regretting the paucity of my behavioural and diagnostic skills, because the more I thought about it, the more I could see that Emms was exhibiting signs of some type of anxiety-related condition. My dissertation had been on non-verbal psychological cues and, if I say so myself, I'd done some good work on the subject, but it was no use in helping Emms because I was a theorist. Not a therapist. But you didn't need a degree to see that the amulet tapping was caused by anxiety. Whether it was a passing stress-related condition or a harbinger of something far more serious, I didn't know. But I was worried enough to experience a constant tightness in my solar plexus, and there lay the big joke: I was absorbing her anxiety by osmosis.

'What are you thinking about?' Richard asked. 'I can almost hear the whirring and clicking of your brain.'

'I was just wondering whether I should have the classic or the burger with avocado and bacon.'

'I don't believe you,' he said, looking at me across the top of his glass of beer.

'How do you know?'

'Something about your eyes,' Richard said, as his own narrowed thoughtfully. 'I can't quite describe it.'

I pulled my specs down off my forehead.

'Maybe I can't help looking into your eyes and I'm hypnotised like a rabbit in headlights? Did you ever think of that? Did you? Don't forget Richard, I'm the psychologist round here, and you're just the joint and cartilage doctor.'

'Fair comment.' He thrust forward his lips as he considered what I'd said. 'You're also holding the menu upside down.'

It was our third date since Richard had moved into his one-bedroom flat in Surbiton, thus satisfying my conditions for meeting again. I turned the menu the right way up and applied myself to my choice, concealing (I hoped), a smile. At least this part of my life was going well. No pressure was the deal and that's the way it was.

Richard and I were in an unpretentious burger chain that suited us both. "Us"? Get me. "Us" - first sign of coupledom, a notion that was more than a little premature, given my allergy to intimacy. Even if I'd momentarily thought "us" because of some inadequately buried reflex, I wasn't about to share my thoughts with him. I barely knew the man and, what's more, I needed to preserve my emotional resources.

'How's your week looking?' Richard said as he laid down his menu with an air of decision.

'Not great. I think I'm going to have the classic. How about you?'

It was the night before the inquest and that subject was none of Richard's business. All I really wanted now was an early night, an easy-to-digest meal and some stress-busting sex.

The waitress came up to us, and Richard nodded at me to start the order.

'I think I'll just have a salad, please.'

The coroner's court in Woking was a room that reminded me of a register office, but without the flowers and ribbons. There were red upholstered seats on either side of an aisle and, at the top of the room, three desks and a plaque with the royal coat of arms behind the black executive central chair. It wasn't just the aisle that made me think "register office", it was the air of expectation as twenty or so people crowded into the room.

We made our way to the front and sat in our allocated chairs. 'How're you doing?' I said to Emms.

She nodded and brushed her newly cut hair off her forehead.

I took her nod to mean okay given the circumstances. I went on, 'Just remember, it's a legal formality because Tony's death was sudden. That's all it is – a formality. It's not a trial, it's not about guilt and the police have signed off on the file.'

The only other person I recognised in the room was Sheila, who was accompanied by a lightly bearded man in a snappy suit. He could have been some friend or relative, or he could have been a solicitor. It didn't matter. Okay, this was an ordeal for the already anxious Emma, but in half an hour, the "i's" and the "t's" of the accident would be appropriately dotted and crossed and we could put it behind us and concentrate on the other matters that were making Emma anxious: the business and Mairi. One thing at a time.

I splayed my fingers and examined my heavy ringed hand. The snatched coffee I'd gulped with Richard before leaving home had left a bitter taste in my mouth but my tiredness was a small price to pay for the sense of wellbeing.

I nudged Emma and pointed at my ring. 'Still working,' I whispered.

She nodded and swallowed.

'Please rise for Mrs Madeleine Linber, the coroner.'

We all stood and a pleasant-faced woman with a helmet of lacquered grey hair took the black executive chair at the desk.

The process was business-like and swift. Tony's identity was established, the place of death and the exact injuries that had caused Tony's death. Happy that my glib confidence was bearing out, I let my shoulders drop. As I thought, it really was just an unpleasant formality.

'I'd like to call Mrs Emma Harens as a witness,' the usher said. Emms made her way to the witness table and swore on the Bible that the evidence she gave would be the truth, the whole truth and nothing but the truth.

'I'm Emma Susan Harens of 95 Summerbrook Road, Darkbridge, Surrey.'

'What was your relationship to the deceased?'

'Employee,' she whispered.

The coroner smiled kindly. 'Would you speak up a little, please?'

'Worked for him,' Emma cleared her throat. 'I worked for him, he was my employer.'

Emms' hand was crawling up to that bloody pendant. I glared at her. I'm not sure that she noticed but she did manage to pull her hand down and keep it by her side.

'Would you describe the events of the morning in question?'

'The morning in question,' Emms said. Her hand was up again as she brushed the hair off her forehead. I wished she'd stop fiddling and keep her hands on the table. She continued. 'I drove... I was driving Tony - a meeting. His car was being serviced. The car... my car skidded...' She pressed her lips together and locked eyes with the coroner.

'We all appreciate that this is deeply distressing for you. Thank you. I'd now like to call Mrs Sheila Day or her legal representative. As the wife of the deceased and in her capacity as a properly interested person, she has the right to ask the witness questions.'

If Emma could have gone any whiter she would have been transparent. So he wasn't a relative or some helpful friend after all. The bearded solicitor referred to his papers and asked Emma about the meeting she'd been driving to, when she'd had her car serviced, what the driving conditions were like on the day and other questions that were designed, I knew, to soften her up before he built up to where he was really going. The bloody seatbelts.

I could have kicked myself. If only I'd told her about the stupid conversation I'd had with Sheila, she'd have been able to prepare. Here I was trying to protect Emms, and now I'd made the stupid ordeal a whole lot worse - and for what? For nothing. And all because Sheila's grief process needed closure.

Poor Emms. Seeing the solicitor question her was like watching a cat play with a mouse. Actually, it was a whole lot worse. At least a mouse knows what's going on. Emms was stammering and stuttering with no idea where this was going. I took off my specs and rubbed at the lenses with my scarf. Listening was bad enough; I didn't have to watch.

'I understand that the airbag on the passenger side had been disabled. Why was that?'

Oh yes. Another lovely open-ended question. He knew his stuff.

Emma said, 'Why was that? I have ... ever since ... ever since the twins were born, we have two children, you see, aged three.' She was speaking slowly, and then she suddenly speeded up as if the words were like bullets that she had to rattle out. 'Of course, we disengaged the airbag, it would have been extremely dangerous if an airbag had gone off and it could have suffocated one of our children if they happened to be in the front of the car, so we have always turned it off. Anybody with children who leaves the airbag engaged is risking a disaster.'

There was a tingling in my chest. I hauled myself to sit up straight in my seat to concentrate on Emms, not on what she was saying, but on her delivery. There was something wrong with it; my hand went to my mouth as I studied her.

I can't believe this. I'm wound up. I've had a bad night's sleep and Emms is anxious.

I waited for Sheila's solicitor to ask the next question. He was leafing through his papers, and the rustle of the sheets seemed to echo. Was he doing it to try to rattle her further? I tried to read the solicitor's face; had he noticed what I thought I'd seen?

He found what he was looking for, held up the paper and prepared to ask the next question. I could feel the undigested croissant and bile rising up in my oesophagus and swallowed down.

'How do you explain that the deceased wasn't wearing a seatbelt when he was apparently very safety conscious? Can you explain that, Mrs Harens?'

'Can I explain that? Of course, I can explain.' Emms spoke slowly, as if she was deliberately placing each word.

I shifted in my seat. She was doing it again. Repeating the question to give her time to think. Starting slowly while she held the solicitor's gaze and looked only at him. Only at him. Then, as she'd done with the last question, Emms picked up speed and justified her actions. Listening to her, I felt sick.

'Tony undid the belt because he was trying to take his coat off,' she said. 'It was hot in the car. How could I possibly know that I'd skid the car? How could I possibly tell him to keep his seatbelt on? He was the boss; you don't tell Tony to buckle up. I respected him. I wouldn't have wanted him to die for anything.'

It was like listening to the section in my psychology dissertation on verbal cues and deception recognition. There was no doubt in my mind, no question, no possible misinterpretation.

Emma was lying.

eleven

The verdict was accidental death. Somehow, Emma and I made our way to the car park. I say 'somehow', because my knees felt as if the cartilage and bone had been replaced by bendy rubber. I could have toppled over at any time. Fortunately, we were in a rush to get Emma to Woking train station as she had a central London meeting, and I was more than happy to drop her off without discussion. From her set expression, she wasn't interested in chatting, either.

Only at the station, when she got out of the car, did she make eye contact.

'Thanks.' She leaned into the car's open window. 'Thanks for the lift -- and thanks for everything.'

I watched her disappear into the station; overhead, the metal canopy glinted in the sunlight. It was only midday but I was exhausted. I headed back to the office via Ripley, gripping the steering wheel as if it could give me some stability in an uncertain world.

A wave of dizziness hit me as I turned into Ripley High Street, so I pulled up at The Talbot, a former coaching inn. I needed to eat and I needed to think. On the way in, I couldn't avoid the plaque that said that Nelson met Lady Emma Hamilton there for a bit of extramarital how's your father. Given the circumstances, how bloody apt.

I sat by the open fire in the bar and ordered a burger and a diet coke. Dark panelling, low ceilings, small windows and a corner by the fire where cheating lovers might have met. Emma Hamilton. Emma Harens. I sipped at my diet coke. I actually smiled. Talk about a sign. How could Emms possibly have fooled around with Tony? But there was no other explanation.

A barmaid brought my meal.

'Thanks, that looks great,' I lied. Now that the food was in front of me, I knew I would struggle to swallow. I took off my specs to shut out the world and focused on the plate. I cut small mouthfuls, chewed carefully and tried to get it down. For a few terrifying moments, I sat with fork in hand, frozen, and I was mentally back in the past to a time when I couldn't eat because of anxiety. My hand shook as I put the fork in my mouth, chewed and swallowed. I wasn't going down that road. No fucking way. I had to think.

If Emms had been having an affair with Tony and accidentally caused his death, it would explain a lot. But I still struggled to believe it. I mean to say, Tony? That was enough to turn anyone's stomach.

Not only was he a deeply unpleasant human being, he was also a good fifteen years older than Emms. Old. I never had old boyfriends. The alleged attraction of old blokes was a total mystery to me. But back in the day, Emma had a phase of them, Lord only knows why. Probably something to do with her ghastly father and a quest to replace him with a responsible male.

I remembered a riotous evening in an Italian restaurant. We'd finished eating and were drinking liqueurs. Emms had been applying lip-gloss to the mouth of a Scot who was down here for some sort of conference at Sandown Park. From across the table I could see him whispering in her ear. He was attractive, I gave her that - salt and pepper hair, blue eyes. He was also probably married (whatever he might have told her). He had that look. Emms and I had a conflab in the loos. She was swaying from the booze, fluffing up her hair and her eyes had the shiny look I associated not only with heightened excitement but also with her being irrational and intransigent.

'I've called a cab,' I said. 'It'll be here in ten minutes. You really don't have to go back to his hotel, you know. He'll survive, you'll survive. Nothing bad will happen if you get in the cab and come back home with me.'

'I must, I must, I must,' Emms leaned back against the sink. 'He's got this really cute accent and he's been saying the wickedest things to me. He's so hot.'

Next morning, my phone rang and, of course, I heard hangover voice in her groan.

'Where are you?' I said. 'Your mum's here, waiting to see you. I've just let her in and told her you've gone down the shops to buy fresh bread.'

Emma groaned. Again. 'Oh God. Why did you let me.... I'm looking out of the window, I can see a fucking red bus. I'm in London. How am I going to get back?'

We always laugh about that. The guy who wafted her off to London, how I covered for her and told her mother that Emms had nipped out to buy fresh bread, had a flat tyre and had to call out the AA. Who knows whether her mother knew, but that's the way it was. We covered for each other and kept each other's secrets.

But now I had to confront Emms and find out the truth about her and Tony, no matter how unpalatable it might be.

For a few days I tried to find the right moment to ask Emms, but the timing was always wrong. For one thing, we were racing towards the finishing line on what Emms called "the business plan of the century". But by the end of the week, the document had been both emailed and fedexed to our new boss in Canada, Marcus. It would be studied over the weekend and our budgets approved for the next three years. Not just our budgets, but also Sheila's pay-out. More than ever, this seemed like a priority to me. If Emms had been shagging Tony and this sordid affair had led to his death, then the least I could do was work towards the process that would make Sheila's financial future secure.

So "the conversation" was set for Friday lunch and I'd even prepared a crib sheet. That's how nervous I was about approaching the subject of Emms' fling with Tony. And I hoped it was a fling and nothing more.

My plan was to open with work chitchat, ease on into the personal with an update on Richard and enquiries about the twins and possibly the prevailing situation with mad Mairi, although I didn't want to get side-tracked on that subject. Bearing in mind the circumstances, I couldn't bring myself to ask about Greg. That would be much too difficult. I didn't want to hear any personal moments, good or bad. I didn't want to hear excuses or justification. I just wanted to know the truth.

But how to ask was where I kept stumbling. I thought of a dozen different ways I could phrase it. A dozen different styles, from the jokey inquiry to the interrogation. In the end, it just tumbled out. So much for my psychology smarts.

We were at Martin's, and had given our order to the Polish waitress. I'd bagged the table in the bay window and over Emms' shoulder I could see the busy little street and the metal tables and chairs refracting the sharp autumn light. As soon as she'd wriggled out of her coat, Emms positioned her phone to her right, where it sat on the red and white tablecloth. She brushed her hair off her forehead and unravelled the burgundy scarf around her neck, and then I could see the amulet at her throat. She must have been sleeping in the bloody thing.

By the time our food came, we were winding up the work-related part of the conversation. Sue, our receptionist, was gunning for a rise; she'd been hinting and testing the waters.

'I didn't say no,' Emms said. 'I said give us a few months to see how everything works out and in the meantime, write a job description and include what else you could be doing to justify a rise.'

'Fair enough. And a lot more reasonable than Tony used to be. Remember when you asked if you could work from home one day a week?'

Emms' head went back and she nodded. 'Oh yes ... how could I ever forget? He called me a part-time popsy and an ungrateful tart.'

'And we were all listening outside, but then it went quiet,' I said. 'And it went quiet because you'd thrown a cup of cold tea over him.'

'It shut him up,' Emms said. 'At least, for the moment. And I got my day a week working from home.' Emms looked thoughtful. 'Poor Tony. He really brought out the worst in me.'

I put my baguette down on the plate. The beef filling spilled out from the slices like a gossip's tongue.

'Emms ... were you ...? Was there something going on between you and Tony?'

'What do you mean?' She took a mouthful of soup.

'You know.' I gave her a look. She understood the question and although she didn't choke, she certainly had some difficulty swallowing.

'Me? Shag Tony?' Her raised voice and the urgency in her question made two middle-aged blonde walkers turn their heads. Emms was oblivious. Her eyes were shining and they bored into me. 'You are joking, aren't you?'

I shook my head. 'I could quite understand it,' I lied. 'He wasn't bad looking and he could be quite fun when he wanted to.' I was trying to help her and trying not to judge.

'For God's sake, Liz. Is this a wind-up? Regardless of Greg, that's absolutely gross. I can't think what would make you imagine that I would have entertained Tony in a million years. It's nightmarish.'

'So why wasn't he wearing his seatbelt?' I said.

'Okay, now I understand.' She put her spoon down and fixed me with an appraising look. 'You think that Tony and I were having an early morning canoodle on the way to the new offices. Is that it? Liz, credit me with some taste, and, more importantly, credit me with honouring my marriage vows. I love Greg. He's the best thing that's ever happened to me. The idea that I would cheat on him to fiddle around with Tony, of all people ... It's grotesque.'

'So why wasn't he wearing his seatbelt?' I repeated.

Emms sighed and leaned in to me so her lips were close to my ear. I felt her hot breath.

'He was having a go at me, you know how he was,' she whispered. 'He was going on and on, saying the usual stuff about being surrounded by idiots and how he had to carry us all, how we were nothing without him. And then he started rubbishing my driving, telling me to indicate, telling me to put both hands on the steering wheel, telling me to slow down. So I,' I heard Emms swallow before she went on. 'So I put my foot down and took both hands off the wheel. That's when he went berserk and called me a fucking crazy bitch.'

I pulled away for a moment and looked around the café. The walkers had gone, thank goodness. I glanced at Emms' face. It was quite white and her eyes were oddly black and shiny. Her hand was on my arm, maintaining our connection, and I felt the moist heat from her palm through my shirt as she squeezed and held on.

'Liz ... Liz ... I've been desperate to tell you ever since it happened. Remember in the hospital, when you said it wasn't my fault? You were wrong, Liz, it was my fault, because I lost it,' Emms said. 'When Tony called me a fucking crazy bitch, I just ... I don't know what happened. Yes, I do ... I slammed my foot down and went even faster, because I could tell he was getting really scared and I thought, I'll show you, you bastard. Just once, Tony Day, I'll show you what it's like to be scared of someone else. So I took my hand off the steering wheel again and he was totally freaking out, screaming and swearing and shouting. And the car was bucking and bouncing on the speed bumps. And then I ... I put my hand down and unclipped his seatbelt, just to scare him a little more. Just to see if he might piss himself. I wanted him to piss himself with fear. That's when the car went into a skid and ...' Emma let go of my arm and looked me in the face, squaring up to me, looking into my eyes. She pushed the hair back off her forehead. 'I really didn't mean to kill him, Liz. I just wanted to scare him till he pissed himself.'

Somehow, and I don't quite know how, I managed to give Emms an empathetic smile - the therapist's nod, as if to say, 'I'm cool with that; how do you feel?' But it was as fake as fashion. The expression "gob-smacked" comes to mind as I searched around for an appropriate response, but in the end I said nothing. Why? Because I didn't know what to say to her.

At the very least, Emms had admitted to manslaughter and dangerous driving, and this was not simply someone on a cell phone, phoning home to find out what time dinner was and driving into some hapless pedestrian. Emms had undone Tony's seatbelt. What's more, everybody knew Tony was a bully, and it wouldn't take a top-ranking crime prosecution unit to turn the events into a charge of murder. Even worse, I'd supported Emms' account of the events in the police interview at the hospital.

I'd happily agreed with her that Tony was a wild kind of a guy who wouldn't wear a seatbelt and was forever undoing it. What did that make me? An accessory? Fantastic.

Given that we'd also inherited the company and were already benefitting financially, the police might even think we'd planned it together.

I had every reason to be "gobsmacked".

twelve

An hour later we were both back at the office. I was sitting at my desk staring blankly at a document that made no sense, but Emms seemed relaxed. She was locked into a relationship with her keyboard and the screen, inputting figures and shifting them around with her mouse. A small smile crossed her face. For a few seconds, watching her moment of absorption in what she was doing, I felt resentful that she had passed this pile of shit on to me to deal with. It was like an obscene pass-the-parcel, and I'd been the one who had unwrapped it and found the truth about Tony's death inside.

I sighed and the outtake of breath released some of the stress in my body. The reality was that I had asked Emms. In other words, I had held on to the parcel and I had opened the bloody thing. It was now my responsibility to deal with what I found there in whatever way I could, because if the situation had been reversed, I knew that Emms would have done the same for me.

I cancelled my date with Richard by text, saying I felt under the weather – a statement which was the understatement of the year. He sent back a flirty, 'I'm a doctor, I'll rub your back' text but my libido was somewhere around my toenails and I certainly didn't want to respond to any 'How was your day?' questions.

After thirty minutes more at the office, I left, muttering something about research, and drove home. I wanted to take a bath. It's something I only do when I feel lousy, and never in the middle of the afternoon on a weekday. But there I was, lying in the water, blinds down and drinking tea, the warmth seeping into my flesh, soothing and softening my muscles. I gradually relaxed and found some focus.

Of course, I should contact the police. However much of a shit Tony was, he didn't deserve to die. That sounded ridiculous. Didn't deserve to die? Who the hell does deserve to die?

I pulled myself up out of the water, my body squeaking against the sides of the bath. Through the blur of my spec-less eyes, I could still see the ring that Emms had given me. It was on the little chest of drawers where I stuff my toiletries. There was no point going to the police. It wouldn't bring Tony back. Emms and I were working round the clock to make sure that Sheila got her pay-out; if we were defending ourselves against a manslaughter or murder charge, it would achieve absolutely nothing except make Sheila into not just a widow, but a poor widow. But I couldn't ignore what Emms had told me. I couldn't let it go, pretend it hadn't happened, pretend I hadn't heard.

Or could I?

In fact, when it came right down to it, right down to that hard line, I could. Because that's what friends do. It was like that old clichéd joke, 'Does my bum look big in this?' Men have learnt that the answer must always be 'no'. Well, women already knew the answer; they have always known; pretending is one of the deep truths of friendship. We do it in the playground: 'Let's play pretend,' little girls say to each other.

There were times, back in the day, when Emms was drinking a fair old bit and doping just a tad to keep going - to pay the mortgage, to get to work, to have a bit of a life - when she was wild. Actually, we both were. There was a conveyor belt of boyfriends, we played loud music and our neighbours loathed us.

I remember once, when it was wintertime and there was a rare, deep snowfall outside the house. Stalactites stuck to the guttering and our world had become monochromatic, like an old photograph. On the street outside the flat, cars slipped and slithered across the ice. I was indoors. I didn't need to go out except to play in the snow, which was our plan for the afternoon, when Emms came home after her Saturday morning bookkeeping job.

From my first floor bedroom window I was watching for Emms to return and I saw her trying to manoeuvre her low-slung Honda into a space, driving over the banked-up snow, skidding then reversing. Her wheels spun and I cast around my mind, trying to think of something we could use to break up the ice. Then, I thought of a bread knife. Still looking out of the window, I was pulling on my boots when some woman in a 4-wheel drive deftly nipped into Emms' spot, turned off her engine and climbed down. I saw everything. With her bag over the shoulder of an ankle-length coat, the fur-hatted woman marched down the road in her snow boots, completely unaware that Emms had thrown open her car door and was struggling to catch up with her. Emms was wild. Finger wagging, face contorted and through the window, over the snowy sound-muted air, I could hear her shouting.

'Come back here and move your car! That's MY space!'

Without thinking, I ran out of my flat, scuttled down the stairs and was outside. I slipped on the icy path and righted myself just in time. Up ahead, I saw the woman's face. It was contorted with fear as Emms pointed her finger and shouted.

'Emms,' I called out. 'Leave it!' I managed to get to Emms in time and I pulled at her sleeve, 'Come away,' I said. 'It's a parking spot, that's all. It really doesn't matter. There are others - look. Come away Emms, leave her alone.'

I felt Emms' rigid muscles under my fingers but she turned to me. After a couple of seconds her set expression melted. The rage in her face softened and her anger seeped away. Up ahead, the woman unfroze, and then sheepishly sidled off, no doubt relieved that the threat was over. Arm in arm, Emms and I walked back to her car.

We've always laughed about that incident. Emms' red mist rage and my tugging, pulling, wheedling her back to reality - saving her before she nutted a complete stranger. At the time, we put the irrational fury down to exhaustion and an amphetamine hangover, because that's what friends do. We all do it: we reassure each other and we put the negative down to externals - to traffic, bad luck, star signs, biorhythms, other people. We tell our friends, 'It's not your fault - it's him. He's the bastard,' 'It's not your self-indulgence and sloth that makes your arse fat, it's your metabolism.' And we don't just do it about being fat or picking the wrong men. That's the problem. We accommodate our friends to the point where we nurture each other's illusions, we're complicit in our friends' view of themselves, and we play "pretend" to protect each other's vulnerabilities. So, I could and I would pretend that Emma hadn't told me that she'd unclipped Tony's seatbelt.

Marcus, the Canadian general manager, had come back to us with detailed notes on the business plan, and we had a scheduled time for a Skype conference call to discuss the numbers. Although I was physically present in my capacity as joint managing director, this was Emms' territory and we sat in our new meeting room with the smart TV on the wall, ready to beam us across the Atlantic, waiting for the call. The room was mostly white, the meeting table a white laminate surrounded by white swivel chairs with arms that tilted and twisted. The only colour was a massive, gouache painting; a turquoise tossing river ran diagonally across the canvas with a green wriggling bank and blue stick trees against dark rocks and red blobs of indeterminate origin. It was a nightmare landscape, another world, another planet, but it was an arresting image, all ominous energy and distorted turbulence. I wondered who'd sourced it and whether it was supposed to stimulate our business nous, or if someone had simply liked it. On the other side of the white laminate table, Emms flicked through her colour-coded folders, and as the minutes ticked by, I could see her straighten her spine and square up her shoulders, ready to do battle with Marcus.

At the agreed time, the phone on the big screen trilled and it was party time; I saw Emms in her element. She really is rather good at this. Confident, fluent and fast. She and Marcus had a willy-waving mental arithmetic interchange when they discussed composite blah, and even though I didn't have the faintest idea what they were talking about, I could tell that they had shared a special moment in the most positive way. Marcus was even smiling, showing his perfect North American orthodontic work, and if you liked his type of preppy symmetry, he was quite attractive. After about fifteen minutes the call was winding up.

'Thanks, Emma, if you could just reshape this and come back to me with a new version, we can sign off on it when I come to the UK next week.' Marcus said. 'I'll even buy you guys dinner, eh?'

'Terrific,' Emms said. 'That will be great.'

'So I've got a window on October 31 7pm Manchester. The airport. I'm flying back at 11pm so we can have a bite before I catch the red-eye.'

Emms stiffened in her seat; she twitched to attention as if she'd just been shot with a rigor mortis drug. I pulled myself out of my distracted slump. What was this all about? Why was she so suddenly tense?

'I hear what you're saying, Marcus,' Emms paused and her hand went to the amulet, where she tapped out her sodding stress semaphore. 'The thing is, Marcus, we're pitching to a new client on the thirty-first and we won't be able to get to Manchester in time.'

'So let Liz do the pitch. You're the numbers maven. She's the performing seal, eh.'

Thank you very much. I smiled pleasantly, more interested in Emms' agitation and her lies. As far as I knew, there was no new client pitch scheduled for the thirty-first.

'Unfortunately, I really need to be there for this particular client,' Emms said. 'It's in the financial sector and I don't think Liz will be comfortable with the terminology.'

Thank you very much again, Emma. Not only was she lying but she was also using my financial ignorance as an excuse. Nice work. Even though I truly don't give a monkey's what people, least of all Marcus, think of me, I was ever so slightly peeved. What's more, Emms needn't have bothered rubbishing me. Marcus's hand stretched towards the camera, 'In that case, you'd better reschedule the client pitch. See you on the thirty-first.' The screen went blank. Emms said nothing.

'Emma, would you care to explain why you just lied to try to get out of –'

'It's Halloween, Greg and I have been up till 1am every night this week, secretly making costumes for the kids. It's the first year we've thought they were old enough to go trick or treating and I didn't want to miss it. What a total bastard.'

I took off my specs and cleaned them on my tee shirt. I wasn't sure whether the total bastard was Marcus or Emms' reflection on the turn of events. She abruptly stood up and jerked into a pace across the room, her gaze bouncing around as if she was looking for something that wasn't there. Then she stopped, inhaled and slowly exhaled.

'You were right, Liz, this is pay-back for the Faustian pact of becoming MDs of the company.'

'Faustian pact? Lighten up, Emms, that's completely ridiculous. Next you'll be saying it's the evil spirits of Halloween who are going to come out wrapped up in sheets or whatever they're supposed to do.'

'You're right. It's the demands of the business. It's what I signed up for, I can't whine about it now.'

As fast as the tension had come it had gone, which was a good sign. Emms collapsed into the chair and threw her legs up on the boardroom table. I noted that she had even polished the heels of her dumb black courts. She took a swig from the water bottle, wiped her mouth with the back of her hand and stabbed the air as she pointed at me.

'That's what makes you a good friend. That's what makes you the best of friends. You warned me this was going to happen and that the business would take over. And now that it has, you haven't said, not even once, "I told you so". Not even once. For that one thing alone, I love you, Liz Verrall. You are the best friend anyone ever had and I'm bloody lucky to have you. I know you'd never let me down.'

'I haven't done anything, beyond allow you to call me a financial half-wit in front of Marcus.'

'You know what I mean.'

Emms' mobile pinged with an incoming text, and she reached for it, 'That's Greg. He's going to be so disappointed if we don't all go together; he went to three shops yesterday to get red lining for Robbie's black Dracula cape.' Emms read the text, shut her eyes, pulled her arm back and hurled her mobile at the painting on the wall. It hit the canvas and clattered onto the wooden floor.

'And now we've got Mairi coming for dinner tonight.'

thirteen

The drive to Manchester is boring, and since Emms was keen to do the long run in her new Golf, I didn't insist. Yes, there was a moment when I thought about Tony, in another passenger seat, in another car, when I wanted to tug onto a hanging thread of fear, and pull at it, but I didn't, because it would unravel my calm and there would be no benefit for either of us. As we hit the charcoal-grey asphalt of the M1 and swirled into the traffic, I could see Emms relishing the activity involved in powering along, anticipating traffic ahead and feeling the car respond to her commands. She's a good driver, and she was enjoying the new car, not to mention the new mobile we'd picked up that morning to replace the one she'd smashed against the wall of the meeting room.

So Emms drove, leaving me to enjoy the changing landscape, trees in leaf and colour, green to gold, gold to red, red to copper, and the sheer, clear sky.

'You know, we haven't done anything like this for years,' I said, searching through her alphabetised CD collection and finding children's nursery rhymes and a yodelling CD that looked like a holiday souvenir.

'What? Had a Thelma and Louise moment? But without the attempted rape and murder.'

We were quiet for only a moment, but it was long enough for me to realise that Emms must have been pretending that everything was okay just as much as me. Neither of us wanted to think about Tony and how he'd died. For a moment, it was like being back in Hersham Road, where my marriage and Emms' family were on the unmentionable subject list. With the ease of muscle memory, we knew what the other was thinking; that if we don't talk about it, it can't hurt us.

I took a deep breath, 'Anyway, if Marcus approves the new figures, which I'm sure he will, then Sheila gets paid out – handsomely. And then we can put the whole thing behind us.'

I didn't need to say any more. Emms took one hand off the steering wheel and scrabbled in the door compartment. She pulled out a bag of liquorice and chucked it into my lap.

'Open it. Let's chew on that,' she said. 'To Sheila's big fat pay-out and her happy future.'

The packet crackled as I ripped it open and the liquorice was sweet and salty. Today was going to be a good day.

Even the Halloween problem had been resolved. Greg was going to take trick or treating photographs at every single doorstep. Then they would watch them all together when she came home and they'd have a second Halloween evening.

Everything was fine until we arrived at the airport hotel and Emms phoned home.

We had adjoining rooms with an interconnecting door in the grey box, bleak-outlook hotel, and as soon as we'd checked in, I took a fast shower and dressed corporate casual. For me that meant clean trousers, clean tee shirt and ankle boots instead of trainers; if Marcus didn't like it, it was just too bad. Since it was still early, I sat on the side of the bed and texted Richard to say I'd arrived, then tried and failed to open the window to get rid of the over-circulated air that was like stale breath.

By then, it was almost time to meet Marcus, so I knocked on the unlocked communicating door into Emms' almost identical room. It had the same grey walls, the same grey and red carpet, the same flat screen TV attached to the wall, the same complimentary tea set and no doubt the same Bible in the bedside drawer. It was any-room, in any-hotel, in any-town, on any-continent. But for one difference. Her room stank.

I sniffed; it smelt tangy, of chemicals. Then I spotted a bag of anti-bacterial wipes and Emms with one in her hand. She was wiping the surfaces and door handles as she paced up and down with her new mobile phone clamped to her ear. How long had she been secretly cleaning? How many wipes did it take to make a room smell that foul? This was a bad sign; I resolved to take it up with Emms, but only after the meeting with Marcus.

Besides the whiff of disinfectant, Emms had made the room her own in other ways. She had exchanged the pillowcase on the bed (I recognised the raised pattern, it was part of my wedding gift to them). The hotel's discarded pillowcase was folded up on the coffee table. Was the bed linen exchange simply a nod to making a strange room homely or was it another bad sign? Of course, I knew, and I felt a quiver in my stomach. On the sofa, Emms had laid out the clothes that she would be wearing that evening. They were arranged left to right, in careful, parallel lines, presumably in order of how she would dress: pants, pop-socks, bra, trousers, shirt, shoes, jacket. The tidiness was nothing new, since Emms is organised to the point of obsession but at what point does tidy and clean become OCD?

When it affects your life.

I felt chilled and wanted to get out of her room, away from the tang of anti-bacterial wipes and her jittery presence.

'Ready to go?' I said. 'Let's not keep Marcus waiting, he's not the kind who will take it well.'

'I don't know where Greg is.' Emms took the phone away from her ear. 'I've been phoning and phoning and all I get is voicemail. He should have been back by now, so I can't understand why he's not answering unless he's managed to get the kids in the bath early and is trying to get the face-paint off them.' She looked at her watch, then at me. 'I haven't got time for a shower now, have I?'

'Not unless you can shower in five minutes. Don't worry, you'll be fine. It's not as if you're going to get up close and dirty with Marcus, is it?'

Emms sighed. 'Okay, a bit of lippy, splash of scent and I'll brush my hair, but if I can just get through to Greg, I'll have time to say goodnight to the kids. Let me try his mobile one more time, I'll put it on speaker phone and they can say good night to Aunty Liz.'

In the smelly, grey hotel room, Emms' mobile trilled three times before Greg answered it.

'Thank you, that's very kind of you.' Greg's voice spilt out of the handset. In the background, I heard a buzz of other voices and a peal of excited adult laughter. I knew that laugh. It was Mairi. Mairi was laughing. Mairi was with Emma's husband and children, and she was laughing.

I could barely stand to look as Emms' white-knuckled hand gripped the phone and she rocked from one foot to the other. We waited for Greg to speak and overheard a muffled, but explanatory conversation.

'Really kind of you,' Greg was saying to someone who replied faintly. And then I heard Rob. 'Thank you Mrs Atkins. I hope we didn't frighten you –'

'Too much!' came a disembodied voice that could only be that little minx, Tessa.

At the sound of her children's voices Emms' knees buckled and she sat back down onto the edge of the bed, her grip on the phone loosened and she held it in her lap, white-faced and wide-eyed. Only then did we hear Greg's voice leaking out of the phone.

'Emma, Emma, are you there?'

She lifted the phone as if it was a heavy weight and spoke into it.

'Yes ...'

'How was the drive?' Greg said. 'Sounds like you made good time. What's the hotel like?'

Emms' voice was flat, cold and tired. 'Why are you trick or treating so late? Why aren't you back home? It's nearly seven o'clock, Greg. The children should be in bed.'

I frowned at her. Why didn't she say what must have been uppermost in her mind, which was what the hell was Mairi doing there? It's not her family; they're not her children. Why was Mairi going around Emms' neighbourhood with Emms' husband when Emms was a three-hour drive away?

'I know,' Greg said completely unaware of Emms' distress. 'But Mairi turned up in her very own witch's outfit. It's hilarious. And they're all having such a great time. I've taken some amazing pictures.'

I took off my glasses and polished the lenses against my tee shirt. I felt like plugging my ears with my fingers or going back into my own room, but I couldn't leave Emms. I couldn't leave her listening to Greg. There was an ache in my throat as I heard Greg's disembodied voice, along with the children's excited squeals in the background and the gurgling, throaty, peals of Mairi enjoying her night out.

'And don't worry Emms, we're keeping a tight rein on the sugar consumption. I don't know what I'd have done without Mairi holding on to the bootie in her witch's bag.'

I really couldn't believe it. What on earth was the matter with the man? Greg was talking about Mairi and him as a team, as "we". As two people who do stuff together, who share things, ideas, plans, adventures, experiences and children. He was completely unaware that traipsing around the neighbourhood with his kids and a woman who was hitting on him was in any way inappropriate.

I shrugged and smiled at Emms. From being white, her face and neck were now flushed as if she was sunburnt or, as was actually the case, heart burnt. I tapped my fingers against my watch and nodded towards the door. Emms nodded back. Her voice when she spoke wavered.

'Greg, Greg, listen to me a minute. I don't care how good the pictures are or how much the children are enjoying themselves –'

Another peal of Mairi's laughter escaped the mobile and spilt into the room like a noxious stain.

'Take the children home, Greg.' Emma's voice broke. 'Please take them home.'

'Are you okay, Emms? What's the matter?

fourteen

By drinking more than the single glass of white wine I usually allow myself when entertaining clients, I survived dinner. In other circumstances, it would have been a pleasant evening in the wood-panelled restaurant, with its white starched tablecloths and bustling serving staff. Marcus seemed determined to be charming and share spreadsheet moments with Emms. But of course, instead of swapping format minutiae and debating the benefits of business algorithms, Emms was, if not clinically catatonic, certainly brain-fucked, as a direct consequence of her phone conversation with Greg, out on the Halloween strut with his frolicking sidekick, Mairi.

Ever since Emms had first introduced me to Greg, in a Thai restaurant in Fulham, I thought he was as close to perfection as any man could be. He wasn't just a good guy, he seemed to get her and love her for what she was, but either he hadn't noticed what Mairi was doing or, worse, he didn't care. Was Greg really that stupid or so unfeeling?

So, for the duration of the dinner, I had to cover for Emms and be the life and soul of the party, which is why I drank far more than I normally do and overate as well. Fortunately, Marcus contradicted my expectation of a buttoned down preppy who only drank green tea, necked vitamins and worked out to a schedule on his computer. Maybe he was as anxious as I was, sitting next to catatonic Emma and opposite my wine glass-toting self.

By 10pm we'd bundled a squiffy Marcus into a cab to the airport in plenty of time to catch his flight and had negotiated our way back to the hotel. Once or twice, I had to steady myself on Emms' arm and even in my sense-dulled state, I was aware of the muscle tension in her body. Taut sinews stretched beneath her arm, and she walked with a stiff, jerking gait.

'You okay?' I said as we parted outside my room.

'I'm just fine,' she said.

'Sure you are? Do you want me to come in with you?'

'I'm fine. I'm going to phone Greg and you get some sleep. And you'd better drink some water before you do. I'll see you in the morning. Thank you.' She stroked my cheek with her finger as she held my gaze.

I don't know how the conversation went because I did as I was told and gulped back half a litre of water from the hotel's minibar. I tore off my clothes, left them in a heap and staggered to the white-tiled bathroom where I threw up, partially down the loo. The remainder of the undigested chocolate pudding and wine spattered the toilet seat, the walls and my feet. It was hot vomit. But I did feel better.

It took quite some time to clean up both the bathroom and myself but once I'd had a shower, brushed my teeth and was in bed, under the clean sheets, sipping more water, my thoughts turned back to Emms. Everything was quiet next door.

It was still quiet next morning when I woke up, mouth like picked-over road kill, craving salt and sugar. I tapped on the intercommunicating door but there was no reply.

'Emms?' My voice was croaky. I cleared my throat and tapped again before I opened the door and stepped inside. The room was empty. No luggage, no clothes lined up on the sofa, no special pillowcase. And no Emms.

My head was thundering and my hands went to my temples as if to steady it on my neck. Where the hell was she?

Not only was there no Emms but also the bed hadn't been slept in. The only evidence that she'd even been in the room at all was the tell-tale tang of disinfectant and the waste paper bin that contained her discarded anti-bacterial wipes. Emms' current chemical signature scent hit the back of my throat and made me want to puke again.

I lurched back into my bedroom and found my specs. Maybe she'd sat up all night and was now downstairs having breakfast. Or she'd packed up, left her bags with the concierge and gone out for a walk to clear her head. Or maybe, the unthinkable. Something had happened to her.

I tried to swallow and my throat closed. Get a grip. She's okay. Clenching my jaw, I slumped onto my unmade bed, still warm and crumpled. If something had happened who would I call first? Greg - three hours away? The police? How long do I wait before I say that my friend, who was exhibiting signs of acute anxiety and had had an emotionally disturbing episode, had disappeared? Reaching for my phone, hand shaking, I checked the time and my messages. It was eight thirty; there were a couple of texts from Richard and, blessed relief, an email from Emms.

Sorry. I didn't plan to drive off and leave you but I just had to get home. After dinner last night I had this really stupid conversation with Greg on the phone. He just didn't get it. He said she just turned up on the doorstep and he thought it would be unkind to turn her down. Yep – unkind. Can you believe that? But that's my Greg all over.

I just lay in bed and I thought, if she's half the scheming bitch I think she is, she's not going to miss this heaven-sent opportunity of me being away overnight. So I packed up and checked out, had a dreadful drive back and then found Greg fast asleep and snoring.

So now I'm upstairs, back in Darkbridge, having abandoned you, my best friend in Manchester and convinced Marcus that I'm a useless prat who is struck dumb in a social setting.

Liz – tell me ... big, big question ... you know me, I've known you for many, many years. It's time for that 'what your best friend can't tell you' moment. But you have to. You have to tell me. Do you think I'm losing it? Am I going bonkers imagining things that couldn't possibly happen? Or do I have reason to be suspicious?

Get the plane. It'll be faster. I need to talk to you.

Always love,

Your friend, Emma

Faced with the bald question, I didn't know how to respond. Yes, Emma was behaving oddly. Let's face it, undoing Tony's seatbelt because she wanted to terrify him could certainly be considered to be on the outer reaches of odd behaviour. I might be pretending that it hadn't happened but there's only so far that make-believe can go, and I'd reached the limit. The facts were that Emms had lost control of her temper and driven Tony through the windscreen. Did that make her bonkers? Did it make her insane? If the definition was being a danger to herself or other people, she had certainly been a danger to Tony, to put it mildly.

My head was hammering as if someone holding an earth thumper to my right eyebrow. With eyes barely open, I felt my way to the bathroom and found some paracetamol in my wash-bag. I gulped them down with water and returned to the bed to lie with my eyes closed, in the dark of the bedroom, waiting for the painkillers to work.

Listening to my breathing, I went back to the puzzle. Was Emms' behaviour actually mad? Of course, there was the issue of her obsessive superstition and rituals surrounding the amulet round her neck, never mind the potential OCD of her wiping every bloody surface with foul-smelling anti-bacterial wipes. But loads of people do stuff like that and continue to function. What is the fine line that you have to trip over to be considered bonkers?

I sipped some more of last night's lukewarm water and felt it slither down my throat as the tablets began to smooth out the throbbing in my temples. Soon I would get up. Not now, but soon. A steaming shower would unknot my neck, a full English breakfast would settle my stomach, and then I just might be able to start thinking about how to get back to Darkbridge.

Meanwhile, my mind drifted from Emms to Mairi. It had only been a couple of weeks ago that Mairi had been bleating about it being her birthday and that nobody loved her or would care if she died. At the time, I was amazed by how patient Emma had been and how kind to tell Greg to buy something. I wouldn't have done anything like that. I would have told Greg that if Mairi stepped in the house, I'd step out. Or would I?

Who knows? You never know until you're on the spot. Would I have undone the clip on Tony's seatbelt? I certainly had violent and hostile feelings towards him when he was bullying Sue. And I relished seeing him wet and contrite when Emms threw her cold tea over him. But what would it take for me to risk his life? Was she even thinking that at the time?

Eventually, I got myself up and into the bathroom and then down to breakfast, and I thought about what I was going to say to Emma all the way from Manchester to home. When I arrived in the office after lunch I was still undecided - which was just as well, because Emms had completely forgotten.

Before I could put my coat down or pick up the mail, Sue pounced on me.

'What's up?' I said.

Sue shifted around on the spot as if she had done something wrong. 'The BACS payments with our wages haven't gone through to our accounts and they're supposed to be there.'

'Of course they're supposed to be there.' The effort of speaking was bringing on my headache again.

'Then everything's okay? Because Brendan and I thought that maybe if the payments hadn't come through then there might be something ... something ...'

'Emma forgot. I'll deal with it now.'

I still hadn't taken off my coat and, don't forget, I was also hung-over. I threw Emms' office door open and she looked up from her computer and nodded. 'You've gotta see this, Liz. You have got to see this.'

'What? The bank's been blown up, which is why you didn't put the payments through?'

'No. I'm doing something much more interesting. I'm trying to find out who Mairi Sondergaard really is. You're not going to believe this but she told Greg that she changed her name to honour her dead sister - that's why I haven't been able to find out anything about her. Mairi Sondergaard isn't even her real name. Who changes their name? It's nuts, completely nuts.'

'Emma, listen to me for one bloody second!'

I never shout. I never, ever shout, but I was shouting at Emma. 'You forgot to do the payroll. Sue and Brendan and the rest of them are imagining that we're going under because you forgot to authorise their salaries. What's the matter with you? How do you think they're going to pay their mortgages if you're obsessing about this bloody woman and anything else you can find to act out on.'

The fog lifted from Emma's face and she pushed back in her chair.

'What day is it?' she said.

'What day is it? You are asking me what day it is when you drove me mad with this Halloween performance. You wanted this company, Emma. You wanted to run it. You said you had a million ideas to make it better, and now you're pissing it down the drain starting with not paying the people who work here, the people who are trying to support you, and that includes me.'

'I'm sorry. I'll do it now.' Her hand darted to the mouse and she clicked and tapped, dancing with her fingers, skipping across the keyboard, rattling the plastic keys. She sighed. 'I've done it.'

She stood up and walked past me to the door, opening it and put her head out.

'Sue, I'm so sorry. It won't happen again, I promise. Please tell Brendan and the others.'

Emms came back in and sat down. She clasped her hands in her lap. 'I'll make it up to them in their Christmas bonus. They shouldn't have had to worry because of my cock-up. I told you I was losing it, didn't I?'

I stood watching her, trying to understand her.

'How's everything at home?' I said.

'Big row with Greg this morning when he caught me checking his mobile for messages from that woman. Nuclear row to be precise. I told him that I thought Mairi was fake because I couldn't find out anything about her and when you Google her nothing comes up, and I mean nothing. And then he comes out with Mairi bloody Sondergaard isn't her real name anyway. Like I said, she changed her name by deed poll to honour her dead sister. I mean, come on, Liz – is that nuts or what?'

Emms' face was wide open, begging me to understand her point of view.

My mouth opened to speak, and then it shut again. I nearly told Emms, but I just couldn't find the right words. And it didn't feel like the right time to tell her that eleven years ago, I changed my name by deed poll.

fifteen

It had been easier than I expected.

The court hearing had established a non-molestation order but my ex-husband had continued to phone and harass me and hang around outside the flat where I was staying. He would phone thirty times a day and say nothing when I picked up. I just heard his breathing at the other end. Hot, raspy breathing and the wet, gulping sighs of the drunk. And then he sent flowers, left them outside the house with messages, 'I will never give up,' 'Till death do us part,' 'Love transcends life'. Those were a few of the favourites. At first I took in the flowers, but because they arrived daily, it didn't take too long before my flat looked like a funeral parlour, and living among the flowers did little to help me maintain my tenuous grip on sanity. It scared the shit out of me.

He'd dumped her. Or so he said. The woman he'd been fooling around with, the woman he'd moved in with. I didn't believe him. I didn't believe for one second that he'd wised up and realised what he was doing when he kept disappearing with increasingly poor excuses. I knew with total clarity that once she worked him out, she'd turf him out. And of course, she was right. If he'd screwed me over, then it was only a matter of time before he would have done exactly the same to her and to whoever came after her. John was that kind of guy.

I knew a bit about her. She had a huge job in the city and he'd met her at some work-related function. She was a power fuck. In other words, a million miles away from my struggling post-graduate student status. A million miles from the sad sack he repeatedly put down and, on occasion, physically hurt.

After she dumped him and he came back, I wanted out, more than anything I'd ever wanted in my whole life. But he wasn't having any of it and he made my life a misery. So I changed my name by deed poll.

One of the most satisfying moments in my entire life was when I'd packed up and left the house, I had my new name and I phoned him from a phone box to ensure that there wasn't the slightest chance of him tracking me down.

'I've left the keys under the mat, John, because I'm leaving you – for good.'

'I'll find you, you know that: I'll find you wherever you are,' he said.

My throat closed up and the hand holding the phone was soaked with sweat. 'No, you won't. I've made damn sure of that. Make the most of this phone call, John, treasure the moment, because this is the very last time you will ever hear my voice.' And I put down the phone.

In that way, Liz Verrall was born. Verrall means truth. And that was one truth I'd never told Emma, because it belonged to another time, when I was another person. A mad, scared, jealous person, who behaved irrationally, did things I regretted, and needed a friend. Desperately needed a friend.

Now it was my turn to be the friend I wish I'd had back then.

The truth about my identity was another thing I wasn't going to tell Richard. If I hadn't told Emms, I certainly wasn't going to tell him. What for? Why rock the boat? He didn't need to know that Liz Verrall was a made-up name, particularly when I am and have legally been Liz Verrall for eleven years. And especially when he'd texted to say that he'd booked a table for a proper Saturday night dinner date. Why ruin the evening?

It was the day after Guy Fawkes' Night and the air was cold and damp and stunk of sulphur as we headed down the A3. Inside Richard's car all was sleek and humming; the leather seats were smooth and even heated, giving me the sensation that I'd wet my pants, but in a good way. I closed my eyes and for what seemed like the first time in a few days let pleasant thoughts fill my head.

'Where're we going?' I said, eyes still shut.

'I thought I told you,' he said. 'An Italian restaurant near Newlands Corner. I thought we might be able to watch some fireworks go off from the top of the hill before we eat.'

Newlands Corner is on the edge of the North Downs and from the top there is a real sense of the landscape tumbling away into the lush green valleys of England. This was where Emms dreamed of living in the house on the Shere Road with the massive oak tree. I shuddered, remembering what Emms said about being buried under the oak tree.

'Are you alright?' Richard said.

'Of course. Did you know that when Agatha Christie disappeared, her car was found pushed over the edge at Newlands Corner?'

'No and I can assure you that I have no similar plans.'

'I love it when you sound stuffy.' I saw him smile in the dark of the car. Things were going well between us; we were developing our own private language of jokes and glances and shared moments. And also no-go areas.

'There are a few lovely villages around here,' Richard said. 'Shere, Albury, Abinger Hammer, Friday Street. Did you know that Stephen Langton, the Archbishop of Canterbury who pushed through the Magna Carta, was born nearby?'

'I prefer my Agatha Christie mystery.'

'Funny girl.' He caressed the words and I skipped a heartbeat.

After a cursory walk around the car park at Newlands Corner where the damp, cold air ate into my bones and my empty stomach growled, we settled at Carlo's. Of course, I knew that there was something up with Richard. He was fiddling with his napkin in an uncharacteristic display of tension and swallowing slightly more than usual.

'So what is it,' I said. 'You've either got some news or you want to ask me something. Let me think, you want us to be in a pub quiz but you're frightened to ask if I can handle the music questions. Is that it?'

'No.' He put the napkin down. 'I have some news and a suggestion. Actually, not even a suggestion, a mere thought that I'd like to put to you.'

'Go on.'

'I know the arrangement was that I didn't talk about my soon-to-be-former wife; however, I want you to know that I will be legally single in six weeks.'

I folded my arms. I'm not sure what I expected him to say; in my defence there had been a few other things going on in my life. But I wished I'd known this was coming up before I was faced with Richard across the table expecting some sort of positive response. I felt cornered, got at and uncomfortable. Richard was watching me carefully,

'So I was thinking,' he said. 'What if we became a bit more of what I believe is colloquially termed "an item"?'

'Meaning?' I knew I sounded aggressive, but I couldn't help it.

'We could go away for the weekend or even, perhaps ... I could come with you at Christmas to Florida.'

He'd been dropping hints ever since I'd told him I was going, saying how much he'd always wanted to go to the Florida Keys and follow in Hemingway's footsteps, how he loved the humour of Carl Hiaasen, the romance of Key West, the drama of Key Largo, but I'd been unequivocal that it was a big step. A really big step - and he was technically married.

I didn't want to get hurt. I didn't want to start relying on him being around and then for it all to go tits up. Better solo, single and strong, and a holiday of shared memories was too much, too soon.

'Can I think about it?' I said. 'I mean, it's only been, what, five weeks, six weeks. You know very little about me, you haven't even met my friends.'

'Easily remedied. How about next weekend,' he said. 'We could come back here if you like?'

So that's how I found myself, a week later, to use another colloquial term, "double dating". It had been a good week all round. My row with Emms after the trip to Manchester seemed to have settled her. Perhaps, like a child, she needed some tough love in order to establish a sense of security. She had assurances from Greg that he loved her and was not about to embark on an affair with Mairi. And she had boundaries set down by me to stop obsessing about Mairi, whatever her bloody name might have been, otherwise the business was in danger of going down the toilet.

Before the double date, there was some to and fro. Greg suggested that he cook dinner back at theirs but I was insistent that I wanted to be somewhere neutral. I was concerned that Greg would be overly protective. Or overly welcoming. Or just overly. Let's face it, I was nervous. This was the first time I had ever introduced Emms and Greg to a man I was sleeping with, and it mattered. I wanted them to like Richard and for Richard to like them.

We'd had a lovely day. Richard had done his Saturday morning outpatient clinic at St Luke's and then come over. We'd had a walk along the towpath, coffee and a sandwich in a café, we'd watched the swans and the people, speculated about who they were and what they were doing and then we'd gone back to mine for an afternoon nap and afternoon sex. Afterwards, Richard wrapped his arms around me and kissed the tops of my ears, muttering incomprehensible words. It was as if I was his very own cuddly toy and he was sharing a secret language.

Is this what our life would be like if we lived together? Would we share a haven of laughter, warmth and safety? Or would it all unravel?

When we arrived at Greg and Emms', we were ushered into the sitting room, where Greg had laid out home-made canapés and a bottle of Prosecco in a bucket. Greg and Richard shook hands in what I can only describe as a hearty, manful manner, and I could see Greg sizing up the taller Richard as he poured him a glass of fizz. It was the inspector's glance; the examiner's crinkled brow; the teacher's raised eyebrow. But Richard did well: he didn't look flustered, he didn't look irritated. He was consciously trying to get Greg on side. Only the small detail of his raised shoulders indicated that he knew he was under scrutiny and felt uncomfortable with it.

'Home-made canapés,' I said to Emms when the men were out of earshot. 'I'd have preferred a packet of crisps.'

Emms shrugged and whispered, 'Be grateful you've only got a few nibbles, I'll go up and settle the kids. Mairi is babysitting, which has been enough of a bribe to make them promise not to come down.'

'Mairi?'

'It's term time and it's Saturday night.' Emms said. 'She's the only one available. It was either Mairi or Greg's seven-course tasting menu.'

After Emms left the room, I helped myself to one of Greg's fancy bites and looked at the little pools of light filling the small room and the fire spitting sparks in the grate. It was domestic and harmonious, and I was regretting the decision to meet there. However, on the plus side, Richard and Greg were almost talking properly, without circling each other like animals on a wildlife programme. Besides Mike, the blind date gym jock, Greg and Richard had found someone else they both knew, as well as a shared interest in Hard Rock. I could see from the set of Richard's shoulders that he was starting to relax. Equally, Greg had stopped gibbering - stopped asking questions and not waiting for the answers and seemed much less suspicious. Greg had even told Richard about his new business venture and how the nursery would soon be in profit.

Since everything was going so well, I took the opportunity to go to the loo before we left and I was heading towards the end of the narrow hallway just as the doorbell rang and Emms clattered down the stairs.

'It's the sitter,' Emms said. 'I'll get it.'

Through the closed door of the downstairs loo, I heard Mairi's voice raised at its usual pitch of excitement. For a moment, I pondered about what her real name might have been. It had to be something more prosaic than Mairi Sondergaard, which was a handle that suggested icy fjords and Viking maidens. But then, who was I to talk when I'd buried my own birth name?

I washed my hands, careful not to jog the kids' animal toothbrushes in their pot, and applied a little more lipstick. Just a dash; Richard had already expressed his preference by saying he liked to kiss lips, not petroleum-based chemicals. I looked okay, bright eyes, that sex-exfoliated clear skin look. My hair might not have been in alluring tendrils, but it was shiny and bouncy. I'd pass.

I pushed open the lock and stepped out into the hall, just in time to see Emma closing the front door. Her face was contorted, eyes squeezed shut and yes, she was tapping the amulet. Something fluttered in the base of my stomach. Not now, Emms. Please not now.

'What's up?' I said. 'Are you okay?'

Emms' eyes were still shut, but she did nod.

'You're sure? Everything's okay with Mairi? She hasn't let you down for this evening at the last minute?'

She nodded again and opened her eyes, 'No, Mairi is here but -'

'No buts. If Mairi is here then let's round up Greg and Richard and get going. It's going to take a good twenty minutes to get there. Come on, I'm ready for food.'

From upstairs I could hear thumping feet, squeals and Mairi's yelps of delight confirming her presence. Just then, Greg appeared in the hall carrying a tray with the finished drinks.

'Nice bloke,' Greg said as if Richard wasn't there.

I looked at Emma's face and at the front door.

'Did Richard just go?' I said to Emma.

'Yes. That's what I've been trying to tell you. There was an emergency at the hospital. He said he would call you later.'

'Really?'

'Yeah,' Greg said. 'Who'd be a doctor? No chance of me running out the door to attend to someone's tax return.' He squeezed past us with the tray, but Emms was still holding my gaze. Something was wrong.

We were locked together watching each other. Noise came from the kitchen as Greg loaded the dishwasher and noise came from upstairs of Mairi reading a bedtime story. Snatches of magic and beanstalks and princesses wafted down the stairs as we stood in the darkened hall, a pool of light from the table lamp casting Emms' face in hard sculpted shadow. It was as if we were in a world between the worlds, a no-man's land away from the warm domestic clatter in the kitchen and story-time upstairs with the kids.

'What the hell's going on?' I said.

Greg appeared in the hall, a silhouette against the light from the kitchen. He was waving a flyer in his hand. I prayed that it wouldn't be a flyer for the new nursery and I was heard.

'Since Richard isn't going to join us, how about we put the whole evening on hold and order some takeaway? I think it would be nicer not to go without Richard. What do you say?'

'Fine with me,' I heard myself say. I wasn't hungry and I didn't give a rat's arse what or where we ate, I just needed to get Emms in a corner and find out why she looked as if she'd found a dead body in the bath. Was she going into meltdown? Had the last few days just been remission before she really started to lose it?

Greg grabbed his leather jacket from the newel and called up the stairs: 'Mairi, change of plan, we're having a takeaway, would you like to join us?'

'Greg, no, please,' Emms hissed. Greg looked at his wife and frowned, then grimaced an apology.

'Sorry, I just thought it would be friendly –'

And he had no time to say another word. At the top of the stairs Mairi appeared. From our vantage point, she towered over us as if she was taller, mightier and more powerful than us.

'That would be lovely,' she said, descending the stairs, one step at a time.

'Any preferences?' Greg said, standing with the door open, no doubt anxious to escape Emms' baleful glare.

'I'm sure whatever you choose will be perfect,' Mairi said. 'You always know exactly what I like.' There was palpable energy emanating from her, waves of emotional static that made my scalp tingle, and with each step, her musky, earthy scent first flowed, then wrapped itself around us like a dark mist. Cowardly Greg nipped out, closing the door behind him. The latch clicked. Mairi had reached the bottom and now looked up at us.

She was wearing a long skirt and peasant blouse that made her look like an extra from Ben Hur and as usual, she stank of some really sickly scent.

'Shall I put some plates in the oven to warm? I know Greg loves to eat off hot plates. Come on, you two,' Mairi said in her nursery school voice, as if she was getting us out of the sandpit. 'Let's all sit in the kitchen and have a nice glass of wine before Greg gets back. How naughty would that be? We can have a girly chat and I can tell you all about Richard.'

Richard? Ice water spread through my veins. I looked to Emma for help, for her to deny, laugh, or mock, but her face said otherwise. Emms shut her eyes whilst Mairi gaily went on: 'Who'd have thought that Liz's new beau would turn out to be Richard, my ex-sex-monkey?'

My ears were ringing and I grabbed the bannister to keep myself upright. I heard Emms' voice. It was clipped and cold.

'How come you've stayed alive so long?' Emma said.

I didn't have to look at Mairi to know that she would be smiling. And I didn't want to see it. I wouldn't.

'Oh, have I spoken out of turn?' Mairi said. 'I'm so sorry but I thought Liz would have known about Richard's previous relationships. Surely he told Liz about us?'

At that, I lurched to the front door and stepped out, fishing for my car keys in my pocket. The dizziness hit me like a plank of wood as I walked to my car, those sodding high heels clicking, tapping, and echoing in my ears. To my right, it was dark, the dark of the green, the pond, the trees and the weeping willows overhanging the pond. For a second, I stopped and looked into the comforting gloom. Right across the green, lights were on in the social club and cheery voices carried in the still night. But immediately ahead it was dark, quite dark. Only the quiet black water of the pond.

I had to get to my car. If I got to my car, I'd be okay. Breathless, I struggled to inhale and although my hands trembled, I unlocked the car and collapsed into the seat, locking myself in, against I don't know what.

'NO!' I pounded my fist against the steering wheel. The pain shot up through my arm. I stopped and forced damp air slowly into my lungs. I exhaled as I rubbed my hand to ease the pain. This was all so unreal; how could Richard have been hooked in by that grubby troll? It was ridiculous, but it was the sheer impossibility of her claim that convinced me.

The hospital where they both worked: opportunity. His dysfunctional marriage: motive. And the means? Her little fuck-pad in West Molesey where they met when he lied to his wife about after-hours consultations. It was too much. Much too much.

My hand still throbbed. Trembling, I pushed in the key to start the engine and felt the car's vibrations through my body. In spite of the residual pain in my arm, I was clenching and unclenching my hands around the steering wheel. I didn't know who I wanted to hurt more: Richard, for making me think that it just might be okay to trust someone again and then dismembering that trust as efficiently as anything my ex-husband had achieved, or Mairi. If she'd had an ounce of humanity, she wouldn't have goaded me. She wouldn't have taunted me. What she'd done was cruel. It was more than cruel - it was sick, it was deviant. Yes, that was the right word – deviant.

I slipped the car into gear and edged out onto the quiet road, heading out of the village towards the

High Street. The restaurants were brightly lit, filling up with Saturday night revellers. Who were they? Where were they going? Were they being betrayed? My thoughts were like a merry-go-round, coloured horses, discordant music. Got to get a grip. Got to stop the music. Got to get control. Control the thought. Control the feeling. Deviant. That was the key. Deviant.

And then the music in my head stopped.

Mairi was deviant. I took a logic step forward and searched the catalogue of my memory for diagnosis. Narcissist, a primitive hysteric. Yes, that was about right – I placed Mairi in a box with a window for me to study her through; she was a specimen to examine, a sample to analyse. At that thought, a warm cloak of detachment settled on my shoulders and enrobed me in a cashmere caress. As for Richard, there really was no decision to make, except to control any emotional echoes of our affair. And an affair is all that it had been. How could I possibly describe it as a relationship, when that would imply a level of honesty that was simply not there? What was the matter with me? I sounded as stuffy and as stuck up my own arse as him. For a moment, the cloak slipped off - I had to gulp back a glob of pain and focus. Pull the detachment cloak back onto my shoulders and focus. Focus. Focus. Focus.

I took a huge breath of air. Summary. The sex was good enough, he was decent company, and we'd had a few nice dates. Nothing was lost. I still had my flat, my job and my best friend, Emms. Those were the things that mattered. They were the constants in my life that grounded me. Everything was going to be just fine. I was not going into a tailspin after a six-week shag.

sixteen

By the time I drove into the car park under my flat, I'd achieved some measure of equilibrium. In other words, I was functioning normally, which gave me a sense of satisfaction. Inside the flat, I threw open the balcony windows to the night air and listened to the distant hubbub of a party boat on the river. I let the noise of the revellers fill the flat with other people's lives. Once again, I was part of and apart from what was going on around me. It felt safe. Why should I put myself through the emotional wringer? What was to be gained?

I stripped the bed; I didn't pull the pillowcase to my face to smell his scent. Not this time. I turned on the TV and let it settle on some nameless game show where an audience was excitedly cheering a performer, a celebrity or some other joyous person. And I made myself a cup of hot chocolate. Then and only then did I check my phone and computer. I was pleased with myself.

Predictably there were missed calls and text messages from both Richard and Emms. Only hesitating for a second, only hovering my finger over the keypad for a moment, I clenched my fist and deleted all Richard's messages without listening.

But I did open Emms' email.

Dearest Liz, dearest friend.

Please tell me that you got home safely. A text will do, phone call better or email. I am still processing Mairi's announcement. I knew there was something seriously wrong as soon as she turned up. You were in the loo when she waltzed into the sitting room and Richard turned grey. He looked as if he was going to throw up and she did this sickening coquettish, head on the shoulder smirk and when Greg was doing his polite introduction thing, she said, 'Oh, Richard and I are old friends.'

So Greg, as ever oblivious, assumed they know each other from the hospital, offers her a glass of fizz and treats her like the human being she isn't whilst Richard was totally dumbstruck. But I really have to hand it to Richard. While Mairi was gushing about Greg's snacks, Richard muttered something, and asked me to tell you that he had to go and he would call you later.

And as said, Greg was completely oblivious. Amazing really.

Anyways, you would have been proud of me, I showed enormous restraint, besides which I wasn't going to tear her limb from limb with the children upstairs. After you left, I told her that we didn't need a babysitter and I asked her to go. There was a funny moment when she looked like she was going to insist that she stayed, but I opened the front door and stood there until she went out.

So by the time poor Greg came back with an Indian meal for four there was just me and, you know what ... I didn't tell him. I'm still not sure why. But it's a first, a first secret.

The thing is, I don't think it's Richard's fault and, key point, it happened before you met him. You did stuff before you met Richard that was in a different time and place, so why let the past screw up the present? Why not bury this stupid thing, forget it? Chances are, all it was a drunken fumble at the hospital Christmas party that Mairi built into some big romance. I mean, can you seriously see Richard being interested in her?

Anyway, love, just let me know you're okay and if you want me to nut her, it will be my pleasure.

Don't forget, I'm here. I'll always be here for you.

Always love

Emma

I typed back:

I'm okay. Promise. I can't talk right now and I can't explain why, but it's better for me if I dump Richard. Thanks. You're a good friend.
xL

In the darkness, I heard the email whoosh off and sipped at my hot chocolate. I needed to walk. In swift moves, I shrugged into my parka, grabbed my keys and reached the door. I'd walk to Kingston Bridge and back. I'd watch the river and the sky and find my space again. It was still early, not even chucking out time at the pub. An arm-in-arm couple marched past me, heading for Hart's Boatyard, no doubt. Hart's Boatyard - where love or, to be precise, lust took me by the hand and delivered me to Richard. Hardly. But a convenient way of making myself feel like a victim, if I chose to pursue that thought. And I didn't.

My head was full of questions like, do I tell Emma why it's better for me to dump Richard and why it would be damaging to try to make it work? Do I tell Emma my birth name and explain why the name Liz Verrall is unique? Do I tell Emma that giving Richard another chance would go against every single thing I've achieved during the last ten years? Do I explain that it would be like digging down to a time capsule, opening it with pathetic hope, but finding inside only misery and madness ... and I don't mean for one moment, the let's be wild and crazy kind of madness, I mean illness and pain.

Do I tell Emma that I was mad?

There'd been weeks of waking up in the morning, feeling fine for a moment and then having a suffocating pall descend on me. I was frightened to go to a cinema in case there was a fire, I eyed up emergency exits in restaurants, calculating the time it would take to get out if there was a bomb. I was scared in the Tube, sweating, trembling, imagining the weight of hundreds of tons of yellow clay crushing down onto the tunnel, the train and me; if I heard a low-flying plane overhead, my heart would start pounding as I imagined the bomb bays opening and the terrorist releasing his attack.

I went to the doctor.

In the crumbling waiting room, I had a moment's respite because I was doing something. The doctor would fix it, because that's what doctors do. They make it all better, don't they? But the balding middle-aged man was brusque, hurried.

'I'm having panic attacks,' I said.

'I see.' He delved into his scarred wooden desk drawer and extracted a sheet with small pink stickers. 'How long have you had these episodes?' I watched his white fingers peel off one sticker and fix it to the top of my patient's folder. He pressed it down, securing the pink round marker. It was now official. I was nuts.

'Two months, ever since things have been going really badly with my husband.'

'I see,' he said again, and then he reached for his prescription pad, scrawled and ripped and handed a script to me. He avoided making eye contact.

'Take these twice a day for two weeks. Don't drive and come back if there's no improvement.'

Truly, I don't know what I expected him to do in terms of making it all better, but a pink sticker on my notes and a script for tranquilisers wasn't what I'd hoped for. I emerged onto the grey street and caught the bus back to the house I was sharing with my husband. The big, inappropriate house that we were renting while John did his six-month posting. It had acres of parquet flooring that seem to attract dust. The washing machine had broken beyond repair and we were miles from a laundrette. I was a student, he was the breadwinner, and he dictated where we spent money. Have you ever tried washing sheets by hand? Don't.

That particular evening, after my visit to the doctor, it was raining. The car headlights swept across the window as John roared up the drive. I'd made a fire in the sitting room and was wrapped in my dressing gown and a blanket, trying to keep warm in the draughty house whilst I read one of my course books.

I don't remember what sparked off the row, I just remember John holding my shoulders and shaking me as if I was a doll, and I remember his face - his angry, scrunched up, booze sweating face.

'I've been out working, while you're sitting here all day and doing what? What exactly are you doing?'

'Studying' I said with a calm I did not feel.

His face was inches from mine and I could see the pores in the red skin. He pulled the dressing gown off my shoulders and started tugging at it, pulling it off me.

'Sitting around all day. I hate that fucking thing.' He threw it on the fire and walked out of the room. I heard the fridge door open as he helped himself to a beer. I scrabbled up from the sofa and pulled my dressing gown off the fire. It smelled, it was singed, but it was intact. I took blankets off the bed and made a nest for myself in the loo, where I could lock the door until I heard the front door close again and knew that he was going off to see his girlfriend. I knew he'd be back eventually, I knew he would stink of drink and of her. I still heave whenever I smell Samsara, that musky sexy scent; he carried it on his jacket, mixed with the smells of sex and soap. I debated whether to grind up the tranquilisers that I'd got from the GP and put them in his food. I even got as far as going to the library and looking up the effects of the quantity of pills I'd been given. I finally settled on putting a turd in a Tupperware container and posting it to his girlfriend, with my compliments.

But only after I left him.

And it took months to leave John, months of fear and shame, never mind the organising. I was not going to go through that again.

But it wasn't the violence or the shame that I feared the most. It was the madness.

seventeen

I suppose I have become adept at the skill and art of compartmentalising, closing down bad feelings, putting them in files, burying them in inaccessible corners – in other words, pretending. For Chrissake, I'd been pretending for two months that Emms hadn't unclipped Tony's seatbelt, so by comparison, relegating Richard to the post of non-person, into "Richard Who?", was a walk in the park. I told Emms his name was never to be mentioned again and I ignored his phone calls, deleted his texts and contact details. After two weeks, the calls stopped coming and I felt as if I had cleaned a piece of shit off my shoe. Easy to step into, a little harder to clean off – but nonetheless, it was do-able. Well, that's what I kept telling myself.

On good days I reasoned that what made me so angry was his appalling taste in shagging Mairi, but of course, I knew the anger was at myself, for letting him get close enough to hurt me. And like any grief process, I had to let it take its time. And life wasn't all bad, because I was going on holiday.

By now, it was a Saturday morning and mid-November. The build up towards Christmas was escalating and I was anticipating the seasonal hysteria with some satisfaction, because my ticket to the Florida Keys was booked and paid for. At 8am. I set off to the centre of Kingston to buy presents for Emms, Greg and the kids that would be distributed before I jetted off to the sunshine, to the Florida Keys, and a bloody good rest.

Greg was always easy to buy for - any food-related gadget or the latest cookery book would win a smile from him. Emms was harder and as for the children, that was the toughie for a non-parent, which was why at eight fifteen I was driving down the ramp into the car park at John Lewis so that I could grab a coffee and be first inside the store without being trampled by fellow shoppers.

In the semi-subterranean gloom, I found a space, and only moments after I'd locked my car, I was striding towards the lifts.

'Liz?'

My muscles tensed. I didn't turn round but I stopped, aware of the footsteps approaching. Before I turned round, I composed my features.

'Richard, what a surprise, isn't it Saturday morning clinic?' I could have kicked myself for remembering. 'Did you cancel it in favour of Christmas shopping?'

He looked his usual buttoned-up self but I noticed his lips were tight and white and around his eyes there was a new strained look. Or maybe that was the light.

'I followed you,' he said. 'I've been sitting outside your flat since six thirty this morning and I've taken the step of following you because I have to talk to you and you've ignored all my messages.'

'Really. Given that I have ignored your messages, did you consider that I just might not want to talk to you?' I said. 'Whatever you say isn't going to make the slightest bit of difference to the way I feel about you, so you may as well save your breath.'

'I do not expect – ' Richard broke off as a people carrier parked in the next bay and a family prepared to unload. 'Liz, I'm not asking you to understand, neither am I asking you to resume our ... to resume what we had. I'm not even asking you to forgive me, even though what happened was before we met ...' Richard raised his hand to make his point. 'Anyway, I'm not asking for anything like that. I just want to buy you coffee.' He looked over at the family who were now approaching - pram, toddlers, bags, and a family mass. 'I just want to buy you coffee somewhere,' he nodded in the direction of the family. 'Quiet.'

They trundled past us, the couple glancing our way and then at each other. It was obvious we were having a fight. I would have liked to have told Richard to fuck off and die, but if I yelled at him, ran off, or even got back into my car I would be the morning's entertainment and that didn't sit comfortably on my shoulders. I nodded at Richard.

'Okay.'

In silence we shared the lift with the family, and five minutes later, I was sitting in the near-empty café looking out over the river, watching swans manoeuvre through the choppy flow, whilst Richard brought the coffees. He placed the coffees down on the table and lowered himself with one movement. He didn't smile or attempt a charm offensive, and I couldn't help but appreciate that he wasn't trying to humour me. I certainly wasn't prepared for his statement.

'I want to warn you about Mairi.'

'Mairi?'

'To be more precise, I want you to warn your friends Emma and Greg about her. I know how important they are to you and I wouldn't forgive myself if I said nothing.'

I picked up my cup and swallowed a mouthful of the milky drink. Of all the things I'd been expecting Richard to say, this was not it. Pleas, remonstrations, excuses, but not this melodramatic warning.

'Go on,' I said. 'What do we need to know?'

Richard let out a long breath and pursed his lips before he spoke. 'She's dangerous, in that she manipulates people and is destructive - but that's not all. I think she's mentally ill.'

Hearing Richard confirm what I'd been telling myself - that Mairi's behaviour was deviant to the point where she could be diagnosed - had the oddest effect on me. I wanted to deny it. Because it was Richard telling me, Richard who had dangled the notion of a trusting relationship in front of me, made me slaver for it, and then snatched it away. Why should I trust anything he said?

'Are you suggesting that she's not safe with the kids?' I said. 'I understand she has all the necessary clearances and references.'

'If I had children, I wouldn't be comfortable leaving them with her. But it's really Greg you need to be worrying about.'

'Greg? I really don't think Greg is likely to fool around with Mairi, if that's what you're implying' I said. 'Besides the fact that he's devoted to Emms, he's a genuinely good man and not the type who's angling after a bit on the side and would shag anyone with a pulse.'

Richard's colour changed and I had the immense satisfaction of knowing I'd hurt him.

'No excuses. I thought I could help her.' He spread his hands out and looked at them, eyes down, not making eye contact. 'That's how it started. She was helpless, trying to get some computer skills, so I coached her and one night and only one night, I ... and then, and then, and then.' He shook his head as if could shake the memory away.

Finally he looked up: 'The thing is ... she stalked me.'

'You mean she sat outside your house and followed you? Let me think about that for a minute. You did say you were outside my home at 6.30, didn't you?' I couldn't help myself and he closed his eyes, obviously exercising some control, and thought about what he was going to say next.

'No,' he said. 'It was a completely different situation, because after this conversation, I will accept your decision and I will disappear from your life. The point I'm trying to make is that Mairi didn't accept my decision. She threatened me, she said she would write to the GMC and say I'd raped her, she left notes and letters on my car, she let down my tyres and she stood outside my house, under a lamp post, looking up at the house. Not just once, but night after night.'

'So she was angry, very, very angry because she thought there was something going on between you.' Part of me couldn't believe that I was actually defending Mairi, but that didn't stop me. I was pissed off at Richard.

'There's reasonable anger and there's aberrant behaviour. And you're right, she was entitled to be angry, so I met her and I tried to reason with her,' he said. 'But all that did was increase her psychosis.'

'Psychosis?' I said.

'Psychosis. She's been on and off anti-psychotics and anti-depressants most of her adult life.'

'So what? Half the population is and I think you're exaggerating,' I said.

'Do you think it's an exaggeration to tell her workmates at the hospital that we were secretly engaged, that we were going on holiday to find the perfect location for our wedding? That I'd introduced her to my family, who adored her, that she was going to have my mother's engagement ring, that my wife had already left me? And wherever I went in the hospital, I knew that she'd been spinning another tale. But I ignored it. I ignored the phone calls, the letters and the lamppost vigils. But the final straw was when Mairi door-stepped my wife and asked if she could look round the house to see how she'd redecorate when she moved in. I've never been angrier in my life. I wanted to kill her and I told Nicci the whole story. That's largely what precipitated me moving out. But the point is, Mairi suddenly stopped harassing me, she went quiet. At first I thought that having successfully brought my marriage to an end, Mairi had lost interest in stalking me, but I now think it was because she'd met Greg.'

'It's only a guess, though,' I said. 'I accept that Mairi's got a significant personality disorder or two, but what makes you so certain that Greg's in the line of fire?'

'Because Mairi is a prolific letter writer, and about a month ago she left her latest rambling missive on my windscreen. It described how she was starting a nursery business with her new boyfriend who was raising the finance, and how things were going so well between them that she expected to announce their engagement any time now. At the time, I thought it was a positive outcome for all sorts of reasons, not least, I have to admit, that she had transferred her obsession to someone else. And I did have a vestigial hope that perhaps she had found someone who might care for her, since I don't believe her to be evil, just – anyway, I even texted her to say that I was happy for her. But of course, you realise that I now believe her boyfriend is Greg.'

eighteen

Thanks to Richard's revelation, I'd completely lost any interest in Christmas shopping. What was the point of trying to find the right gift for Emms et al to open with glowing faces round the cheery Christmas tree? If what Richard said was true, maybe there would be no Christmas tree, maybe they'd be holed up waiting for Mairi to morph into Glenn Close in her immortal bunny-boiling role. As I plodded back to the car park, all I could think about was what a total bastard Richard was to dump this on me.

'Now what am I supposed to do?' I muttered to myself, loud enough to startle a passer-by. Once I'd got home, I took a pad and started jotting down notes with a pencil held between clenched fingers. It was a way of trying to organise my thoughts and also a way of delaying action. 'For fuck's sake,' I said aloud, this time satisfied that I wasn't startling anyone.

The obvious solution would be to take Greg aside and have a quiet word with him, tell him what Richard had said about Mairi and let him draw his own conclusions. But that notion was a complete non-starter, because Greg, living in his own happy bubble where Mairi was a sad little fairy that needed friends, was completely unaware that anything had happened between Mairi and Richard. If I told Greg about Mairi, I would be breaking Emms' confidence and that didn't feel right.

I was pressing so hard on my pencil, the end snapped and left a graphite powder trail on the paper. I flexed my hands, stretching out the tension, and the ring that Emms had given me caught the light. The pink of the stone was marbled, cool to the touch and rough. For a moment I stroked it.

I couldn't possibly tell Emms. I'd ruled out that idea way before I'd got back to the flat. Poor Emms, with her paranoid cleaning and superstition, was right on the edge of reason. I couldn't put more pressure on her. She was too fragile.

I uncrossed my legs and walked to the window to look out at the street and the cars down below. Mid-morning and it was overcast with a smothering blanket of cloud. There was something else that was nagging away, making me fidget. How did I know that Richard wasn't exaggerating? Everything he told me was hearsay; other people told him that Mairi said they were engaged and all the rest of the nonsense. Even the visit to see his wife might not have been exactly as he described. Ridiculous as it was, I found myself empathising and sympathising with Mairi, who'd obviously thought that their moment of love was significant.

And, of course, there was another issue that made me empathise with Mairi. Even though I wasn't dumped after a one-nighter with a married bloke, I had been upset, disturbed, devastated, okay, deranged enough, to follow my then-husband to find out where his girlfriend lived. What's more, I had threatened him, I had written letters saying I would kill either myself or him, I had phoned at 2am and not spoken to him and, yes, when I found out where he was shagging his girlfriend, I had also stood outside the flat. And what about the apogee of my anger, the turd in the Tupperware episode?

So what if Mairi was on medication? Loads of people are on something: it doesn't make them bad. It just takes the edge off overwhelming emotions so that a person can function. I'd been offered my own pharmaceutical solution during a difficult time. The only definite as far as Mairi was concerned was that she was incredibly annoying and she had a crush on Greg. She'd also been a spiteful fucking bitch when she told me with great relish that Richard had been her sex monkey. I wasn't going to deny that.

But what if Richard was stretching the truth to make it sound worse than it was so that he could punish Mairi for screwing up not just one, but two relationships? It wouldn't be very nice of him but, I'd only been seeing him for a couple of months - how well did I know him, anyway? Maybe Emms was right when she'd said I shouldn't shag him that first night and I should wait and find out more about him. Maybe he was a vindictive man who always had to have the last word?

Heat was rising round my neck, so I tore off my fleece to try to cool down and decided to put the washing on. I stomped around the flat and gathered up a basket, savagely stuffed dirty clothes into the drum, rammed soap into the container, and set the controls. Anything not to have to make a decision. I decided to go out, get some food in and watch a film and then I would decide what to do.

Of course, as I left the flat for the supermarket, I already knew that I wasn't going to do anything. It was like pretending that Emms hadn't unclipped Tony's seatbelt. Call it procrastination, call it cowardice, call it fear, call it hope that things would work out for the best if I didn't meddle – call it anything you bloody well like. I promised myself that I would watch what was going on, if necessary I would get Mairi into a corner and talk to her, but I didn't want to dance to Richard's tune and be the messenger who warns Emms and Greg. Why stir up a load of unnecessary anxiety for Emma by making unsupported claims based on what Richard had said? The way I saw it was, if I ignored what Richard had said, everything would be okay.

Of course, it wasn't okay.

I'd reckoned without Emma's cavalry-charging energy. As far as she was concerned, Richard was an entirely innocent victim of a scheming husband-grabber, and that was without even having heard his version of the events.

It was Friday, and we were having our regular lunch catch-up out of the office, but instead of

Martin's we were in Côte in Esher having a treat. Why? Because the numbers were looking good, we had won two new clients, our existing clients wanted yet more of what we had to offer, little Sue was going to get her rise and Tony's widow had just received another large cheque, with more to come. As Emms said, we deserved a treat for being good.

Côte is a British version of a French brasserie. It's got all the dark wood, banquettes and a little brass here and there, but the waiters are well-spoken English kids and it's a sharp operation. I made a note to contact their head office. You don't become that slick in terms of customer care and attention to detail without some significant internal training programmes.

We were late lunchers because the plan was to go home afterwards, so the restaurant had emptied out and we were spread out over a table for four. I'd ordered duck confit and, as ever, Emms had ordered soup of the day - but, because it was a celebration we started with kir royale. By the time the drinks came, Emms had done her ritual cleaning. Out came the anti-bacterial wipes from the depths of her workbag and she did both the table and the cutlery. The tang rose off the wipes and I winced: the stink was hardly an appetite-enhancing aperitif.

'Are you aware that stuff only works on colds and flu? It does absolutely nothing for Norovirus, which can live on surfaces for days and days,' I said, as I gulped a mouthful of the pale pink fizz.

'Killing cold and flu bugs is better than killing nothing, Liz. We can't afford time off, not when everything's going so well.' Emms had finished her knife and fork and was waving the wipe at me. 'Do you want me to do your cutlery?'

'No thanks, I'll take my chances.'

Emms placed the used wipe in a special plastic bag that she carried around in her workbag for this, and only this purpose. At the end of the day, she put the bag in the bin at work, and the next day she started all over again. Was it getting worse? It was hard to say. I reckoned that if her OCD was restricted to tapping her amulet and some extra hygiene, it was manageable, and, frankly, I had enough on my plate not to work myself up about getting her to see a therapist. I'd live with it. In two weeks I would be off to the Keys. My fantasies had ceased to be sex-related, but were all about driving along the Seven Mile Bridge. I just wanted to get through the next two weeks with the minimum of anxiety.

'So what are we going to do about Mairi?' Emms said.

'Nothing sounds like a good plan to me.'

Across the table, Emms put down her soup spoon and brushed her hair off her forehead. Here it comes. I forked some duck into my mouth and closed my eyes, not only to enjoy the dense texture and gamey flavour, but also to shut out Emms. If I could have, I'd have covered my eyes, ears and hummed a song.

'She dissed you,' Emms said. 'The bitch totally dissed you, never mind what she did to poor Richard.'

I snapped my eyes open. 'Poor Richard? Give me a break. He was cheating on his wife. Anyway, you promised not to mention his name. That was the agreement, wasn't it? Because I really and truly do not want to discuss it. I appreciate that Mairi is spectacularly annoying and a spiteful bitch to boot, but I'm not going to "do" anything about her.'

'Oh go on. We could send her a letter from the goblin world and tell her that her three wishes are up and she has to come and live with the little people. Or ...' Emms paused, thinking. 'I know, we hire some really big bloke, dress him in a green outfit and get him to stomp up and down outside her house and do "Fee Fi Fo Fum, I smell the blood of a Mairi's bum". She'll freak.'

I had to laugh. I pitched in. 'Okay, I've got a better idea. How about we get a mirror and stick a voice-activated recording behind it so that when she goes, "Mirror mirror on the wall who's the cutest girl of all?" it talks right back at her and gives her an earful.'

'I like that,' Emms waved at a passing waiter. 'Two more kir royals please.' Then she turned back to me. 'We're on a roll here. What if we stand outside her house dressed as pink pigs and try to blow it down?'

'Maybe ... might get arrested. How about re-enacting Sleeping Beauty? I'll be the fairy godmother and –'

Emms interrupted: 'I'll stab her so she falls asleep and doesn't wake up.'

I paused. Emms wasn't smiling, but then she did and everything was fine again. 'Just a joke, but my, those fairy tales are violent.'

We had two more kir royals after that and ordered a taxi to take us both home. The car dropped Emms off first and outside her house there was a dirty purple Clio.

'The witch is already here,' Emms said heavily. 'Now you really have to come in and share. It's Christmas cake-making day, and the kids insisted that Mairi should come round to stir the mixture and have a wish.'

'I'm going home,' I said.

'Please,' Emms took my hand. 'Just come in for half an hour. I don't want to go in on my own.'

At the front door, Emms stretched her lips into a smile and took out her keys. Even through the coat, I could see her muscles tense, and her knuckles were white as she turned the key in the lock. Seconds later Tessa barrelled towards us squealing with pleasure, arms outstretched: 'Mummy, Liz, come, come now. You have to make a wish.'

Emms knelt to the floor and buried her head in Tessa's little arms. When she stood up, she let the three-year old hang round her neck and carried her through to the kitchen.

'Hi, everyone,' Emms said. 'Look who I've brought back with me.'

I surveyed the scene and took it all in. Greg was standing at the kitchen table with the bowl of mixture in front of him and a big wooden spoon. He looked flushed; it was hard to say whether it was the heat, alcohol or something else. Nearby, Robbie stood on a chair supported by Mairi, who bled energy and joy. Everything from her sparkling eyes to her soft skin and the tilt at the corner of her mouth telegraphed inner bliss. I glanced at Emms to see how she was taking it. Her jaw was clenched, the skin was bunched around her eyes and who could blame her? This was the first time I'd seen Mairi since date night, and if she'd been in my house, I couldn't have stood it.

With one hand around Robbie's waist, Mairi guided his spoon round the cake mixture.

'Good boy,' Mairi said, as if Robbie was a performing dog. She looked up at Emms, smiling full on, head thrown back. Was it my imagination? Did Mairi look triumphant? Emms' hand stole to the amulet and she tapped it. 'Well done,' she croaked.

All concentration and effort, Robbie stirred the mixture using both hands, tongue poking out of the corner of his mouth, as if to steer the spoon in the right direction.

'Your turn next, Emma. But first of all we're all waiting on Robbie ... you have to make a wish now. A big, fat, juicy wish, with bells and songs and happy, happy thoughts.'

All my carefully contained emotional management went south. How dare that bloody woman stand there in Emms' house with Emms' children and Emms' husband as if she had the right be there? It was outrageous. Emms was catatonic and I don't know what the matter was with Greg, he just looked like a rabbit, hypnotised. But there was no stopping our Mairi, oh no: we were all in pantomime land with the magic princess.

'Close your eyes, darling,' she said to Robbie. 'I'll hold you safely in my arms and whatever you do, you mustn't tell us what the wish is or it won't come true.'

Robbie closed his eyes and his long lashes kissed his soft cheeks. His tufty head of hair and check shirt was like Greg but there the resemblance ended because Greg, with his hands stuffed into his jeans pockets and his lip biting, was a picture of anxiety and something else. Guilt? Was I wrong about Greg being a paragon? Was he as flawed as Richard?

'Well done, Robbie,' Mairi said. 'Isn't this great? Now it's your turn, Mummy and Liz, but before you stir the cake, you have to have a strawberry-covered chocolate, we saved them for you, didn't we?'

'Thanks.' I accepted the warm strawberry and slightly melted chocolate from Mairi's hand and couldn't help noticing her gnawed, grimy nails.

'I'll save mine for later,' Emms said and placed the chocolate on the wooden worktop. 'I think it's my turn now, I've got a big wish.' She caught my eye.

'Have one for me, Emms,' I said.

Emms took her turn at the bowl and accepted the spoon handle from Mairi. She closed her eyes as she shifted the spoon round the beige lumpy mix. Around she went, three times and I had no doubt that she was wishing with all her heart that Mairi would drop down dead.

'What did you wish for?' Greg said.

'Now, you know I can't tell you that,' Emms said. 'Otherwise it won't come true, will it?'

Greg slipped his arm round Emms' waist and squeezed it; he was murmuring something into her hair. Something warm and intimate and loving, the type of easy affection they had between them that was usual to see at the end of their dinners when Greg had drunk a lot of wine.

'You been at the cooking sherry?' Emms said as she pulled away.

'Cooking rum looks more like it,' I chipped in, pointing at the bottle of Morgans on the worktop. 'Never mind, Greg, your wife has been at the kir royals this afternoon, so don't take it.'

'I confess,' Greg said. 'The rum went into the cake and I spilled some.'

'Really?' Emms made full flirty eye contact with Greg. 'Did you happen to spill any into your mouth by any chance?'

'Maybe ... cook's prerogative and all that.' Greg kissed the tip of Emms' nose. It was a sweet moment, and I glanced across at Mairi to see how she was taking it. Both Mairi and the children were watching, the children in expectation of whose turn it would be to stir the cake and Mairi with an expression that I couldn't fathom. She was still. Quite still. But she was thinking, thinking about what to do next and then, as I watched her, she slowly raised the wooden stirring spoon to her mouth and licked off the cake mixture with a red tongue.

'This is unbelievably delicious. Oh my God, it's so good,' Mairi said. Emms and Greg were still holding each other so Mairi went on, 'I think it's Greg's turn, isn't it?' And with that she stuck the spoon back in the mixture.

Result. Emms sprang away from Greg. 'You can't do that. You should never, ever lick a spoon and stick it into anything. How do you think germs are spread in the kitchen if not by poor practice like that?'

'Oh ...' Mairi looked at the spoon, now stuck upright in the mixture. 'Any bacteria will die when it's baked ... won't it, Greg?'

'Why are you asking Greg?' Emms was almost hissing, teeth clenched and I could tell she was trying not to shout, because the effort of not shouting was making her scarlet. 'You do not do that, Mairi. It's poor hygiene and that's not what I want my children to learn.'

'Easy, Emma,' Greg said. 'But you're right. So what I'm going to do is take the spoon out of the mixture, like this and ... ' Greg took a spoon from the drawer and scooped out the mixture around the wooden spoon. 'There we are, that's all the bacteria and germs.' Holding the spoon aloft, he carried it to the food waste bin and shook off the mix. 'There. Problem solved.'

'I'm so sorry,' Mairi said, once again, directing the comment to Greg. 'How incredibly stupid of me. I'm having a terrible day apologising to you, aren't I?'

Greg turned red. I glanced at Emms but she had her back to me as she was at the work surface, bagging up the bacteria-laden cake mix to take out to the bin. She missed Greg's stricken blush. But I didn't. What the hell had been going on?

nineteen

Do you ever have the feeling that you're trying to blot out the pictures in your mind and they keep crowding back in, bigger and brighter, and with more detail? Much more detail. That's what was happening to me. Images of Mairi's red tongue, her winsome expressions and Greg's guilty look shifted and slotted around my mind like a split screen film with Richard's voice-over about Mairi's stalking and threats. The more I tried to distract myself, the more they flooded back with preternatural colour and sound bites. I heard myself groan. How could I have been so stupid, stubborn and self-obsessed not to see it?

I was lying on my sofa, under the throw, with only the light from the TV in the room. Head against the end of the sofa, I was near the cushion with the faded pattern where, during a babysitting episode, little Tessa had her Jackson Pollock moment with a magic marker and I had to use bleach to lift the stain. I hadn't told Emms about that, either.

I was trying to watch TV, trying to concentrate on colour, moving images and the fictional dilemmas of the characters in Downton Abbey. The narrative made absolutely no sense to me; I simply couldn't follow it. The remote control was on the shelf above the TV and I was too stupefied to get up and change channels to find a programme that was less challenging and where the patterns were clearer for my distracted mind.

Ultimately, it was all about patterns. I had been so busy looking out for the repeated patterns in my own life, worrying that Richard was another man like my ex-husband, that I hadn't supported Emms enough as Mairi wormed and wheedled her way into the family. As Emms had presciently said, "Just like Aunty Jane."

I'd only met Aunty Jane once and that was after Emms' mother's funeral. For some reason that I don't remember now, we were meeting Emms' father, Kenny, at a solicitor's office in central London, Piccadilly. Aunty Jane's little business suit was slightly too small, her red nails slightly too shiny and her curly fair hair slightly too fixed and glitzed with hair spray. Every time Kenny said anything, anything at all, Aunty Jane either put her head to one side, frowned and nodded or, if it was supposed to be amusing, tinkled a laugh.

And that's what the pattern was: Aunty Jane – Mairi. Mairi – Aunty Jane. But Greg wasn't Emms' father. So why had he gone red?

I took off my specs and rubbed the bridge of my nose. I couldn't do anything about Aunty Jane. I couldn't do anything about my husband's ex-girlfriend, but I might be able to do something about Mairi.

But what?

I'd have to tell her to back off or else. The "or else" needed to be significant and also something that I really could deliver. I sat up from my supine state and turned off the TV. What would make Mairi back off? She wouldn't care if I told Greg about her affair with Richard, because she would still have her connection with the nursery. I'd have to threaten to close it down. Could I really do that? It didn't matter. I just had to convince Mairi that I could, tell her that I would hire a detective, dig up the dirt, present the evidence to Greg and, more importantly, to the parents of the February intake at the nursery. Would you want your child to be at a pre-school run by someone who had a history of mental illness and stalking married men? It was dirty, but I was sure it would work. Of course, if I had to deliver on the threat, Greg would never speak to me again, but I was prepared to do it, because it would break the pattern. It would break the pattern of the past destroying the present.

In the course of twelve hours, the weather ratcheted down from cool autumn to cruel winter, and when I woke up the next morning I could see snow-filled grey clouds billowing with the moisture that was forecast for the morning and the weekend. After I'd read the papers and was watching the first snowflakes drift down, I phoned Emms to suggest a Saturday morning coffee and to tell her that I'd come round to the idea of doing something about Mairi and I had a plan. But I was checked.

'Can't talk,' Emms said. 'I'm at the garden centre, shopping for Christmas and I've got to get back before the snow. Have you seen the forecast? There's a storm coming in. Have you got food?'

Heavy snow would mean that the minor roads would be impassable for days. I would just have to tell Emms when I saw her but as it happened, that wasn't to be. As predicted, the snow came, the temperature dropped, there was black ice, warnings to avoid unnecessary journeys, plus another big snowfall dump on Sunday night, and I had to get to Kent for a two-day training course with a new client. By the time I got back to Surrey, it was Thursday and I was on my way to the children's Christmas concert, which would be the last time I'd see them before I went to the Keys.

Even though it was bitterly cold, the main roads were now clear and most of the minor roads were passable. My presence at the Christmas show was part of my godmother duty, because Tessa had the lead role as the Christmas Tree Fairy.

We were in the village hall on plastic seats and it was bloody cold; overhead bar heaters pumped out warm air, but all they did was take the temperature from icy to uncomfortable. But on stage Tessa shimmered and sparkled like the snow outside in a dove grey and white tutu and the palest grey tights. She pranced around the stage, pointing her wand and bringing the Christmas presents to life. She glittered, and it wasn't just the sequins. I nudged Emms, who sat rigid by my side.

I whispered, 'You know she's actually rather good.'

Emms just nodded. Her profile was taut, grim. Maybe she was worried that Tessa might tumble or she was controlling motherly pride, or there was something else going on. I didn't know. By her side, Greg was holding up a camcorder and recording the action, a smile on his lips. Next to him sat Theo and Daphne, Greg's parents, rugged up in coats and hats and scarves, looking uncomfortable. And at the end of the row, by special invitation from the children, Mairi sat, with her lips partially open, knees tucked under, apparently mesmerised. She yelped and squealed at the appropriate moments and at the end, she stood up, arms overhead, clapping, trying to lead a standing ovation for Tessa, which was exactly what a star struck, wilful Tessa needed. And I don't think.

By the time we reached Pizza Express in Esher High Street for the post-show supper, Robbie had ditched his beribboned Christmas present costume. However, no surprises, Tessa refused to change, with a level of determination that was non-negotiable. The compromise was for her to wear her grey fleece over the tutu and Ugg-style boots, so now she looked like a cross between a teddy and a fairy with her red hair tumbling down her back.

A server showed us to our table and Tessa skipped ahead, holding her wand aloft and pointing at the other tables. She was attracting a lot of attention, and the minx loved it.

'Tessa, come and sit down,' Emms said. 'We need to order some food.'

Tessa hesitated, assessing the situation and just how much she might get away with. A table of Christmas revellers were exhibiting all the signs of admiration and a woman, slack-faced with drink, was nudging her workmate.

'What a beautiful little girl. Are you a fairy, sweetheart, are you a Christmas fairy?' the woman said.

This was all the encouragement Tessa needed to do her prancing, wand-poking dance around the table.

'Tessa,' Greg said. There was a warning note in his voice but absolutely no reaction from the little diva. Then Mairi sprang forward and before Emms, or, indeed, anyone else could respond, she was scuttling across the floor. 'I'm coming to get you, fairy princess,' Mairi said as she grabbed Tessa in a cuddle, gave a quick curtsey to the delighted table and carried her back to the table.

I caught Emms' expression. It was frozen, and that wasn't just the cold. Her face was a mask of pain and I knew I would fail as a friend, fail as a protector, fail as a human being if I did nothing. Before the afternoon was out, I was going to lay it right on the line for Mairi; her attempt to move in on Emms' family was over. This was not going to happen again.

So for the duration of the meal, whatever Mairi did, however often she referred to herself and Greg as "we" and kissed and touched and gushed over the children, it didn't bother me. Even when Mairi talked at embarrassing length about how grateful she was to be included in family celebrations, I was sanguine.

'Thank you so much,' Mairi said, eyes filling with tears. 'You are all so kind.'

I looked across the table at Daphne, Greg's mother. She smiled and nodded.

'Sweet of you to say so, dear,' Daphne said clearly not meaning it. Oh yes, Daphne had her number. Emms may have been unlucky with her own father, but her in-laws are the best. Daphne was frowning as Greg reached for the red wine bottle and filled up his glass again. Trust Daphne to notice that Greg was knocking it back, more than usual. Meanwhile, Theo looked out of the window at the gathering dusk. In many ways Theo is Greg's mirror image, but balding and slightly hunched, as Greg will be in thirty years' time. Like Greg, Theo is droll, kind and apparently susceptible to Mairi's brand of helpless femininity.

'You're more than welcome, Mairi,' Theo said. 'Too bad you're both going away for Christmas.' He smiled at me. 'You might have joined us for dinner. Our other son and daughter-in-law are coming down from Scotland. Mind you, who knows if Liz will be able to get to Florida and you to Devon if there's another front of snowy weather.'

Mairi laid her hand on Theo's arm and kissed his cheek. In spite of my good intentions to remain unmoved, I winced, noticed by Daphne.

'You are a dear, dear man,' Mairi said. 'I'm honoured that you would even think of including me.'

'Why not? You're one of the family,' Theo said. 'Now if we can just get the bill and get to the car, we might have a chance of getting home before it snows again.'

Five minutes later, we were standing outside the restaurant watching Theo and Daphne pick their way across the icy pavement: hunched figures, eyes on the ground, searching for the next treacherous step back to their car. Now was my chance. I would walk Mairi to her car and put the hard word on her. In words of one syllable I was going to explain to Mairi that whatever Theo may have said this evening, she was not, and never would be, one of the family.

Outside Pizza Express Greg was stamping his feet, 'Wow, how cold do you think it is?'

'They said it would go down to minus five tonight,' Mairi said. She was looking even more eccentric than usual in a bobbled hat with reindeer around the top, blonde strands escaping and a white quilted ski coat, under which she had a thick jumper with yet more reindeer across it.

'Where are you parked?' Greg said.

'Near the town hall,' Mairi said.

'So am I,' I chipped in, even though I was actually on the green. 'Come on, Mairi, let's get going before we freeze.'

Mairi knelt down to be at the same height as the children. 'Goodbye my darlings,' she said. 'You were both utterly brilliant. Magnificent. It was the best Christmas show I've ever, ever seen.'

Tessa and Robbie smiled, one shyly, Tessa as if it was her due. 'Bye kids,' I said. 'Have a great Christmas.' Hugs and kisses were exchanged, and then Greg picked up Rob. 'Let's get going before we freeze. Speak tomorrow, Mairi.' He was moving off.

'Oh God,' Emms said. 'I'm so sorry, I nearly forgot. Just in case we don't see you before you go to Devon.' Emms pulled out a box from a plastic bag and thrust it at Mairi. 'They're chocolates. But please don't wait till Christmas, as they are far too good to share.'

How typical of Emms to feel sorry for Mairi and give her a present, no matter what Emms was feeling. Myself, I wouldn't have given Mairi a glass of water in the desert, never mind homemade chocolates.

'Thank you so much. That is so unbelievably kind of you,' Mairi said.

Greg was five yards away. He called back. 'Come on Emma, we really have to get indoors before we freeze to death.'

And now it was my turn.

'Mairi, why don't I buy you a Christmas drink?' I said.

twenty

We were silent during the walk from Pizza Express to the nearest bar. It was too cold to talk. Even through scarf and gloves and hat, you could feel ice fingers clawing at your skin, trying to peel it away, trying to reach your bones. It may have been -5 but the wind chill made it seem a whole lot colder. As I glanced by my side, I saw Mairi bobbing along in her white snow-boots and white quilted coat like a little snow-woman. I stumped my boot on a gob of frozen snow and nearly lost my footing. Recovering my balance, I felt Mairi's hand in the crook of my elbow, steadying me, supporting me, saving me from another tumble. Being so close to her made the hair on the back of my neck do the can-can.

But dancing neck hair or not, I was going to make Ms Sondergaard, or whatever her name really was, abundantly aware of the consequences of her actions. Shit. That sounded like a Richard expression – the sort of pompous, up your own arse comment he would make. And I thought I was over him, that I'd dragged him to the trash and emptied it.

I <u>was</u> completely over him and I wasn't going to discuss him with Mairi.

Here was the plan: Step One. Buy her a drink. Step Two. Spell out the facts of life regarding Greg and threaten her, leaving no possibility for misinterpretation.

We fell into the warm, glowing Lebanese bar and restaurant and found a corner spot with soft cushions and low chairs. There was no one else in the bar – only the sound of a solitary table of Christmas revellers firing off volleys of laughter broke through from the restaurant. Mairi had shucked off her coat, but she still wore her darling hat with its herd of forever prancing reindeer and the cosy earflaps. Standing, she picked up the cocktail menu and was peering at the list.

'What can I get you?' I said.

'Please may I have a Mango Fizz?' She gestured at a non-alcoholic cocktail. By the time I got back from the bar, the hat was off, thank God. There she sat, perched on the low brown leather sofa, neatly poised, right at the edge of the seat, in a demure little Miss Muffett position. And yes, I know I keep using nursery rhymes to describe Mairi, but that's what she was like. Even though I was supposed to be thinking about how to pitch my, "back-off Greg, or else", spiel, I couldn't help wondering if she'd spent years practising those girly-girl poses in front of the mirror. She must have. It was the only way she could pull off this level of perfection.

I settled myself down and tried to put on my psychologist/negotiating hat. Nothing was going to be gained by showing emotion or anger. Detach, observe and explain in words that she will understand, making it clear what will happen if she continues to hit on Greg. But before I could speak, she smiled.

'I know exactly why you wanted to have a drink with me. It's because of Richard, isn't it?'

She reached forward to touch my hand, but I was too fast for her. I pulled back – right back. Her empty hand settled in her lap.

'Liz, I want you to know that I felt so bad about what I said, about him ... about Richard being my ex-sex monkey. It was stupid. I was trying to be funny and ...' Her eyes started to tear up and she glanced at me, through the lashes, to check my response. She shrewdly and suddenly stopped, no doubt after spotting my appalled expression.

'You need to understand, it wasn't a big romance,' she said.

'I'm really not interested,' I said. 'And that's not why I suggested a drink.'

'But I want you to know. I want to make things right between us. I respect you.' Before I could tell her to shut up and get my two pennyworth in, the drinks arrived. Her mango fizz had a maraschino cherry in the top and the bubbles sparkled up the fluted glass. Mairi clapped her hands at the sight of the drink and I was reminded yet again, as if I needed reminding, just how irritating she was, and how disgusted I was with Richard for being attracted to her.

I took a pull on my tomato juice.

'Like I said,' Mairi went on. 'It wasn't a big romance, but I really did care about him, and afterwards he said it would be better if I left the hospital because it was embarrassing. Well, I thought that was a bit mean and I was pretty cross, actually. So cross that I ... did a few things to annoy him even more.' Mairi shrugged. 'I told one or two people at the hospital that we'd had a thing and then he really got nasty. I was actually rather frightened. He's not a bad man, but there is a coldness about him.'

She shook her head as if she was remembering. As if, for the moment, for that one isolated moment in time, she wasn't faking. Then she popped the mask back on and was smiling brightly; Pollyanna was back, living, breathing, and walking among us, without a care in the world. La la la.

'I want you to know that, Liz. I want you to know that I never, ever thought it was a serious thing, not like Greg and me.'

What? Greg and me? Her bald comment was like a punch in my stomach and it took me a second to catch my breath.

'There is no Greg and you.'

'That really isn't for you to say, because you can't possibly know.' She clasped her hands together neatly. 'Liz, sometimes people connect, and that's it. There's nothing they can do about it, and that's how it is with Greg and me. So I wanted to talk to you. I want you to make it easier for Emma.'

'Well at least we're on the same page there,' I said. I pointed my finger at her. 'Now, listen to me. I've seen what you are trying to do with Greg, I know it hasn't happened and it isn't going to happen.' This was a bit of a punt because I didn't know, but it was worth a shot. And I was right, I could tell from Mairi's response.

'Some things you can't stop,' she said. 'It's inevitable. The way I see it is, you and Emma have got great jobs that are really fulfilling, so now it's my turn. I deserve a family ... I've never really had one, you know. Not really.'

Once again, Mairi's comment belted me in the guts. It's all very well realising that she was narcissistic and a primitive hysteric but sitting across the table, hearing her say, 'It's my turn'. I couldn't help it - I barked a laugh.

'Are you actually suggesting that you deserve Emma's family, as in her husband and her children?'

'Can't you see ... it's my turn?' Mairi said.

'How can you say, "It's your turn?" It's not a fucking skipping game where we all take turns.'

'I know that. Of course I know that but you see, the children love me, Liz. There's nothing you can do about it. It's too late. They love me because I'm there and Emma isn't. And where they love, Greg will follow, because he's that kind of man.'

'Now hear this,' I said. 'You don't know what you're talking about.' I stabbed the air; any attempt at not being angry had long gone. I was angry because I could see the logic of her thought process and I didn't know if she was right. In the face of my stabbing finger, Mairi shrugged.

'I'm really sorry if I'm upsetting you but it's already happened. You can't get rid of me. I'm part of the fabric of their lives now. I'm part of their childhood memories. Robbie will grow up and choose a wife like me. And when Tessa grows up, she'll want to dress like me. They'll remember the games, the stories, the outings, the trick-or-treating and all the fun we have. Because when you and Emma were away on business, I was there – she wasn't. Neither were you – their godmother. Do you know what Tessa's favourite book is at the moment? How about Robbie – do you know which toy he takes to bed? Of course you don't. Why would you? But that's why they'll forget you and they'll forget Emma. But they'll remember me. Just like today – Tessa will remember I was there when she was the Christmas Tree fairy and Greg will remember our first kiss.'

Besides not getting angry, Liz Verrall also doesn't make scenes in public places. It was the old me who did that sort of thing, the me that I have tamed and I now control. But for a good three seconds I was close to turning over the table and leaping on top of Ms Mairi Sondergaard and smacking her round the face. She was pressing all my anger buttons. Smack her face? Shake her till her teeth rattled? No, I wanted to squeeze her fucking neck.

I took a deep breath and became Liz Verrall once again.

'Tomorrow you are going to Devon and I am going to Florida. I strongly suggest that you use your month in Devon to think about just how unpleasant I might be. And when you come back, keep your distance from Greg; keep a low profile and back off. And, believe me, I will know if you don't. And I will act. Because if you don't back off, your little nursery school business will not happen. I will make absolutely sure of that and that's a promise.'

Mairi shrugged again and smiled at me as if I was an idiot not to understand what was patently obvious. She spoke quietly and with absolute certainty. 'I won't need the business when I've got Greg.'

My throat was dry and there was pounding in my ears. 'If you don't back off, Mairi, I promise I will find a way of making you.'

twenty-one

I was trembling when I left Mairi in the bar, twitchy, edgy, bursting with spiky energy. I stamped on the icy snow and wished that I were crushing Mairi's head. How dare she sit there and say that she deserved Emms' family? In spite of the sub-zero temperatures I was burning hot. I kicked at a chunk of snow, sent it flying; I wanted to smash and shatter and whack, and I'd have loved to kick her head in. I stopped, breath visible in the cold, the sound of my exhale ragged in my ears. Why should I run away from her like a scared child? How hard would it be to go back to the bar, wait for her to come out and then beat her to a bloody pulp? Let her say, 'it's my turn' through a couple of broken teeth.

Ahead I saw a couple of shadowy figures. The sight of other people on the street brought me back down. It was hard to see how old or even what sex they were because they had so many clothes on, but they were walking arm-in-arm, laughing as they slipped and slid on the icy path. As the figures drew closer I saw that it was two women, probably sisters - they looked alike, they were certainly friends. Friends like Emms and me, having a laugh, sharing a moment. And you know what? These two total strangers were the only reason I didn't go back, and lay into Mairi, and even now, I really don't know whether it was because of their humanity or because they would have seen me. The women drew abreast and passed me by, exchanging a cheery smile, and my rage shifted down a gear.

'Are you okay? Do you need help?' one of them said. She had blonde curls peeking out of a beanie and a slight accent that wasn't English.

'No, I'm okay,' I said. 'Thanks. I'm fine.'

I moved off. I had to get home. If there was any justice in the world, on the way to her car, Mairi would break her leg and get hypothermia. But, failing that happy outcome, I had to get back to warn Emms just how dangerous Mairi really was.

As it happened, it was me that nearly ended up in A&E. It started snowing again, and I had a terrifying drive home, slipping and sliding up to the main road and then crawling and edging the few miles back to the safety of my flat. The fifteen-minute drive took an hour and I had both hands clamped to the steering wheel, my brain swirling like the snowflakes in front of my windscreen.

'Concentrate, you stupid cow,' I said aloud, as a Mini up ahead shimmied like a lap dancer on the icy road. All the way home I battled, windscreen wipers squeaking and smearing the white as the heater blasted hot from all the vents. The moment I got inside, still wearing my coat and hat, I tore off my gloves and picked up the phone. Then I stood there, like an idiot, before replacing the phone in the cradle.

I had to warn Emms, but I didn't want to scare her.

Shedding coat, hat, boots and fleece, I padded across to the window and looked out at the unfamiliar landscape of clustered snow on the branches of the trees that hung over the river. Streetlights shone orange on the white surface of the road, and the snow smothered the sound. It was quiet. Only the whirring chug of my boiler bit into the silence.

I knew why I was hesitating about calling Emms: I felt guilty that I hadn't said anything earlier but I couldn't deal with Mairi on my own. Not now that Mairi had laid out her plans. Emms had to know what Richard had said about being stalked by her and also just how unhinged Mairi really was. Who knew what she might do to the kids if Greg rejected her – or, worse - if he didn't. At that, an even worse thought lumbered into my head and sat there like a dark mass – why did Mairi change her name? I'd stupidly assumed she was a fellow victim of domestic abuse, but for all I knew she might have been the abuser.

By now, I was hyperventilating. I heard my own panting breath and it sobered me up. Picking up the phone, I keyed in Emms' number. She needed to know, but at the same time I didn't want to panic her. She answered after the third ring.

'Hey, lovely, I was just about to call you. Telepathy eh?' She sounded fine; she sounded like she was eating something. Now all I had to do was spoil her evening. 'Hold on a minute,' she said and I heard her calling out, 'I'll be up in a minute,' and then she was back to me. 'Did you get back okay? Crazy weather. I just hope you can get to the airport tomorrow, have you checked?'

'It's supposed to stop at midnight.'

'Good, are you all packed and ready to roll? Any room for me in your suitcase?'

I ignored the question, 'Listen, Emms, I had a really weird conversation with Mairi. I don't know what you're doing giving her Christmas presents when she's ... Emms, she wants Greg.'

'Of course she does.' I heard Emms swallow whatever it was that she was eating. 'Tell me something I don't know, but it's okay. Honestly, it's okay. I'm on top of it, and Greg's not that type of guy.'

'How do you know?'

'Because we've talked about it ... GET BACK UPSTAIRS, TESSA - you've got no socks on and you will catch cold. Won't she, Aunty Liz? I promise you, Liz, I know what's going on and I'm sorting it out. Go off, have a lovely time, and relax, I'm just going to carry this lump up to bed.' I heard happy squealing in the background and my breathing began to slow down.

'You're sure?'

'Yes.'

After I'd put the phone down, I took off my specs and polished them against my thermals. My breathing was slowing and I was starting to think again. I was going away for two weeks and Mairi was going away for a month - she wouldn't be back till the end of January. This meant that we had a breather. There was time to do some serious checking when I got back, and time to present Greg with some hard-core information, unpleasant as that might be. And it was Christmas – if ever there was a time of the year when they would all be together and busy – in other words, safe from Mairi – it would be during Christmas. For the two weeks that I was going to be away, they'd be safe.

Some forty-eight hours later, I was sitting on the deck outside a waterside eatery in Fort Lauderdale, drinking a Becks and marvelling once again at the magic of air travel. Ahead of me was powder blue sky and indigo water; above, shrimp pink parasols keeping off the lunchtime sun. Outside in the parking lot, my convertible hire car waited, and somewhere in the kitchen, they were preparing a plate of crab claws. Whilst I listened to the rhythmic slap of water against the hull of a docked boat, the sun worked away at the knots in my neck. Cold beer hit the back of my throat and I closed my eyes. Of course, I'd checked my email. Emms' pre-Christmas messages were brief, but entirely normal and there was no mention of Mairi.

The sunny days passed and I drove slowly down the Keys, buying tee shirts at Mrs Mack's in Key Largo for Emma and the kids, and a cookery book for Greg. I crossed the Seven Mile Bridge and had the sensation of driving into nothingness. I stayed in quaint pre-booked guest houses where I sat in a hammock and lost myself looking at the sea, the blood-red sunsets and the birds. I didn't even read. I just melted. Did I think about Richard? Did I wonder if he would have enjoyed the trip? Of course I did, but not for long. I was finding my place again, the place in my head where I'm in control.

By the time I'd drifted down to Key West, I was feeling more sociable. Christmas had come and gone and I had seven more days before I had to drive back and catch my homeward-bound flight. The last week of my holiday was going to be spent in a colonial clapboard B&B within walking distance of Duval Street. Outside, there was a lush garden tended by two middle-aged gay men, one of whom made the best banana pancakes in the world. After breakfast, I sat in the garden and checked my mail on the iPad. There was one from Emms.

Hey Travelling Girl

Thanks for the postcard. It arrived today and is up on our newly bare mantelpiece as I am dismantling the tree and packing everything away for next year. We survived Christmas without casualties. Greg's doing bath and bed – sounds like a herd of elephants upstairs, but we're good. All good.

Greg showed me a crazy letter from Mairi that would have been worrying if I doubted him. It was all about her childhood and teen pregnancy – I'll spare you the details but it's grim. What's more, after all her plans to go away for Christmas, she didn't go in the end because she got norovirus. I can't help feeling sorry for her. We've taken some soup over but she still can't keep anything down.

She's so ill that the nursery opening is going to be postponed till after Easter and if Mairi doesn't perk up soon we're going to bring her over to stay in the spare room.

Have you had a great time? I hope so. The only downside of the break was thinking about my mother and imagining how she might have been upstairs in the spare room because she'd have been staying over Christmas. I do miss her. And I miss you, too.

See you Sunday week.

xE

I sipped my second coffee of the day and re-read the email. Emms sounded fine, but the idea of bringing Mairi into the house was crazy, never mind how contagious Mairi might be. What was Emms thinking?

The blanket of worry settled over my shoulders as I ran my fingers along the edge of the tablet. What possible trick had Mairi played to get herself invited to stay over? Was it part of the plan? Had she made herself seem so unbelievably pathetic that Emms was going to look after her? Take her home and nurse her back to health. Was that part of Mairi's next strategy - move in to the spare room where Emms' mother would have been, and stay there till she nailed Greg?

'Shit.' I said it aloud and looked around to see if there was anyone skulking in a corner of the lush garden who might be offended. If I'd told Emms chapter and verse of what Mairi had said or even passed on Richard's views, the notion of Mairi moving in would never have happened.

All the muscle-softening benefits of the holiday dissolved as my jaw tightened. There was ringing in my ear. I re-read the email. Surely not. It was just an email; Emms said 'might' which meant that it hadn't yet happened. All I needed to do was find out exactly how ill Mairi really was, and if she was faking it. Then I'd expose her for the husband-grabbing fraud that she was. And how was I supposed to do that four thousand miles away with a five-hour time difference?

The most obvious idea was to phone Emms and repeat the conversation I'd had with Mairi, but after all Emms' OCD behaviour over the months, and the way she now sounded - relaxed, chilled, in control; just like the Emms of old - why rattle the Mairi cage when there may well be nothing in it? This entire anxiety jag might really be about me. My humiliation, my fears and my crappy relationships. Why should Emms suffer because of my neuroses?

There was only one person I could ask, to find out if Mairi really was ill enough to need care: Richard. He was a doctor, and if she really was sick, maybe he could get her into hospital, which was a far better idea than Emms' spare room.

Three hours later, I was sitting cross-legged on the bed in the cool, high-ceilinged room. The blind was down and it flapped in the breeze, banging the edge against the frame, knocking as if it was someone trying to get in.

I booted up Skype and pressed call. The trilling sound filled the room and we connected. He answered, and he came into frame as an out-of-focus, ghosting, Richard replica. After all that had happened, I was not going to get upset: no yammering, and no ranting. But I still felt the blood rush and the heat rising in my body.

'Where are you?' he was smiling. 'This is so much better than a postcard. Show me your room. You are about to miss the biggest storm for years. By the way, you look great. When are you coming back?'

Behind Richard, I could see a pile of books and magazines on a table. It looked cluttered and untidy. This must be the rented flat that I'd never seen, because he said it was a tip.

'I've got seven more days, and then a slow drive north,' I said. 'I'm ... Richard. I'm not just calling for a chat or to hear the weather forecast.'

'Something wrong?' He leaned in to the camera as if he could see me better by getting closer. His face filled the screen. 'Liz, are you alright?'

'I'm fine. Listen. The day before I came away I had this conversation with Mairi. What she said doesn't matter but ... you were right. She is after Greg, she said so. Have you heard from her? Have you heard about what her plans are? Emma says she's got norovirus and she's really ill.'

'Norovirus? So what?' He leaned back in his chair away from the screen and steepled his hands. 'Twenty thousand people a week are going down with norovirus. It's a particularly virulent strain this year. I really wouldn't waste your time worrying about how she is. That woman has a habit of managing to look after herself whatever disaster she spreads around.'

'Listen to me, I'm not worried about Mairi – I don't care how sick she is, I just think she might be using an illness to move in with Greg and Emma.'

'Then they'd be bloody fools. If she has got it, it's highly infectious and if she hasn't ... ' I saw his expression change as he actually listened to what I'd said. 'I see what you mean. If she projects an air of hopeless vulnerability and she moves in to be nursed ... she could do that. Yes, she really could.'

'You don't think I'm imagining it or over-reacting? I've been starting to wonder whether I see Mairi threats when there's nothing there.' I closed my eyes, then opened them and blurted, 'You were right. I should have believed you. She thinks that she and Greg are about to set up home. She said it was her turn and she deserved a family.'

'When did she say that?'

'The night before I came away. I sort of told Emms but I don't think she realises just how unhinged Mairi is.' There was silence on the line; outside the room I heard the high pitch of a bird's chirrup. It was a sunny, incongruous sound.

'I'm sorry, Richard. I'm sorry I didn't believe you.'

'And I'm sorry that I allowed her to continue to spread her poison. Knowing what she was capable of, the responsibility was on me to do something, not to bleat to you. You didn't deserve that.' He was quiet for a moment or two, 'I need to stop this, don't I?'

'Listen, if she really is ill then maybe you can get her into hospital.'

'If she really is ill,' he repeated. He looked tight around the lips. 'I'll find out what's going on and call you back.'

He ended the call in that abrupt way of his. I noodled around, wondering when he would call me back, how long it would take him, whether he'd phone her or go round to hers. And exactly what he would say and do.

I waited.

He didn't call.

twenty-two

For the last week of my holiday, I regressed into the archetypal dumped teenager, checking to see if the Internet was working, sitting in front of a screen in case Richard was trying to get through, looking at my phone for text messages, and anticipating all the possible and probable reasons why Richard didn't contact me. According to the news, there'd been a big storm with hurricane-strength winds throughout the UK. Maybe Richard had computer problems; maybe a tree had fallen on his car; maybe he'd broken his arm; maybe there'd been a family illness and an emergency dash across country. And then I started imagining the conversations. You know what I mean. We've all been there once or twice - or even more. Waiting for the phone call that never comes. It may hurt less than the gut-wrenching pain when you're fourteen, but it's still enough to make a grown woman want to knife someone. I emailed Emms but, of course, I couldn't say anything about Richard's mission to see Mairi nor my fears about Mairi's intentions, and Emms' response was anodyne and rushed.

I was still checking my mobile - just in case - when I was sitting in the grey departure lounge at Fort Lauderdale Airport. Why hadn't he phoned? What could possibly have happened to stop him from, at the very least, sending a text message to say everything was fine? Or not. Right at the top of the list of reasons was that Mairi's norovirus wasn't a ruse to move in with Greg and Emms, but a neat way to put the moves back on Richard, and I had played right into her hands.

The package of newly single Richard might be more attractive than Greg, even with his ready-made family. Don't forget, Richard was a doctor; she'd already told people they were an item; and even better, she didn't have Emma as an obstacle. If ever there were a good plan for Mairi, hooking up with Richard would be the one to choose.

The plane rumbled down the runway and took off, giving me a moment's distraction as I was pushed back in my seat. And then the thoughts started crowding back in again. Fuck Mairi. She'd been a total pain from the very first moment I'd met her hovering over Emms' bedside like the archetypal evil fairy who bobbed up in the worst possible way at the worst possible time. And now she'd done it again, ruined my holiday. Atta girl.

I clamped on my headphones and switched on the white noise that reduced the roar of the aircraft. I couldn't be distracted by film or music. I just watched the back of the headrest in front and the LED display that showed the little airplane inching across the ocean, getting closer to the UK, closer to a mountain of work, and a mountain of Mairi mess. I know holiday endings are always depressing, but this one was particularly tiresome.

In an attempt to aid my detachment, I took off my specs and let the world around me blur. What with the headphones blocking out the noise and the specs blurring the sight, it wasn't unlike being underwater. At least I had the next few hours all to myself. All I needed to do was spend the time putting my shit aside so that I could look out for Emms and protect her. What's more, if Richard wanted to hook up with Mairi, as his silence seemed to suggest, then good luck to him. It bore out what I'd thought when I'd found out that he'd shagged her – he was an arse. And in the cold light of flying thirty thousand feet above the world, it was the best possible solution. The pair of them would be out of our lives. Emms could calm down and get on with building the business, Greg could find some other outlet for his congenital kind heart and I could get back to the place where I'm comfortable: being part of but apart from other people's lives.

By the time we'd landed and I'd hoicked my case off the carousel and wheeled it through customs into the arrivals lounge, I was ready. Or at least I thought was. What I wasn't prepared for was the sight of Richard, standing next to the minicab drivers, with a bunch of red and pink carnations and a handwritten sign: 'VERRALL'. What the hell was he doing there? And more importantly, what was he doing to me?

Even though my knees were rubbery, I'm pleased to say I affected a casual stroll towards him.

'Moonlighting?' I said. 'Trade slow in the upper limb trauma industry?'

'Precisely.' He took the trolley and looked me in the eyes. I managed to swallow.

'How was the flight? You don't have to tell me how the holiday was – you look illuminated.'

'Sun damage,' I growled.

We started walking towards the lifts to the car park. I had that slightly disorientated post-flight dizziness.

'Why are you here?'

'To pick you up and take you home after a nine-hour flight. I've also got you some milk, coffee, smoked salmon and bagels.'

'No I mean, why are you here?' I put my hand on his arm to make my point and I felt the fabric of his navy jacket and a shot of static.

'I wanted to see you,' Richard said, as if it was obvious and didn't merit comment. 'I wanted to have the opportunity to improve my standing in your eyes and I thought that if you were jet-lagged, my chances would be improved.'

And he was right. I couldn't find it in myself to ask him what had happened when he went to see Mairi. Neither could I ask him why he hadn't Skyped me. All I wanted to do was get home, get unpacked, regroup and not end up in bed with him. And I failed in that endeavour, too.

But it was fine, I suppose. He was tender and loving and he whispered and muttered the usual incomprehensible endearments in my ear. Afterwards, he insisted on making breakfast and bringing it back to bed.

'I am going to prove my worth,' he said. 'I can drive, I can shop, and I can cook.'

'Smoked salmon bagels? Call that cooking?'

'I can make fresh coffee.'

'Go on, then. Get to it.'

I heard him clattering in the kitchen and reached for my mobile. After checking the time, I texted Emms. Sunday morning at 10.30 - she might be around.

'Just back. How u?'

I pressed send.

OK. All good.'

'You around or taking soup to Mairi?'

No soup run. Mairi's gone.'

My finger hovered over the keyboard, trembling. Then I typed.

'Gone?'

'Gone. Gotta go. Kids back. Plsd ur back. Speak later.'

I pulled the sheet around me: my shoulders felt chilled. I kept looking at the phone and the message, trying to read something into it that wasn't there. On the face of it, everything was fine, wasn't it? Emms was fine, Greg was fine, the kids were fine. And Mairi was gone.

twenty-three

The next day was supposed to be my first day back at work after the Christmas break, but instead of being energised and full of snippety-snappety action plans, I felt as if I'd come back to a foreign land that only looked like the place in my memory called home. At the heart of this sense of disconnection sat Richard; asking him anything about Mairi was like talking to a tree in a gale. He kept shifting, changing the subject, finding some interesting comment to make or asking me questions about the trip.

At 2am, I woke up. His body was warm against mine, back to back. I could tell that he was awake and also that whatever he was thinking about, he wasn't going to share it. I started to mull over how little I actually knew him and it frightened me. By 5am, he was finally asleep and that's when I pushed back the duvet and swung round, stealing out of my own bed into the bathroom, where I could get dressed and creep out of the flat.

Twenty minutes later I was at the front door of the Brooklands office, pressing the night bell in the pre-dawn darkness of a winter's morning. With only the wool fabric of my trousers to protect my legs, the damp cold bit into my thighs. I kept ringing, shuffling from foot to foot, until a red-eyed security guard meandered up to the door. I meant to barrack him for leaving me to wait in the cold but when I saw his sleep-worn face, I really didn't have the heart.

'Sorry, I've got a presentation to do and I need to get in,' I said. He wasn't interested; he keyed open the door and shambled away, back to whatever dark little cupboard he spent the night in. Soon I was in our empty office, and I sat in reception, at Sue's desk, absorbing the silence. I was trying to sense the building, identify the hum of fluorescent light and the sweet smell of a decomposing apple core lodged at the bottom of Sue's bin.

Was Mairi really missing? Or had she got herself better and buggered off to Devon? For the umpteenth time, I re-examined my mental list and associated thoughts about Mairi being "gone". It wasn't jet lag, it wasn't neurosis, there was something about Richard and Emms' reaction that made me feel uneasy, even if I didn't know what it was.

After I'd made a coffee, I shifted into the office that Emms and I share. I sat at my desk sipping at a cup of foul liquid that made my mouth feel claggy. My desk was a tangle of papers and cuttings, but Emms' was completely clear, apart from three piles of torn-up paper. I went to examine them. It was a mountain range of confetti-sized paper. Was this another one of her OCD rituals? I'd thought she was better and that the panic attacks had abated. The email she'd sent when I was away sounded calm and relaxed, but if she'd been making paper mountains, that was not a good sign.

The office door flew open and Emms breezed in with a gust of air that sent the piles of paper floating like snowflakes. Relief washed over me. She'd barely glanced at the paper, because it wasn't important to her. What she did was open her arms to welcome me home.

'Look at you! Welcome back, you look great.'

'Thanks.'

Emms hung on to me, squeezing my arms hard as if she wanted to make sure I was really there.

'What are you doing cutting up bits of paper?' I said.

'Occupational therapy.' Emms pulled away, smiling. 'It's my new thing. I tear up the bits of paper into smaller and smaller pieces and my problems get smaller and smaller.' She looked me square in the eyes.

'Problems?'

'Problems.'

She pulled a big buff folder out of her workbag and dropped it on the desk; it thwacked when it hit the surface and the remaining tiny bits of paper sprayed everywhere. 'Here's one problem,' Emms said. 'A Marcus suggestion that we get into consumer retail. We need to know if this company is worth chasing and I haven't the faintest idea where to start. What's more, he wants to know today.'

'What about Mairi?' I said.

Emms opened her hands and flexed her fingers, like two starfish. I knew what she was doing. There it was: a twitch in her right hand as if she was stopping her hand, holding it back, keeping it from beating out the safety tattoo on the amulet.

Emms shrugged. 'Honestly, Liz, there's really nothing to tell. But I promise to fill you in on everything that happened whilst you were away at lunchtime, okay? Martin's? My shout? By the way, the kids loved the toys, my scarf is brilliant and Greg's been cooking from that baking book you gave him for the last two weeks.'

'What about your text message saying that Mairi had gone?' I said.

'Exactly that. She's gone. Remember she was going to see those friends of hers in Devon for Christmas? Well, she got better and I presume she's gone there. What is with it you, Liz?'

It was as if I was at a noisy party, I'd misheard a comment, said something in response and then watched everybody trying to interpret what I'd said. Was I wrong? Was there truly nothing sinister about Mairi disappearing?

I felt cold and shaky, and it wasn't just the change of temperature. There was a tap on the door and Sue, God bless her, peered into the room.

'Happy New Year,' Emms said. 'Welcome back, did you have a good one?'

Sue nodded shyly. 'Shall I put the kettle on?'

'Great idea,' Emms said. 'Liz, coffee?'

I picked up the file and headed towards the door. 'Not for me, but thank you, Sue. Lunch time,' I said to Emms and walked out of the office.

I went to Martin's on the pretext of reading the file quietly, but I was distracted and out of kilter. I could put some of that down to jet lag, but sadly not all. If I really was starting to weird out and was seeing shadows where there were none, then I would have no choice but to go to the doctor. On the other hand, my feeling of unease might have absolutely nothing to do with Emms. It could be fears about Richard. I've known Emms for ten years - yes, there have been incidents, and yes, there's the business with Tony, but she's never lied to me. Could I say the same for Richard? No. But I also couldn't worry her with my anxieties, not when she was still vulnerable.

By the time Emms turned up, I'd read most of the file. We air-kissed, which seemed a little odd, but I slapped myself down for over-analysing, and watched Emms do her little security ritual of placing her phone to the right on the red and white table cloth, her bag to the left on the wooden floor and her jacket over the back of the chair. Then Emms brushed her hair off her forehead and sat down.

'How did you get on with the mystery shopping?' Emms said.

'Give me a break, I've only just read this load of stuff.'

'If anybody can do it, you can,' Emms said. 'I mean it. You may lack the ambition gene but sometimes you're so bloody clever it takes my breath away.'

'I didn't think you noticed,' I said. I was playing with the rose quartz ring she'd given me.

'How's Richard?' Emms said.

'I don't know ...'

The waitress came up to take our orders.

'Your usual?' she said to Emms. 'Soup of the day is minestrone.'

'Just for once,' Emms said, 'I'd like something sweet. Cake. Do you have something like a Victoria sponge cake? That's what I'd like, a lovely buttery sponge with cream and jam in the middle.'

'I ask,' the waitress said and took my usual order of beef salad baguette and cappuccino. After she'd gone, I said, 'That's a first. No soup. Striking out, are you?'

'I really wish you'd stop reading something into every single thing that I do,' Emms snapped and her hand wormed its way up to the amulet.

'It was a joke. Lighten up.'

'Sorry, sorry, Liz, it's been ... There is some stuff going on ... And yes, it is about Mairi, but I didn't want to say anything at the office.'

'What stuff? Whatever it is, it can't possibly be worse than what I've been imagining. I thought Mairi might have got back together with Richard.'

'I don't know about that, I do know that Greg thinks it's weird that she's been gone for so long and hasn't got in touch with us. You know what she's like, texting every five minutes, phoning every ten and now nothing.'

The waitress reappeared with our order. I watched Emms tackle her slice of cake with gusto.

'Have you been round to her house?' I said.

'Not since she disappeared.'

'Well, why don't we do that? We could do our mystery shopping at the same time.'

Emms shrugged, 'Okay'

There was an uncomfortable silence as we ate. For some reason that I can't possibly explain, it reminded me of the pauses in conversation after Emms' mum's funeral when we'd all gone back to the flat for tea and sandwiches. There was her dad, Aunty Jane, Greg's parents, Greg and Emms and a smattering of her mum's neighbours all standing around the food-laden table in the shabby kitchen. I remember the little iced fairy cakes that Greg's mother had baked. The conversation had spattered and paused. Spattered and paused again. People blurted out something and then tailed off into silence as the connection chasms opened up between them and the niceties dropped down, down, down into the bottomless pit of disconnect.

I shook my head to wake myself up from my macabre musing. Bloody jet lag, that's what it was, nothing more. 'Come on, Emms, we're done here. Let's go round to Mairi's on the way back to the office.'

'You're right. Let's get it over and done with.'

Emms stood up and dug into her bag for some money to pay and we marched out of the front door. As I walked down the street, the low January sun made me squint. The people coming in the opposite direction became bleached-out silhouettes with shadows tagged onto their feet like serpent's tongues. We passed the newsagent and I glanced through the open door where I could just see the till and someone standing in front of it. A small figure tipped back her head and a peal of familiar laughter rang out. Mairi?

Emms staggered to her left and whacked her hip into a lamppost.

'Ow!'

Just then, the figure at the till skipped down the steps of the newsagent's into the street. She was clutching her OK magazine and was unaware of me and Emms, hunched like two old ladies by the lamppost. The girl was a teenager, maybe fourteen, blonde hair, like Mairi, small, like Mairi, elfin, like Mairi. But it definitely wasn't Mairi. It definitely wasn't her.

twenty-four

Of course, the real reason why I wanted to go to Mairi's house was curiosity. I wanted to see what her fuck-pad looked like, I wanted to know where she'd seduced Richard - imagine if they'd shagged up against the wall, or maybe on the carpet. See her bedroom and picture him there with her. I also wanted to see if there was any more recent evidence that would explain the brick wall that he'd built to avoid discussing her.

The traffic was light on the way to her house; only a couple of cyclists ahead of us that had to be negotiated as we passed the towering water reservoirs. By my side Emms sat hunched, rubbing her amulet with one hand and, with the other, massaging the thigh that she'd whacked into the lamppost. I couldn't go to Mairi's without her and I didn't want to tell Emms why we were going – it would only upset her.

I tried to lighten the mood by turning on the radio. Radio Jackie filled the car with the bouncy sound of a woman singing about last Friday night. It was the sort of music that Emms and I used to jig about and bop to after a night of champagne and shots. I glanced over. Emms was rigid with tension.

'Look, if you don't want to do this, you really don't have to,' I said. 'But if Mairi's disappeared, don't you think we ought to at least go round to her house? Much as I dislike her, common humanity means we should find out if she's lying dead in a heap.' What I didn't say is that Richard is so weird about Mairi that I'm frightened what I might find. Of course, I didn't say that. I didn't want to voice it. It was bad enough thinking, without expressing my suspicions, which would only make my fear real.

'If you say so.'

Twenty minutes later, we stood on Mairi's doorstep and rapped the knocker. It was a quaint Victorian cottage, not unlike Greg and Emms' but without the loving care that they'd lavished on their place. This was a Dorian Gray kind of a house: at a distance it looked quaint, but close up it had an air of crumbling decay and bitter neglect. A wheelie bin loomed in the front garden, with a mouldy roll of carpet by its side that stank of damp. Scattered around the bin, broken glass glinted, and black weeds sprouted through the cracked and cemented path. We walked up the path in silence and stood side by side, in front of a once white door whose chips exposed rotten wood. Beneath a dusty black knocker, there was a note in round, handwritten letters, 'Bell doesn't work, knock.' There was a smiley face scrawled in crayon that could only be Mairi's handiwork. It was half-peeled off, Sellotape curling and grimy. I hit the knocker, against the mouldy wood. We waited.

'Now what?' Emms said.

'Since we're here, we may as well look around.'

I'd pushed my hands into my coat because I'd forgotten gloves and it was cold standing on the doorstep, but since this little enterprise was my idea, I could hardly complain. After a few moments, I knelt down on the grubby mat and pressed my eye to the open black letter box.

'There's post on the mat,' I said. 'That must mean she's not there, so presumably she's still away.'

'Well done, Sherlock. Can we go back to the office now?'

As I stood up, I noticed that the front door of the next-door cottage had opened. A white-haired woman with a face like a button hobbled out.

'You friends of Mairi's?' She looked worried, or maybe it was just decades of fretting that had worn in the worry creases on her face.

'Yes, we haven't heard from her for a while. I don't suppose she's been in touch with you?'

'Not a word. Landlord's been round 'cause she didn't pay the rent, and I've been worried m'self. I always heard her through the walls, sometimes late at night but it was a comfort knowing she was there. She even gave me a key, just in case she lost hers. I've been wondering where she is.'

'May we have a look inside?' I said.

'Liz, do you really think going into the house is necessary? If Mairi's not here, she's not here. Why don't we just leave it at that and go back to the office?'

'There might be some post for Greg.' I turned to the neighbour. 'Greg is Emms' husband, he and Mairi were in business together. Would you let us in?'

'Don't see why not. You're friends of Mairi's - I can tell.'

Moments later, the neighbour had turned the lock and the front door swung open. It went straight into a sitting room that would have been special if it had sparkled, and cosy if it had been simply clean. The room was neither special nor cosy.

There was a dank, sweet smell of decay, an air of a place where someone couldn't be bothered. The glass coffee table was greasy and smudged, so fogged with filth that it was hard to believe that it had ever been transparent. The waste-basket overflowed with tissues and on every surface there were piles of magazines, clothes dried to a shrivel on radiators. The whole place smelt not only of dirt, but also of the sickly scent Mairi favoured. Emms was pale, looking as if she was trying not to inhale, and I couldn't blame her. She gathered up the post from the floor and leafed through it.

'Mucky pup, isn't she?' Mairi's neighbour said.

'You might say that.' I followed the neighbour's gaze to the fireplace, where grey ashes and a charred piece of wood sat, cold and damp. On the wood surround there were a few Christmas cards, including one made by Tessa and Robbie. I strolled over and looked at the cards. There was nothing in Richard's cramped writing. By the side of the card from Tessa and Robbie, there was a photograph of Mairi with the kids. She was wearing a pink witch's outfit - no doubt the get-up she'd worn on Halloween when we'd been in Manchester meeting Marcus. I glanced at Emms, who followed my gaze. She looked sick and I felt bad for making her come to the house. There was Mairi, a beatific expression on her face, cheek to cheek with Emms' children. All it needed to complete the family picture was Greg, but obviously, the happy photographer was behind the lens.

For a moment, and only a moment, I thought about how lonely Mairi must have been in her grubby house, with the photo of her make-believe family above the fire. How she must have yearned to be needed, to be cared for and to be loved - unconditionally. Emms' voice broke into my thoughts, 'My kids,' Emms said to the neighbour. 'Those are my kids,' I could hear the thickening in her voice.

'Come on, let's go and look upstairs,' I said.

'Why? She obviously isn't here. Why do we have to go upstairs? Mairi,' Emms called out and waited. 'See. No reply. She's not here, Liz, and I really don't think we should be going through her stuff. I think we should go.' Of course, Emms was rattled, and I didn't know what I was looking for: all I knew was that Richard had blanked my questions about Mairi and the answer might be in the house. However difficult this was for Emms, and however bad I felt for putting her through this ordeal, we had to stay.

'We're here now, so we may as well check upstairs,' I said.

Now it was the neighbour's turn to get cold feet. She wrung her hands, the furrow in her brow deepened with fear. 'You don't think that Mairi might be, maybe we should call-'

Emms interrupted, 'We do not need to call the police, for goodness sake. I'm sure Mairi's absolutely fine. But if you insist, let's make sure that there's nothing upstairs.'

My stomach clenched tight. If there was a photo of the kids downstairs, would there be one of Richard by the side of her bed? Or worse, would I see some memento of the fling, or some evidence that he'd been upstairs more recently? I shifted from one foot to the next. Now it was Emms' turn to take the lead, 'Come on,' she said. 'This was your idea.'

Upstairs there was the same chaos, same dirt and same sadness as downstairs but, thankfully, no evidence of Richard. The iron bedstead had a frayed patchwork cover, and Mairi had been testing paint pots on the wall, to get the right colour pink.

In a corner of the room, there was a broken Lloyd Loom chair that you could barely see under a pile of odorous, colourful, patterned clothes and by a free-standing wardrobe, was a pine bookcase, with a selection of self-help titles, mostly about loving yourself and getting a man. Everywhere there was dust and the overpowering smell of Mairi.

'Nothing here,' I said. 'I'm going to use the loo, before we go.' The bathroom might yield some information.

Just like at Emms', the bathroom in the little house was downstairs and at the back of the cottage, where it had been converted from the outside loo. But that's where the resemblance ended. Although I'd never been in Mairi's bathroom, it was everything I expected from the rest of the house. The once-white bath was matt with soapy grime; the sink taps were spattered with toothpaste and lime scale; and there were so many smears on the mirrored cabinet, my reflection was distorted. Inside the cabinet, among the dust, hairballs, gobs of make-up, rusting razors, sticky scent bottles, I saw a couple of cardboard boxes with prescription labels on them. Diazepam and Thorazine.

I closed the cabinet and rinsed my hands, not wanting to use the black, cracked soap.

By this time, the neighbour and Emms were in the kitchen waiting for me.

'Anything?' I said.

'Nothing,' Emms said.

'In that case, I think we can all assume that Mairi's off somewhere, having a grand old time, whilst we're worrying about her, and when she's good and ready, she'll turn up and be less than happy that we've been stomping round her house.'

Emms was hovering around looking through the post. I glanced at my watch, hopeful that it was enough of a hint to wind up things; after all, we'd found nothing.

'Tell you what, why don't we leave a note for Mairi telling her to call as soon as she gets back? Do you have a pen?'

Of course Emms did: she always has a pen, tissues, change for a parking meter and who knows what else in her handbag. I scrawled a few lines about calling us when she turned up, and went out to the car, leaving Emms with the neighbour.

Moments later, Emms followed with a plastic bag that she threw into the foot well of the car.

'What's that?' I pressed the ignition.

'Her post.'

'You can't take her post, you have to take it back. There are some fairly strict laws about tampering with people's post.'

'Who says she's coming back?' Emms said. 'I'll say I'm looking after it and, after all, Greg is supposed to be in business with her.'

Even though I'd instigated the snoop around Mairi's house, somehow taking her post felt like a step too far. 'I think you're wrong. Take it back, give it to the neighbour and ask her to look after it.' I turned the ignition off and sat with my arms folded, waiting for Emms to get out the car.

'Don't be ridiculous,' Emms said. 'You just heard that Mairi didn't pay the rent: what does that suggest? I didn't want to say anything till we're sure, but Greg thinks she may have done a runner with the investment money.'

'I don't believe it. She had no reason to do a runner with the money. Emms, what if something's happened to her?'

'Like what?' Emms looked exasperated.

I started the engine, 'I don't know - ignore that. Put it down to too much ligging around in the Florida sun and not enough work. Let's go and see those supermarket shoppers.

'Are you okay?'

'Everything's peachy.' I pulled out and threaded my way through the parked cars, aware that Emms was watching me. There may have been no visible evidence in Mairi's house that she'd resumed her affair with Richard, but I was sure that he knew something.

What if the reason why there were no traces of Richard in the house was because he'd been there and removed them?

twenty-five

The next day I had to go to Birmingham to deliver a training course at the Hyatt. All the participants were bright and highly motivated, which was just as well as I wasn't exactly at my tip-toppiest in terms of skills. It was more like dragging myself through mud on an uphill trek. The idea of Richard having something to do with Mairi's disappearance was so totally ridiculous that I was fearful that it had even bothered me. How could I imagine that Richard was sneaking around covering up traces of his contact with Mairi? It was nuts. Meanwhile, what about Emms' claim that Mairi had gone off with the investment money for the nursery? I didn't believe that, either. It made no sense for the wretched woman to embezzle when she thought she was getting Greg and his well-heeled family.

As I sped through my presentation, clicking from slide to slide and rattling off the key points, I had a tight sensation in my chest. Was there something in the letters that Emms had grabbed from the house? What was she hiding from me? For the first time ever, I nearly lost the thread of the presentation and suffered a couple of agonising seconds swaying from foot to foot with a completely blank mind, then I hauled myself back, to the room, to the participants and to the presentation.

It was only later that evening, in my hotel room, that I allowed myself the luxury of analysing my thought processes. Fact: there was more to Mairi's disappearance than Emma was telling me, and I was pissed off and hurt that she didn't trust me. And I was also scared. That was the nub of it: fear. I took a sip of the G&T from the hotel minibar. I was shit-scared. There was something going on, and it had to be bad for Emms to say nothing; it had to be worse than Tony's accident.

I allowed myself to imagine what Emms might have done if Mairi had gibbered, in that stupid, winsome way of hers, that it was her turn and it was only fair that she took Emms' family. I pictured them together, tall Emms, angular, in black and Mairi's flowing curls. I remembered how I'd yearned to put my fingers round Mairi's white neck and squeeze. What if Emms had been on the receiving end of Mairi's hopes and aspiration spiel, there'd been nobody around and she hadn't been able to stop herself? After all, she had more to lose and she has that rage of hers. How the fuck would I protect her, if she had done something to the bitch? The alcohol was making me warm and relaxing my muscles. I would protect Emms, whatever she'd done, because she's my friend. In the meantime, I'd wait. As if in answer to my decision, I heard the ping of an email into my inbox.

Dear friend Liz,

First apologies. I know I've been off-message. Like I said when we had lunch, and I was pretty rude to you, there's a lot going on. For starters the kids aren't well. Robbie had a cold and a fever so we're both knackered because we've been up all night trying to get his temperature down. He seems a little better this morning, now I'm waiting for Tess to start snivelling as they always pass bugs between them.

You asked about Mairi. There is still no sign of her and, as I said, Greg thinks she's run off with the investment money for the nursery, which - for some arcane tax benefit - was all in her account. While it wasn't a huge amount by con woman standards, it's enough. She didn't pay her last two months' rent either. Greg is in a terrible state. He's boozing, has dreadful stress-related indigestion and has been blaming himself for being taken in by her. The problem is that most of the money came from his parents, so he had to tell them.

Greg was all up for going to the police, as if they would be able to find a woman who had already changed her name once. Anyways, the long and short of it is that instead of giving Greg a hard time, Theo was positively statesman-like and said that if Mairi was that desperate to screw us out of so little money when she had the opportunity to make so much more, then her need was greater than ours. So it seems that she's lucked out, yet again, and is no doubt somewhere in the country or even abroad, calling herself something different and probably planning to do the same thing. Unfortunately, there are always going to be families that need help with

their children, and it doesn't take much to forge a
CRB form or references. I suppose we all got off
lightly.

The rest of the email was about work and the
course. I tapped back a response but then put what
I'd written into draft and closed my laptop. For a few
moments, I sat in the hotel room, stroking the cool
metal of the laptop lid. More than anything in the
whole world, I wanted to think that, besides Theo
being down a few grand, everything else was back to
normal, everyone was safe and snug, the ramparts
were up around our little world, and above all,
Emms trusted me again and Mairi was a common-
or-garden con woman.

So I didn't send the email that described my last
meeting with Mairi when she'd said that she didn't
care about the business, she just wanted Emms'
family. And I didn't voice my fears to Emms that she
might have lost her temper and done something to
Mairi, because I am old enough to know that night is
when all the dark thoughts come rolling and
crashing on the clear sand of our minds, dragging us
into the churning water and choking and drowning
us. I knew that any doubts I may have had would
have evaporated by morning and I would have
successfully parked all my anxieties about Emms,
Mairi and even about little Robbie's cold.

All I needed was a little more of Emms'
pragmatism and her ability to look at the logic of a

situation. The bottom line was that Mairi was gone. Who fucking cared why or how?

I wasn't going to see Richard till the end of the week, and I was pleased. I still needed to process the trip to see Mairi's love nest and I was keen to have an evening where she was not on the agenda. I had decided that she was history and I had to try to trust Richard and that meant trusting myself that I hadn't picked another bastard. There would always be gaps and chasms, fissures with dark unknowable secrets that Richard kept to himself. And you know what? I didn't really want to find out everything. I didn't want to learn what it was about Mairi that had impelled him to fuck her and fuck up his marriage. I didn't want to go there, and why the hell should I? As I kept telling myself, she was gone. Hopefully forever. Now move on.

We had dinner in a strange little restaurant in Kingston. Strange and expensive. Cast iron artisan-designed candleholders were planted on starched white tablecloths. Odd and old furniture juxtaposed with a futuristic fireplace in the wall. Either they'd run out of money during the refurb or they had friends with artistic aspirations that they wanted to support. The candleholders were like an adult education project and the whole effect was mash-up, lash-up and rather explained why ours was the only occupied table on a Friday night.

Richard had been working, so he was in his charcoal suit and now rather crumpled white shirt. But at least he'd removed his tie to emphasise the off-duty nature of the evening.

'Would you mind very much if I kept my phone out?' He placed his mobile by the side of the cutlery. 'There was a problem during the last operation, and I've told them to keep me informed if there is any deterioration.' This was one of the things that I liked about Richard. The kind and caring and modest side countered the bits that I didn't like.

'How was Birmingham? Did you train them to listen and speak in the most appropriate way, or were there any backsliders who dared to rebel against the customer service doctrine you espouse?'

'Just because you have the bedside skills of an android, don't rubbish people who are trying to be professional about what they do.'

'Fair point. I was actually trying to be amusing and provocative.'

I nodded and took another mouthful of the pasta that was stuffed with something I couldn't identify. It was swimming in a cheesy cream sauce and I had to manoeuvre it into my mouth without dripping gunk down my shirt.

'Actually, there's something I want to talk about, and I know you're not going to like it,' Richard said.

I stopped the fork midway to my mouth and glanced across the table. His expression telegraphed that he was expecting me to react – and he was right on the money. 'Must you, Richard? Can't it wait until

I'm not eating?' The tortellini dropped off the fork into the cream and splashed my shirt. 'Or trying to eat, anyway.' I tried to laugh it off, I tried to joke it all away, but I could feel the cold air around my neck. The cream sauce now seemed cloying in my mouth and I felt a little sick.

'Of all the irritating things about you, Richard, this, "we have to talk" habit is possibly the worst. I've driven 150 miles today, I've been away all week and all I want for my Friday night is to have a decent meal and then snuggle up in front of the TV ... or something. I don't want a big conversation. Why can't it wait till tomorrow?'

The invitation to snuggle, aka have sex, diverted him for the moment.

'Tomorrow? What do you mean, over breakfast?'

'If you're lucky.'

If I could steer him away, I might be able to have the type of evening I yearned for. And come, to that, I damn well deserved. And of course, I knew, one hundred per cent, that "need to talk" actually meant, "need to talk about Mairi," because if it had been about anything else, anything at all, he would have just said it, instead of flagging it up with his ominous tells. And I didn't want to know. I'd parked it, buried it, drowned the fucking thing.

'If this is about Mairi, send me an email, tomorrow.' I said glancing at his mobile, which had maintained its discretion and not interrupted. The inanimate phone highlighted my conflict. I liked the caring side of him, his sense of responsibility and need to do the right thing; what I didn't like was his insistence on telling me things I really didn't want to know.

'It's not about Mairi, I promise,' he laid down his fork, abandoning the risotto on his plate. 'It's about Greg.'

'Greg? What about him?'

'I think he has some significant problems, health and otherwise. For one thing he's drinking to excess and for the other ...'

I changed my mind and raised my hand to stop Richard saying any more, 'No, I don't want to know. Email me tomorrow.'

'I'm not emailing you when you're sitting in front of me.' He looked testy. 'Listen to me for a minute: the reason I didn't get back to you when you were in Florida was that after I went to see Mairi, I took it upon myself to contact Greg via our mutual friend, Mike. I invited Greg out for a drink.'

The phone rang. Not Richard's but mine. I didn't want to hear any more about Greg. Whatever it was, it would be bad news. From the depths of my bag I grabbed my mobile as if it was a life raft in stormy seas. I didn't care who was at the end of the line, junk caller, wrong number, or anybody else.

'Hi,'

'Liz, it's me.' Emms.

'Are you okay?' I said. I heard a crack in her voice. 'What's wrong, Emms, tell me what's wrong?'

For a moment, I heard nothing, except breath, in and out of Emms' lungs, gasping, pained breath.

'Hello ... Emms, are you there, are you okay?'

'It's Tessa.' Her voice was sharp-edged with fear. 'I thought Tessa had Robbie's cold but, but, she got worse, Her temperature went up to 102 and now she's having trouble breathing. I called the GP and they told me to get an ambulance. It's on the way. But Greg needs to stay here with Robbie and I need to go with her.'

'What do you want me to do?'

'Meet me at the hospital, please, the ambulance is here.'

Across the table, I saw Richard's concerned and questioning expression. When I told him, he wanted to come with me to the hospital, but I batted him off. Ironic, I suppose, with him being a doctor and all, but I didn't want him near Emms and me. This was something that we had to do together. And of course, I also didn't want to hear the rest of whatever he thought was wrong with Greg.

So what if Greg's been boozing more than usual, who cares if he's having a wobble? "Significant problems?" what's that supposed to be mean? All it meant is that Greg was stressed about Mairi and the money from the business going down the toilet, and being embarrassed in front of his parents. So what? It would pass, which is more than could be said if anything happened to Tessa.

twenty-six

I left Richard at the restaurant and drove through the dark night towards the hospital. Swilling out my mouth with the water bottle, I tried to get rid of the taste of cloying cream sauce, not to mention the bitter acid of fear. I couldn't bear to think about Tessa. I may not be a mother, or even her mother, but Tess had sat on my lap, I'd whispered stories into her perfect and tiny ears and I'd watched her grow from squalling baby into smart toddler. I'd smelt her sweet scent, I'd bathed her soft skin, and I'd held her, close. If that was never going to happen again, if I wouldn't see her grow to leggy child, cool teen and confident young woman, I'd be bereft, I'd miss out, and I'd be diminished not being able to share some of her first exciting moments. And my selfish loss was insignificant compared to Emms' and Greg's. What's going to happen to them if Tessa dies?

There, I'd thought it, expressed it, faced it off, because that was the cold core of my fear. No two ways about it: if that little scrap of naughtiness and love didn't survive, Emma would either implode or explode, and I didn't know which would be the most damaging to herself, or the people around her.

At the traffic lights by Seething Wells, I took another swig of water and noted that my hands were trembling. There was nothing I could do except be by Emms' side. And if the worst happened, I'd have to protect Emms as best I could.

I parked outside A&E and had a soaring sense of déjà vu while I waited to find out where they were. The woman behind the desk wore a mask of disconnect. Blank-faced and grey-haired, she gave out the information in the order of the numbers above her head, not one moment before. What a lousy job, up close to anguish and shock, not to mention the risk of drunk and fearful people lashing out. As I stood in the queue, I looked around and noted the drawn faces, the hollow eyes, the pain, the worry, families trying to cheer each other up whilst the blank-faced woman behind the desk kept order. Kept the pot from boiling over. Kept the fear in the box. It took twenty minutes of me standing there, tapping my fingers, eyes straying to the sign that said there was zero tolerance of abuse to hospital staff, before I was seen. The sign was another cue for me: whatever happened, I had to stop Emms hurting herself, or anyone else. I had to be her friend.

I found Emms in a side room, on the other side of the hospital, sitting on a hard blue plastic chair, staring into a plastic cup of tea. I watched, before I went into the room, as I tried to compose myself, and I saw Emms' hand tremble too much to bring cup to mouth.

'Emms.'

Her face crumpled, 'Liz ... how could I have let this happen? How could I have left Tessa with Greg, who was either drunk, self-obsessed or worrying about the fucking nursery money? We were supposed to be a family, and now my darling Tess is paying the consequences of my choice of father. Just as I paid the consequences for my mother's poor decisions.'

I took the cup out of Emms' shaking hand and hugged her: 'Come on, stop this.' She sobbed into my shoulder, and as Emms wept out her fear, I dared to look up and across the bed at Tessa. Her red hair lay damp and plastered to her face in strands like stripes of blood. The little tyrant who'd danced to high applause in Pizza Express so short a time ago, was gone. In her place was a shrivelled stranger who looked old. An oxygen tube was taped to her tiny nose and both her hands were connected to drips, as if she was a marionette. Her chest rose and fell, and the sound of lungs crackling made me clench my teeth tighter.

'It came on so fast,' Emms pulled away from me, 'I'm used to the kids getting sick and then recovering but this is outside anything that's ever happened, and it's my fault.'

'It's not your fault. That's ridiculous."

'You don't understand. I should never have given Greg responsibility when he simply wasn't up to it. I am to blame for expecting too much from him. I made my job more important than the family and, if I hadn't been so obsessed with making the business work, then Mairi wouldn't have been the blight on us that she had been, the curse: that's what she was – a curse. And you, you told me how it would be with the business and you know what, I wanted to hate you for being right, but really I hated myself.'

'It'll be alright,' I said. 'We'll get through this. We'll ALL get through this.'

Emms let out a huge sigh and I could see her straightening her shoulders and her resolve. She swallowed, 'Sorry, I'm okay, we'll get through this, I know you're right.'

Emms recognised the game we were playing: deny, deny, deny. We'd done it before, we did it when her mother was first diagnosed with secondaries, and we did it when her mother died. Sometimes that's the best way, when the alternative is that bad. That's what I was trying to give her, the ticket to survive the next few hours.

'Good,' I said, in my matter of fact, disinterested voice. 'I spoke to Greg on the way.'

'Did he tell you we had a colossal row? Greg didn't want to believe there was something wrong, and even when I told him that the GP said to call an ambulance he said I was fussing about Tessa. Did he say anything?'

'Not a word - but then he wouldn't. He did say Robbie wants to come and see Tessa. Thinks it's his fault, thinks he gave Tessa the cold. Greg's promised that he can come in as soon as she's better.'

We were silent for a few seconds. "As soon as she's better," must have been hanging in the air.

'What's happening here?' I said.

'Consultant's coming tonight but the tests are back and it's bacterial pneumonia. One drip is antibiotics, the other is liquid to keep her hydrated, and the oxygen is to help her breathe.'

'And?'

'We wait.'

Outside the window, it was densely dark. We were high up on the seventh floor and in the distance I could see little lights spiking the sky like stars. The cloud of anxiety around Emms was breaking up and although she looked grey and drawn, she was calm. A trill from her phone made Emms' head jerk and she pulled her mobile from her pocket.

'What day is it, Liz? I've lost track of time, I don't remember how long I've been here.'

'Friday.'

'I was supposed to send Marcus the monthly figures and discuss them in a conference call. I'd better tell him not to hold his breath. Come with me, he might want to talk to you, too.'

In the anodyne visitors' room, she found a spot in the corner where she could catch a decent signal. A family group of Asians clustered on the sofa, three generations hovering around each other like bees, offering mutual support during the shared sadness of family illness.

'I just keep wishing my mother was here,' Emms fiddled with the phone. 'When I was waiting for you, I could almost feel Mum, hear her voice, and I smelt her, do you remember she used to wear 4711?' Emms put Marcus on speaker and he picked up within two long North American trills.

'Where the hell are you, Emma?' He sounded angry. 'You realise I've been waiting all day for the figures so that I could present them to the board, don't you? Have you any idea how I felt when I had to say I had no idea where you were because you hadn't called in.'

'I'm sorry Marcus, but I –'

'I went out on a limb for you to take over the company with your pal. We could have easily hired someone else, someone who was better qualified and had more experience, but we didn't. We made a commitment to you because you insisted that you were committed to making the business work. And then you disappear. How can you possibly expect us to take you seriously?'

'Give me the phone,' I said. I held out my hand. 'Come on Emms, give me the phone.' I had to stop Marcus saying any more. He went on, 'You had one supporter who said I should check the hospitals and you know what I said? Huh, I said, "I'll put her in hospital when I find her".'

'Marcus,' Emms said softly. 'I am in the hospital, that's where I'm calling from.'

Even though I know that Emms was tortured by anguish over Tess, she looked oddly satisfied, presumably because she'd shut Marcus up. The sound of his gulp and gasp, at the end of the five thousand miles phone call, filled the room.

'I'm in hospital,' Emms said in a dreamy, calm voice, 'With my three-year-old, who has bacterial pneumonia; she's on two drips and oxygen and we're waiting to see the consultant,' I saw the Asian family look over and send her a collective bolt of sympathy. But it didn't soothe Emms; all it did was justify the anger that was building up to boiling point and energising her. I'd seen her like this before: this was what she was like when she nearly decked the woman in the snowy street. Her eyes were dark and shiny, and she spoke precisely. This was all completely out of my control. There was nothing I could do: Emms was unleashed.

'And you know what, Marcus?' she said. 'I don't care about you, the company, the board or any of it. Ever since you did me the big favour of giving us the care-taking job, you've bullied me. It's all carrot and stick with you, isn't it? What about me, Marcus ... what about my family? Why did you insist on meeting in Manchester on Halloween? Shall I tell you why? Because you're a bully and you've kept me going with promises, and all the while my family has been falling apart.'

Out of the corner of my eye I saw a compact man in a badly fitting suit. There was a nurse by his side, and he was looking at Emms, who was in another place. I put my hand on her shoulder, trying to break the spell.

'I think the consultant's here,' I said.

She nodded, 'I've only got one thing to say to you, Marcus. Fuck off and die.'

Apart from the consultant, who seemed to have found the meaning of life in the papers he was studying, everyone in the visitors' room was staring at Emms. The young lad in the family group was wide-eyed and absorbing Emms with an expression of awe and admiration. Perhaps he had never heard a normal-looking woman swear down the phone at someone. Judging by the expressions of the rest of the family, that would be about it.

Emms pocketed her phone and looked up at me brightly. She nodded as if to say, 'Let's get on with it.' I could see that she had moved on from the moment of pissing off Marcus, that she was charging ahead, leaving behind the wake that tipped and unsettled, making us all bob up and down, and she was unaware that there was anything either notable or damaging in her phone exchange. By contrast, I felt hot, charged up, almost as if I'd told Marcus to fuck off myself. It was exhilarating and distracting, and for a wonderful moment took me away from the drama on the table – Tessa. Maybe it was the same for Emms, too.

Could I talk Marcus down and convince him that it was the circumstances that had thrown Emms off balance? Who cares? If Tess died, then it would be the end of everything anyway.

We followed the consultant back to the Tessa's room, like naughty girls following the headmaster to his office. The moment of excitement had passed; now I was numb and resigned to whatever happened during the course of the next few hours.

Essentially, the first type of antibiotic they were stuffing into Tessa hadn't worked, so they were trying a second variety. But in the meantime, Tessa's immune system would become weaker and the risk of fluid gathering in her lungs would increase. If that happened, they would drain off liquid, but the next six hours were critical. If her kidneys couldn't process the antibiotics effectively, there could be life-threatening damage.

'Sounds as if the cure is worse than the illness,' Emms said to the consultant. I frowned at her trying to signal, "tone it down" to no avail. She went on, 'Let me get this straight. Your strategy is to keep trying different brands of drugs and procedures until you either kill my daughter or cure her, is that it?'

'Emms –' I said trying to check her.

The consultant glanced at me and nodded. He was obviously used to distressed parents.

'We really are doing the very best we can, Mrs Harens,' he said.

'What are the chances of ... ?' I trailed off.

'Hard to say. She's a strong child but she's also extremely unwell. The nursing staff are going to make up a bed in the room, so make yourself as comfortable as you can and I'll see you in the morning.'

Emms asked me to phone Greg and update him while she stayed with Tessa. When I got through to him, Greg was also all brusque practicality, which I recognised as his way of coping.

'Robbie is fine. Don't worry about us, we're absolutely fine, on top of everything,' he gabbled. 'You just need to make sure that Emms gets some food inside of her. It may be hospital rubbish, but it's better than nothing. How's she doing?' I heard his voice crack a little and it made my throat feel tight.

'Bearing up.'

'Tell her ... tell her. Liz, I wanted to go with her but - I'm sorry. I'm so sorry. I thought it was just a cold, I didn't realise ... '

'She knows, Greg; she's supervising the nurses who are putting up a bed in the room. I promise I'll organise something to eat,' I borrowed the handy phrase. 'We're all doing the best that we can and that's all we can do.'

'You're right, Liz. It's in the hands of God now.

twenty-seven

As I went back to Tessa's bedside, it occurred to me that I had never before heard Greg express any religious beliefs. He'd always scoffed at what he called god-botherers and religo-freaks. Given the circumstances, this turnabout was hardly surprising, but it still gave me an unpleasant sense of unreality, as if I didn't know these people because I didn't know what they would do under pressure. They were becoming strangers, and I was starting to wonder if I had ever really known either Greg or Emms, because they certainly hadn't known me. For one thing, they didn't even know my real name. I plodded around the hospital and found the café where I bought a couple of sandwiches and coffee and thought about what's real. I was in no hurry to get back to the room. The real me is a coward, an emotional coward who avoids confrontation, who stayed in an abusive marriage for too long and who would rather stand in a café queue than go back to a room and watch a friend's child, my godchild, struggle to survive. How I wish I had half of Emma's fire. Well, if I didn't really have it, at least I could pretend I did, which I suppose is half the battle.

On the way back to the room, I picked up a little speed and tried to be resolute for the night ahead.

Marching along a corridor, stiff-legged, knees locked, my eye caught the framed artwork from the children's ward, scrawls of crayon, sunbursts, and gardens, little houses, stick people and trees and what were obviously hospital beds where other tiny children were trapped by illness.

I bit my lip till the pain arrested my tears. Dragging my gaze away, I fixed my eyes on the end of the corridor and kept them there. For tonight, I was going to be implacable in my pretence, unswerving in my impersonation of bravery. Maybe that's what we all do, pretend to be braver, better, kinder than we really are, and maybe in the action of pretending we find ourselves becoming the thing we're faking. I bloody well hope so.

Inside the side room, the only light was around the bed where Tessa lay struggling to breathe. Her face was waxy and her little chest went up and down emitting a sound like cracking glass. The nurses had made up a couple of camp beds by the wall and Emms was leaning over Tessa, holding her limp hand. She looked up as I came in and I saw Emms' face. No surprises, she looked awful, deep dark hollows under her eyes, and her beautiful hair hanging limply around her white face with none of the usual sculpting bounce. She met my gaze and the sheer wretchedness in her expression made me walk to the window and look out at the distant lights, to collect myself. I couldn't weaken now; it wouldn't help Emms if I cracked up. I had to fake bravery like I've never faked anything in my life.

'Spoke to Greg, all's well, he wants us to eat something and he mentioned God.' Emms didn't respond. 'Anyway, he said we've got to eat, whether we like it or not.'

'Thanks, I don't remember when I ate anything last.'

Emms gently released Tessa's hand and sat down on the makeshift bed with her back against the wall. I joined her and we unwrapped the sandwiches and chewed and swallowed texture without taste. In front of us, Tessa's bed loomed, lit up as we sat in the dark. The room itself was like an island in space with the lights out of the window in the distance and the strange noises from the rest of the hospital outside, the scurrying feet and the call buttons. Inside, there was only the sound of Tessa's crackling lungs.

'I'm not sure what's in this, but it's salty,' I said.

'Liz, do you believe in God? Do you believe that there is a heaven and sin and retribution and punishment for things we've done? Do you think God would punish me by taking Tessa who's never, ever done anything?' Emms inhaled deeply to stop the sob.

'That wouldn't be any God I'd vote for.' I put my free arm around her shoulders; they felt stiff and bony under the fabric of her tee shirt. Emms shook me off; she was trying to make me understand.

'Maybe we don't have a choice. Maybe the vengeful God is round the corner, waiting to destroy us. Maybe the Catholics are right with their confession and absolution.'

'Hey, come on, Emms. Whatever happens, it isn't a punishment. It doesn't work like that. God, whoever he, she or it is, doesn't smite people down through their children.'

I knew what she was doing, trying to find a reason and a pattern to make sense of Tessa being ill.

'It'll be okay.' I said.

'No, Liz, you don't understand. I did something,' Emms grabbed my hand and gripped it so tight between her own that it hurt. 'When you were in Florida, I went out for a walk with Mairi. It was a really windy day after the big storm. We were by the river on the recreation ground behind the house.'

Her breath was hot against my face and I could smell tuna. 'Mairi said stuff about Greg and the kids and how much they loved her, all of them, and she said I had the business and a good friend and that she deserved to have my family. So I prodded her, but I didn't push her, Liz. God knows, I didn't push her into the river.'

Ears ringing, my voice sounded as if it was coming from a long way, away.

'What are you saying, Emms?'

Fear glittered in her eyes, 'It wasn't my fault. I ... we ... don't deserve to be punished. And ever since then, I've seen her. Here and there, in the Waitrose car park of all places. Outside Martin's café. I don't know if she's alive and is persecuting us or if I'm imagining it. I've been thinking that maybe she got hold of some bacteria and somehow infected Tessa. You can do that, you know. Maybe she's doing it because I told her she couldn't have the children. Whatever she does, they can never be hers.'

Emms clung to me and spoke into my shoulder, rocking. 'I had to protect us, Liz. I had to protect all of us. I shouldn't be punished. I'm a good person, a good mother ....' She was trembling in my arms, shaking; I could sense that her teeth were chattering.

I felt choked, as if a hand was closing round my neck stopping me breathing, but I couldn't let Emms know. Not tonight. Not with Tessa so dangerously ill.

'Of course you're a good mother and a good person,' I said. Now, come on, you've got to lie down, you've been awake for forty-eight hours, you've barely eaten. Just close your eyes and try to sleep. That's it, there's nothing to worry about.' I fought to make my voice soothing, and I must have succeeded, because Emms let me straighten out her limbs on the makeshift bed. I covered her with a blanket, and within minutes her heavy breathing had softened to the sound of sleep. Quietly, so as not to wake her, I got to my feet and walked to the window, where I stared out at the lights in the distance. There was no option. I might be able to pretend that I was brave, but I couldn't pretend that Emms hadn't told me what she'd done to Mairi.

twenty-eight

I knew that Emms was close by, but I didn't know where I was. At least not for sure. In the light and shade of the hospital room, with the sound of footsteps and the clicking pulse of the monitors, I drifted in and out of a nightmarish sleep with vivid dreams in saturated colour. I was inside the picture that was on the wall in the office, the one with the turquoise river and blue trees on the riverbank. First I was on the dark riverbank and then I was in the water, being dragged along, choking for air. Even worse, I knew I was dreaming and I couldn't get out of it, until I hauled myself back to consciousness and found myself sweating and shaking in the hospital camp bed, from where I could see the shape of Emms and hear the sound of her steady breathing.

Over and again, I replayed what Emms had said, trying to make sense of it, trying to interpret where her frantic worry about Tessa might have led her. In the jumble of what she'd said, it was evident that she'd had the same conversation with Mairi as I'd had; the one where Mairi explained with her infinite logic the justification for moving in on Greg. What I didn't know is how Emms had reacted and I feared the worst. For hours I sat on the camp bed, listening to Tessa's crackling lungs, Emms' steady breathing, smelling her prevailing scent of anti-bacterial fluid mixed with Eau Dynamisante, watching the monitors and the lights out of the dark window.

What was going to happen? After the nightmare, I was too scared to close my eyes and try to sleep again, too frightened to think about what Emms would say when we had the inevitable confrontation about Mairi, so I forced myself to stay awake and directed my twilight mind to drift back to other camp beds and a camping holiday we'd had way, way back, when we first became friends. We'd driven down to Brittany in my clapped-out Renault, crossed to St Malo on the pitching ferry, got repeatedly lost, missed turnoffs and ended up in fields, with dusk coming and no idea where we were. During the day, we tramped the red granite beaches and at night we drank red wine and ate tarts from the traiteur. Outside, it rained, and rained, pattering the tent, and we made jokes about being intrepid explorers. I felt safe.

When I woke up, it was light, and for a moment I neither knew where I was nor remembered what had happened. But with consciousness came the terrible weight of memory, right in my gut. It was as hard as a horse's kick. I started, sat up and looked around, scrabbling towards the hospital bed. Standing around the bedside were the consultant, doctor, nurse and Emms, all leaning over the bed in which

Tessa lay still. Emms was covering her eyes with her right hand and her shoulders shuddered.

'What?' I rasped.

'She's okay,' Emms said. 'She's going to be okay.'

I turned to the consultant for confirmation. He nodded. He even looked relieved. 'This really is one very tough little girl.'

Emms was still crying, nose filled with mucus, eyes with tears, she sobbed, 'Tessa, lovely girl.' As if in response, Tessa's eyes flickered open and Emms held her hand and let the tears drop onto the sheet unchecked. With half on eye on them, I talked to the doctors and said all the right things, and let Emms focus on Tessa. First things first. In spite of the relief that Tessa was going to live, I felt like throwing up when I looked at Emms and remembered what she had said the night before and what I had to do today.

After a while, Emms' tears slowed and she glanced around with wide, barely focusing eyes. I couldn't meet her gaze.

'The medics have gone for the moment,' I said. 'They'll be back shortly to change the antibiotic. Apparently, there's a shower somewhere here we can use, or if you want, you can go home and I'll stay till you get back.'

'Are you okay?' Emms said, not waiting for an answer. 'Or just exhausted? I'm sure I stink but I need a coffee before anything else. That was some night, how about you? Do you want to go and get coffee and I'll stay here and wait for Greg to turn up, then we can go and sort ourselves out, or would you like to go home? Once again, you've saved my life, Ms Verrall.'

'I'll get us both some coffee,'

By the time I got back to the room, Greg and Robbie were there and I had the most dazzling sense of déjà vu. Greg was leaning over Tessa's bed and Robbie was in Emms' lap.

'Thank God,' Greg said. 'And thank you, Liz, thanks for being here.' He was unshaven and his hair was standing up in mad, greasy tufts. 'Do you two want to get something to eat while Robbie and I hold the fort?'

'Let's do that,' I said. 'Come on, Emms, she'll be fine and we won't be long.' I put my hand on Emms' elbow.

'Are we sure she'll be all right? I really don't want to leave her, Greg. I'm frightened after all this. Are we sure that's she's on the mend?'

'Liz's boyfriend has already been on the phone. He knows the consultant and half the staff here; he says this is one of the three best units in the country. Tessa will be fine and if there's the slightest change, I'll call you.' He waggled his phone in the air.

Emms brushed her hair off her forehead, 'I really do need some food and the chance to wash my hands and face, and we could also go by the hospital shop and see if they've got any cleaning materials,'

I guided Emms towards the door and we started to move through the rest of the ward, out past the nurses' station. I couldn't look at her; I didn't want to connect or share or sympathise or rejoice that

Tessa was alive. I needed to be detached so that I could ask what needed to be asked and assess Emms' response with a clear mind. Or as clear a mind as possible. As we walked, I could feel my heart hammering and I knew what that was about; I was scared of her.

Even though Emms should have been as tired as me, she had a spring in her step, and she babbled about cleaning materials and the pros and cons of staying in the hospital in terms of infection and stabilisation. She seemed completely unaware of what she'd said the night before, and that made me even more frightened. As soon as she had a coffee and a chocolate muffin in front of her, I launched in with no preamble.

'We're going to have to go to the police,' I said. 'You need to tell them what happened.' I could feel the tension around my mouth but I didn't look away. Emms frowned and then she cocked her head to one side.

'Tessa's going to be fine,' she said. 'Why do we need to go the police? Liz, I don't understand, do you think the hospital have been negligent in any way? That would be awful; we'd need to do something about it. I'm so zoned out that I don't know what's going on.'

'I'm not talking about the hospital; I'm talking about what you said last night. About Mairi. About having an argument by the side of the river,' I looked over my shoulder to see if anyone was listening, then I lowered my voice and leaned forward. There was sleep in Emms' eyes that had crusted her eyelashes. 'You said that you prodded her and she fell in the river behind the recreation ground. You said it was the day after the big storm.'

Emms stopped stirring her sugarless latte. 'Did I say that? Did I really say that last night? I'm not sure if I dreamt it or fantasised about it, but I can assure you that it certainly didn't happen. I must have been completely out of my mind, I know I was distraught last night and exhausted from not sleeping but I didn't know it was that bad. I suppose I didn't know what was real and what wasn't. What else did I say?'

'You said you thought that you kept seeing Mairi and that she might have infected Tessa with bacteria in revenge.' As I repeated what Emms had said, it struck me how ridiculous these absurd statements sounded. It wasn't Emms – it was me who was losing it.

Emms shook her head. 'You'd better not tell Greg, that's all he needs to worry about at the moment, me going crazy. That Mairi, what a job she did on us. Not only did she con us out of the nursery money, but she scrambled our brains to boot.'

'What about her saying to you that she deserved your family? I know that's what she said, because she said it to me too.'

Emms reached across the table and took my hand. She squeezed it, and I felt the strength under her soft skin.

'She said the same thing to me: when I took the soup round to her. She was sitting on her ratty sofa under a duvet without a cover that was stained with heaven knows what. I was standing there with a thermos of homemade soup. After all we'd done for her, it was so nuts and so ungrateful, I almost laughed, but I managed not to. Though, I must admit, I did tell her that I would kill her before I let her near my children again. That must be why I had the dream or whatever it was. There was something about the river but I don't know what it was ...' Emms was thoughtful for a moment, and then she was back and squeezed my hand afresh. 'I'm so sorry I upset you, you do too much for us, Liz, too much for me. I'm not sure what I've done to deserve a friend like you, but I'm just happy you're here.'

Finally I relaxed, the tension drained away, like fetid water down a plughole. 'I've got to admit, it did seem a bit far-fetched, and I should have noted the rant about Mairi deliberately infecting Tess as being delusional. But at least it explained what happened to Mairi. I've got to tell you, Emms – it's bothering me. I don't understand why, if she was after Greg – which she was – and she thought that he was within her sights, she'd piss off.'

'Maybe my threat worked; maybe she wasn't even after him. Maybe she was always hoping to be paid off. Maybe she realised that she wasn't going to get Greg, so she cut her losses. That would be shrewd, and whatever you say about Mairi, she wasn't stupid. She knew how to play people.'

I could see that, I remember the birthday rant, the Christmas concert one-upmanship. She always knew what she was doing and the effect she wanted to have. I nodded. 'Yes, that might be her shtick. Richard said that she threatened to tell the GMC that he'd raped her.'

'Nice.'

'I didn't know whether to believe him.'

'Believe him?' Emms said. 'Why didn't you tell me?'

'Because like I said, I didn't know whether to believe him. I still don't. Even for Mairi, that's a bit extreme. What is she, a small-time con artist or a blackmailer?'

'Maybe both. What's the difference? She's gone.'

'Don't you think we should go to the police and stop her doing to someone else what she was trying to do to us? How are we going to feel if we read in the papers in a couple of years' time that she's screwed some young couple out of their life savings?'

'You know something: you're right,' Emms nodded thoughtfully, 'You're one hundred per cent right, we have a responsibility. I'm going talk to Greg about this. Just because Theo's rich enough and happy enough to write off the con, it doesn't make it okay. Knowing what we now know about her, we wouldn't forgive ourselves if we did nothing about it - she needs to be made accountable for what she did. But first of all, let's get Tessa all better and back home. For the minute, she's the priority. A couple of weeks isn't going to make the slightest bit of difference to Mairi's – or whatever she's calling herself – new con trick. What do you say?'

'Agreed, that's a plan.' As Emms said, a couple of weeks weren't going to make a difference, and it would give me a chance to think about where Mairi might be. 'I'll start thinking about the best way to approach this; we could search for her ourselves or hire a detective. What do we know about those friends of hers in Devon? Didn't she say they ran a pub? They might have a lead into where she might be.'

'You're the ideas person,' Emms said.

'The best idea in the whole world is no good without the execution.'

'Agreed,' Emms said. 'Execution is everything.'

twenty-nine

The first thing I did when I got back to the flat was rip off my clothes and head for the shower, where I stood and finally sat in the shower tray, letting water pour off me until it ran cold. As the water and shampoo stung my eyes, I began to feel something physical that stopped the thoughts chasing each other around my brain. I knew my eyes would be going red; well, Richard would just have to put up with it. He was due to come around with some food. He'd said that he'd cook while I lay on the sofa and watched something suitably soporific and unchallenging on the TV. That was his expression: soporific. I needed that. I felt as if I needed to decompress, as if I was coming up from the murky depths of the ocean where there were wrecks and barnacles and nightmares and darkness. Fuck. I'm just not equipped for this level of stress.

I hauled myself upright and rinsed my hair in cold water before I stepped out and hugged a towel around myself as if it was a friend. How should I start processing all this crap charging around my head? I was starting to feel the way I used to, in the bad old days, when I was married, trapped in a nightmare that I couldn't escape, with my mind rambling and rattling and squawking with mad thoughts. Yes, Emms had explained everything, but I was still reeling from the night, the nightmares and, let's face it, my fear. I took a lungful of the damp shower air; I had to compose myself before Richard turned up. It was hard to believe that it was only twenty-four hours ago that we'd been sitting in that odd Italian restaurant and he was rubbishing Greg with some scuttlebutt gossip. Impossible to consider that in that time, I'd watched Emma probably piss away the business by telling Marcus to fuck off, seen Tessa fight for her life and win, and best of all, or in fact, worst of all, sat in on Emms' dark dreams and fantasies about killing Mairi, and even believed that's what she'd done. No wonder I was wound up like a yoyo. It wasn't just sitting up all night replaying what Emma had said about the river and Mairi: it was the whole shebang. I badly needed to come down, and telling Richard the whole story wouldn't help my frazzled mind.

I rough-dried my hair and patted my face, feeling, as I habitually do, for the ridge on the bridge of my nose. The last glorious twenty-four hours went into the same private box as my broken nose.

Three weeks after John had tried and failed to burn my dressing gown, he broke my nose. For reasons that I am simply not prepared to attempt to understand, even now, and please note my self-loathing, after the dressing gown incident, I had accepted his apology and I was still living in the house. In my benighted state, I actually suggested that we invite the neighbours for supper. For a student like myself, this seemed like a wonderfully grown-up and couple-like activity. I remember, I'd spent the day cleaning and cooking, the table was laid with everything I could find in the cupboards and the glasses sparkled. The dining area was a step up from the open-plan sitting room, its walls were exposed brick and the dining table itself was the smoothest, darkest cherry wood. Like chocolate. My feeble cooking skills just about stretched to a roast dinner, and while the meat was in the oven, pud in the fridge and table laid, I went to have a bath. I hadn't locked the door, why would I? That's when John came back. He was drunk.

'What the fuck's going on here?' John said as he loomed over me. Sober, he was attractive in a rugged kind of way, but when he was drunk, he was ugly, blotchy and fleshy. And from his face, I could see he'd probably been drinking since lunchtime. Drinking and who knows what else. My stomach tightened.

'I told you this morning that Ben and Sophie are coming round for supper. You said you'd bring some wine on the way home, but it doesn't matter if you didn't because I'm sure we've got enough.'

'Who the fuck are Ben and Sophie?'

My stomach tightened and I felt the weight on my solar plexus as if an invisible hand was pushing down on me. Closing my eyes, I tried to compose an answer that wouldn't inflame John, who was obviously looking for a fight. I failed.

'They live next door.'

'Open your eyes!' he shouted. 'Open your eyes when I'm talking to you. Who the fuck are Ben and Sophie?'

'I told you, they live next door. Now please get out of the bathroom' I opened my eyes and then wanted to close them again. He was leaning right over the bath. Before I could do anything, he had his arms under my armpits and was trying to drag me out. He was strong, but I was wet and slippery. My leg came over the side and then I toppled, hit my thigh on the way down and whacked my nose against the toilet. I felt the crack, I heard the crack, and then I saw the blood. There was a moment or two when I lay on the bathroom floor, waiting to see if he was going to do anything else, kick me, punch me, pull my hair, but happily the sight of my blood calmed him. And then I noticed how much my nose hurt. Really fucking hurt.

John called a taxi to take me to A&E and when the neighbours turned up, he explained my absence by convincing Ben and Sophie that I'd had a cooking accident. And I was too ashamed to tell them, or anyone else, otherwise.

But that was then. Now, eleven years later, I sat on the edge of another bath massaging the ridge on my reconstructed nose. When I wore specs, you couldn't see it at all, and even though the reconstructive surgery was unpleasant, to say the least, it was in the past. I towelled myself briskly, trying to warm up my skin before I got dressed. What I had to remember was that not everyone is like John and, what's more, Richard is about as unlike my ex-husband as any man I have ever met. So it was all on me. If I didn't learn how to trust people in general, and men in particular, then I'd have allowed the past to dictate my present, and that would mean that John had won. What's more, if I couldn't trust Emma or Richard, well, what did that say about trusting myself?

Not much.

After dressing in pyjamas, I dashed off an email to Marcus explaining exactly how close to death Tessa had been and proposing that he forget that the phone call had ever taken place. I assured him that I would go into the office and source the figures that he wanted and that he would have them as soon as possible. Not for the first time, I blessed the time difference between the UK and Canada. I read over the email before I sent it, and, if I say so myself, it was masterly. He may have an ego the size of Lake Erie and be a preppie automaton, but replacing Emms and me would take time and cost money. I'd given him enough reasons to get over Emms' phone call.

I looked at my watch. Richard was unusually late, but that was just fine: the minutes allowed me to marshal my thoughts. It was about time that I told Richard about my past and why I'd changed my name. If I really wanted to get over the past, and finally let John go, then it was only reasonable to start off by telling Richard who I really was.

A little later, Richard was bustling around in the kitchen and I was nursing a glass of wine. I'd like to say that he was revealing culinary skills of great prowess, but it was evident that he didn't spend that much time at the chopping board by the way he was reading the instructions on the packet of pasta. But, what the hell? There's more to a man than culinary skills and his attempt at doing something at which he was so unskilled was heart-warming. The least I could do was be honest with him and once we'd got over that, he might even be able to help with tracking down con woman Mairi. My only question was whether to tell him the whole sorry tale of my marriage before we'd eaten or after. I plumped for after, as I suspected that I might disturb what seemed to be an exacting process, judging by the depth of his frown.

'When it says ten minutes cooking time, does that mean before or after it's achieved its boiling point? Then should I wait till the pan reaches boiling point once more, which may take another minute and a half because, if this is not the case, the pasta will be overcooked. Or will it be alright?'

'I'm sure it will be great, and it's very kind of you to do this. I must also thank you for using your hospital connections with Tessa's consultant.'

Not only was the pasta overcooked when it reached the plate, but the sauce was also diluted. I truly didn't care. It was secondary to maintaining my equilibrium and doing what I should have done the first night we'd had sex. Told him the truth.

'Richard, you know that thing you do that really annoys me when you say there's something you need to talk to me about ... well now it's my turn.' I put down my glass and had the immense satisfaction of seeing that I had his entire attention. And then some.

'Go on.'

'I told you I was divorced. What I didn't tell you was that I was in an abusive relationship and that I had ...' This was a whole lot harder than I thought, even though I had rehearsed saying it. His eyes were wide and I swallowed to help me continue. 'I had a couple of physical injuries before I left my husband and, well, I effectively walked out and disappeared because I was frightened of him. And, the thing is, I was completely nuts, actually. I did some very strange things.'

Richard took my hand, raised it to his lips and kissed my palm. It was an extraordinarily un-Richard action, as he's not given to great displays of affection.

'Thank you for telling me,' We sat in silence for a few seconds while I prepared for the next revelation about my name. Before I could speak Richard said, 'I think everybody behaves in an aberrant way from time to time. Indeed, if someone says they are completely sane, they're the people to monitor. There were times with my ex-wife when I was so angry with her, so incandescently furious, that I calmed myself by constructing elaborate fantasies about her dying. My favourite was a speedboat accident – random and violent. I thought about how I would react, I went through the whole sequence of events, her funeral, the condolences, even the order of service. So every time we had a row, and that was a frequent occurrence, I would watch her, listen to her adolescent rant, and then play my version of events all over again, so I might be sitting across the table from her and thinking should the casket be oak or should it be white? I even used to go online and look at funeral director rates.' Richard laughed. It was a dry sound. 'That was about the time I met Mairi. And yes, I know you don't want to talk about her,' he shushed me with his hand. 'But she was lovely, and helpless and vulnerable and she didn't belittle me. She didn't demand, well not at first. But when Mairi shed her charming carapace and started threatening me, my fantasies became even darker. Even more violent and sensory. It rather surprised me.'

Richard was looking into my eyes, but he wasn't looking at me. I felt chilled by his tone but more than that, by his detachment. I don't know where he was but at that moment, he certainly wasn't with me, and what's more, I didn't know who he was or what he might have done or, indeed, might do if the same moment came over him. How could I possibly trust him? As if to confirm my thoughts, he came back from wherever he was and kissed my hand again.

The hairs on my neck stood up and it took all my self-control not to shudder.

'We all have a dark side,' he said. 'The only issue is whether or not we act on it."

thirty

Lying next to Richard that Saturday night, I barely slept, as I replayed not only what he'd said, but also the way that he said it. Wide-eyed, I looked into the dark of the room, frightened to turn because I didn't want to wake him. I didn't want another conversation until I had processed the last one. Who was this man by my side? Long before dawn had outlined the bottom of the curtain, I had constructed my excuse to get him out of the door first thing on Sunday. I said that I had to go and see Emms and the moment that the door was closed behind him, I flopped down on the nearest chair and an exquisite sense of lightness poured through me as the anxiety of the night gave way to relief. So much for making Richard the holder of my secrets; a man who fantasised about his wife's funeral. An involuntary laugh burst from me, and I shook my head in disbelief. I couldn't even tell Emms that her Crippen joke was closer to reality than she had ever thought; not for the time being, anyway. For the moment, it was simply a case of getting through the day with the minimum of anxiety and as soon as everything was settled, easing myself out, out and away.

An image of my parent's backyard in Manley came to me, the slightly shambolic paved area outside the sitting room with the pots of primroses my mother tended and talked to, the pair of them sitting at the metal table, Dad in his gardening shorts, Mum in one of her peacock-coloured tee shirts, having a drink before dinner, while the roast rested. I had to get out of here to a place where the biggest problem was the cricket score and the next holiday destination. But for the moment, it was one day at a time; helping Emms get through the trauma of nearly losing her daughter and convincing Marcus that telling him to fuck off was a quaint British way of saying 'I'm stressed'.

Unsurprisingly, Emms had forgotten about the business and was in hygiene overdrive, cleaning floors, door handles, sinks and toys and anything that might carry bacteria. Part of her heightened health anxiety led to her persecuting the nursing staff in case they brought more germs anywhere near Tessa. Yes, I know it was extreme, but under the circumstances who could blame her? When she told me that she had reported two nurses to the senior sister for not washing their hands for the correct amount of time, I didn't have the heart to suggest that she was over-reacting, and what was the point anyway?

I was left with her other baby – the business. My email to Marcus had bought extra time to deliver the figures, but then the problem became who was going to do it. Guess. I snatched four days' grace and had a hellish time manoeuvring around spreadsheets, all the while wondering why and how I had got myself into this mess, and how quickly I might be able to get out of it. Between her disinfecting forays, Emms talked me through the cells, columns and formulae over the phone and in video conference calls. I'd see her on the big screen in the meeting room, with her blue disposable gloves, a black plastic rubbish bag and anti-bacterial wipes as she wiped and binned all the surfaces whilst trying to explain how to get out of a circular formula on the spreadsheet. On the upside, I was genuinely too busy to either worry or find the time to see Richard. I didn't even have a spare hour to go to the hospital, which was just as well, because Emms had forbidden visitors in case they brought in bacteria. All I did for her was buy the children a fluffy toy dog apiece and then arranged to meet Greg at Martin's to pass them over. I suspected that she'd fumigate the new toys or even dump them, but at least she'd know I was thinking of her.

Greg was late and blamed the parking in Bridge Street in a meandering rant that gave me the opportunity to take a closer look at him. Never a master of sartorial grace, Greg usually looked clean; however, even though Emms had only been in hospital for three nights, he looked as if he had been up through every single one of those nights and had neither bathed nor shaved.

'So this is where the secret society meets,' Greg looked around the café in a fake cheery manner.

'Better roll up your trouser leg,' I said.

He laughed hard, much too hard for it be natural. It sounded as if it hurt. I went on, 'Besides the parking problem, how are you, Greg? How are you dealing with all this? Emms told me about Mairi doing a runner with the investment money for the nursery. I really don't know what to think about all that and I can't imagine it must have been much fun telling your folks.'

'My parents are on a cruise spending three times what she ran off with,' Greg rubbed his shoulder, as if by doing so he could ease out the knots, 'I don't think it's going to be hurting them too badly. I must admit, I was worried about telling them, but they were completely relaxed. Funny, when I remember them arguing about money when we were kids. Dad took a hit in the early 90s, we had to sell the house, and Mum went back to work to keep us at school.' Greg drifted off; he must have been thinking back. I could see he was unshaven and his skin was blotchy. At last his attention returned, 'Anyway, what are you having?' he looked at his watch. 'We could have a drink if you prefer.'

It was two o'clock in the afternoon on a working day. 'We're settled now and I've got to get back to speak to Toronto: perhaps another time, although I bet you need a drink at the moment. How are Emms and Tessa doing?'

'Good. They're taking Tessa off the oxygen today and if she's breathing okay, they'll let her out tomorrow.'

'Wow. Big relief.' The tea and cakes arrived and I gave Greg the presents for the children. Whilst I poured and he ate the carrot cake I took a closer look at him, and he looked like shit. When he lifted the cup up to his lips, his hand trembled and his eyes were bloodshot. But I was not going to make my life any more complicated than it already was, and that meant no questions or statements beyond the polite and obvious.

'We're both very grateful for you spending the night at the hospital.' Greg sounded slightly closer to his normal self.

'As sleepovers go, that was about the worst one of my entire life,' I said in an attempt to lighten up the atmosphere, to absolutely no avail.

'What do you mean? What are you trying to say?'

Greg looked furtive, even shifty. He leaned across the table and I smelled sweat. I realised what the sour smell was, it was alcohol leaking out of his pores.

'Liz, bear with me for a moment, but I want to ask you about Emms. I've been worried about her for months,'

I felt my throat close up and the ringing in my ears drowned out the classical music from the stereo. I removed my specs and started polishing the lenses, hopeful that this might halt Greg's outburst. It didn't.

'Haven't you noticed how superstitious she's become? You knew her before I did, but she never used to be like that. When we first met she always used to laugh at that sort of thing, and then there was all the anxiety about Tony. God knows, I encouraged her to take over the business, but I didn't expect it would be this hard. She never stops working and if she's not working, she's worrying about it. And then there's the cleaning: you must have seen it, wiping the floor, spreading disinfectant on the surfaces, sterilising cutlery. Liz, it really wasn't my fault that Tessa got ill. I thought it was just a kiddie cold, the sort they get all the time, but Emms is holding me responsible. She says it's my fault. There's no point you giving me these toys because she won't let me visit in case I bring in some infection. Christ knows what's going to happen when she gets out of there.'

'Look, Greg, she has been under pressure, to put it mildly. And since you ask, I have noticed that she's become superstitious and also, since you ask, lots of people have mild OCD and have little rituals – it doesn't mean anything. Either it will go away of its own accord when she has a chance to relax, or she can do some therapy. Cognitive behavioural therapy has excellent results, in fact, I was reading about -'

'What about her obsession with Mairi?'

I was silent for a moment, trying to think how to phrase it and then I thought, what the hell. I put my cake fork down and leaned back in my chair.

'Oh come on, Greg, don't you think you're being a little unreasonable? I saw Mairi putting the moves on you, and if you were my husband, I'd have been equally obsessed; I thought Emms was incredibly kind and reasonable. Besides being a con artist, that woman was a total bitch and you don't know the half of it.'

Greg raised his hands, 'She didn't mean any harm; she was vulnerable and had no friends.'

'No friends? For goodness sake, listen to yourself. You're talking about some con woman who cheated your father out of several thousand pounds. And now you're saying that Emms was obsessed. This isn't about Emms: this is about you.'

Greg scraped his chair backwards and stood up. He reached into his pocket, presumably to pull out his wallet, and a hip flask fell out and hit the floor. We both looked at the flask and then at each other.

'Forget everything I said,' Greg said. 'I was out of order, I've got to pick up Robbie.' And with that he snatched up the flask from the floor and shuffled towards the till. As I watched him lean towards the waitress to pay, I thought he looked like a shambling old man and I felt a rush of anger that he was drinking and supposed to be looking after the children. Fuck, how irresponsible could he be? He was driving, too. What was he going to do, put Robbie in the car and drive with him?

I grabbed my stuff and charged after Greg, catching up with him a few steps down the street. He was hovering outside the pub, obviously on the point of going in for a reviving nip of whatever he was drinking. Turning round at the sound of my steps, in the sharp sunlight he looked even worse than in the murky dim of Martin's. A cyclist at the end of a ride pushed past us, forcing us closer and I got another unpleasant wave of Greg's alcoholic odour. Then I had a blinding flash of why it was so familiar. It was beer sweat. I used to smell it on John after he'd been out watching the rugby, with 'the boys'. It was sweet and yeasty, like decay, and it used to seep out of his clammy skin as he snored by my side. That's where I'd smelt it before.

'Oh ... Liz ... did I forget something?' he checked himself, his pocket, his keys, again giving me that milky, unfocused glazed-eye look.

'I just forgot to ask you something, something I didn't want to think about. Were you shagging Mairi? Is that what this is all about? You feel guilty and are trying to blame Emms for whatever shit is going on between you. No wonder Emms doesn't want you to come to the hospital, unless she thinks you'll do a detour and go to rehab. But what about Mairi?'

He tried to turn away, but I reached out and pulled him back so we were eyeball to eyeball. 'It wasn't like that ... you don't understand ...' he trailed off and swallowed hard.

'Oh for fuck's sake, Greg, what happened?'

'I didn't ... I didn't shag her ...'

'You didn't? Then what was going on between you on Christmas cake day? I know something happened, I could see it in her face. You know something? Mairi told me that things were going really well between you two, and that it was just a matter of time before you left Emms and were happy lovebirds, together, forever.'

'Oh Christ,' his hands twitched and his eyes glanced towards the pub. I could see how desperately he wanted to be in there downing something to anaesthetise himself.

'I know, Greg,'

'Why didn't you tell Emms,' he said in a small voice.

'I was trying to protect her, and I didn't believe that you of all people would fuck up your marriage for a bitch like Mairi.'

'You don't understand, you really don't.'

'What were you hoping to achieve by bleating to me about Emms being nuts? Why were you telling me? Did you seriously think for one minute that I was going to take your side against my best friend when I saw what was going on? You were shagging Mairi whilst Emms was working herself to death. You were playing at setting up the nursery business and now you're pissed off that your parents have ended up paying for what was a mightily expensive shag.'

Greg's hands were rammed in his pockets and he was shaking his head through my rants looking like a distressed horse. At the end he looked up with sheer pain in his eyes.

'Whatever you may think and however much you despise me, I didn't shag her. But something happened.'

He turned around and walked off. This time I let him go. There was nothing else to say. This dithering about shagging Mairi was merely semantics. He had just said that 'something happened': I definitely didn't want to know what spin his alcohol-addled brain had put on that statement. It would only be so much shit and no doubt the type of thing John had cooked up on the way home during the course of our marriage. My breath was coming in short gasps and I felt like I wanted to bang my head against something. How could I have been so spectacularly stupid? Everything I'd done in the last few months, from the moment I'd agreed to be joint managing director of the business, had been stupid. Richard was a mistake, the company was a mistake and I should have just said 'no', but I thought I could handle the connection, I thought that being close to Emms protected me in some way. I believed that friendship was important and it was better than being alone.

'Shit, shit, shit.'

For the next three days, I pulled up the digital drawbridge and filtered my calls and emails. The only communications I responded to were work-related. Marcus got my full attention and, hard to believe, I actually started to understand the array of figures on the spreadsheets. This was no doubt due to the hours that I spent at the office and the hours I spent at home working at my serpentine oak desk in the spare room. I hadn't used it since I wrote my dissertation, and I'd always associated it with that struggle in my life so I suppose it was only apt that I was back at the leather top that I had rubbed and polished back into use.

Richard was relatively easy to avoid. We had one date that I was blissfully able to cut short with a conference call from an unhappy client and he was scheduled to go to Baltimore to some conference at Johns Hopkins about prosthetics. Even though Tessa was back home and seemingly improved, Emms still wasn't coming in to the office. Any work she did was shunted around electronically and, although I had to nag her about deadlines, I was happier that she was at home. Leaving the kids with Greg seemed like another stupid idea, and I'm sure Emms had had her fill of hired help.

By March, the yellow forsythia was out and as the days became lighter, there was a hint of promise that, at long last, the endless winter was coming to an end. I'd hired a freelance trainer, a former actor like Tony, who was young, keen and good, and although that meant I wasn't doing the front-end work of the company, the part that I enjoyed, I was at least able to carve out some more time for myself and even look forward to spring and the possibility of summer holidays.

However, milder weather not only brought out the forsythia, the tickly pink blossom and the sticky buds, it also uncovered a darker and decomposing truth.

thirty-one

Some long-lost quote lingered at the edges of my mind: the gist of it was that because the weather in England is so lousy so often, when there's a good day, it's better than anywhere else in the world. Today was one of those days that supported the quote; clear, fresh, glistening like a perfect present. That morning, outside my bathroom, a blackbird seemed to be having the exact same thought - it felt good to be alive - and as I put on my watch and rings, I gave Emms' pink candy quartz, a rub and admired it on my finger.

On the way to work, I stopped at a patisserie and bought a selection of Danish pastries for the troops to chomp through during the morning meeting, and by midday I'd dashed off a couple of new business pitches and spent the afternoon finessing my newly acquired spreadsheet skills. I could bear it. I was actually starting to understand why Emms liked the mathematical side of the business: there was something pleasing about the symmetry of the numbers, and the bottom line took the emotion out of decision-making. There were no grey areas of doubt when something was either profitable, or it wasn't.

Richard was back on the scene, but with some new ground rules. After my night of self-induced terror following his dark side chat, I told him that I didn't want to do sleepovers for the moment, because I had to get as much sleep as possible so I could put in the necessary hours. He wasn't exactly happy about the new regime, but I didn't give a monkey's. That's the way it was, I had to keep my space to myself, and I told him that it was that or nothing at all. Like I said, I didn't care. And I truly didn't. You see, being back in a familiar world, where I didn't engage, was more comforting than I can ever describe. It was like slipping on an old jumper where you've worn down the elbows, the collar's askew, there are threads hanging, but when you slip that jumper over your head, it's as if some old friend has their arms round you. I like to think that I was being Zen, not connecting, not owning, not attaching, and letting it all go. In my heart of hearts, I knew that the truth was bleaker. But there was no way that I was going to go there.

It was dusk when I left work, got into my car and started the engine, I heard the low rumble of the diesel come to life and eased out of the car park. As was my habit, I switched on the radio, looking for some music that I could jig along to. First choice was Radio Jackie. I glanced at the digital clock; I ought to be able to catch the last thirty minutes of the show on thc way home.

'And in local news, a body has been recovered from the River Mole behind West End recreation ground. It's been identified as Mairi Sondergaard, a freelance nursery nurse who had been missing for some months. In sport, Esher will be meeting Twickenham on Saturday for one of the last matches of the season, team manager –'

My head jerked back as if I'd been hit and I started trembling uncontrollably. I scoped around desperately for somewhere I could pull in and somehow managed to manoeuvre the car out of the traffic into a lay-by.

'Jesus Christ,'

Had I really heard what I thought I'd heard?

Images and words crashed in on me, and I was rocking in the seat of the car in anguish, paralysed. There must be some mistake, I must have misheard, it was a trick, a misunderstanding, someone with a similar name. I scrabbled in my bag for my phone and attempted to call the newsroom at Jackie, but my hands were shaking so much that I'd lost all dexterity and I couldn't make the phone work. My fingers seemed like fat sausages at the end of someone else's hands.

I don't know how long I sat there: all I remember is that my over-riding desire was to do what I'd done before, start the car, find a bank, take out all the cash I could access and keep driving. Leave everything behind, the flat, the business and my previous life. I'd done it before. I could do it again.

At last, I stopped shaking enough to be able to drive and limp home. My rationale: whatever I did, whoever I became, I would still need my passport.

Not bothering to turn the lights on, I felt my way to the kitchen, grabbed an open bottle of red wine and emptied it into my morning breakfast mug that was draining in the sink. Then, still standing, I gulped down the wine, feeling the alcohol hit my empty stomach and warm it. Right. Now I was ready to phone Emms and get her take on this interesting turn of events, see what she was going to come up with this time, given the extraordinary coincidence of Mairi's dead body being found in the river, less than half a mile from her house.

Holding on to my breakfast mug, I sat at my dining room table and dialled. The alcohol was spreading throughout my body via the empty stomach, but that didn't account for the heaviness and weight in my body. The phone rang three times before it was answered.

'Hello.'

I could hear the kids in the background and picture where Emms was, in the kitchen, sitting in one of the retro armchairs by the window. The kids would be playing on the floor by her feet and there'd be some casserole in the oven, scenting the air and about to be served to the children for their tea. My throat narrowed, making it hard to speak.

'Hello?'

'Emms, it's me,'

'Liz, are you alright, you sound dreadful?'

'Have you heard the news? I just heard it on the radio,'

'Yes, I should have called you, but we've just had the police round and they only just went. They'll be at yours next.'

'Me? Why?'

'Because you knew her. I think we're something called Known Acquaintances, or something like that. I don't know, but they have a list of all the people she knew. Unbelievable, isn't it?'

Emms was talking as if it were dark but exciting, as if we were discussing the death of someone with whom we had no connection, a pop star or prime minister or a member of the royal family. Someone who was in the public domain and not someone who was the target of her obsession and who she had had murderous fantasies about. I took another hit of wine.

'How's Greg?'

Her voice dropped and she sounded less chirpy, 'Devastated. Absolutely devastated. He's in the most terrible state and I have no idea what to do about it. He's been crying in the loo, for God's sake.'

'Can we ... meet up and talk about this?'

'Good idea, but it's not going to be tonight. I daren't leave Greg on his own. Not kidding, but I really don't know what he might do. Liz, I've never seen him like this,' her voice lowered. 'I've got to go; he's just come back from the offie. I'll call you tomorrow.'

The line snapped dead and I was left in the dark staring at the handset as if expecting it to come back to life. There was something comic about it, or maybe I was hysterical, drunk, clutching a silent phone, waiting for the police to turn up so I could tell them ... tell them what exactly? That I'd known Mairi and because she was a bad fairy there was a long queue of people who were quite happy about not seeing her again. I heard myself laugh. Yes, I was definitely, hysterical. It really didn't bear thinking about.

I stretched out my shaking hand to replace the phone and the pink quartz ring glinted, as if to remind me how happy I'd felt only hours before. Then the phone rang. I nearly dropped the bloody thing.

'Is that Elizabeth Verrall?'

'Yes.'

'This is D.C. Kett at Surrey Police,'

I exhaled and heard the ragged breaks in my breath.

'Hello, I suppose you're calling about Mairi,'

'Yes, this must be a shock,'

'You might say that. I just heard it on the radio, I can't believe it, what ... what happened?' With my free hand, the one with the damn ring on, I pinched myself to stop the gabbling.

'We don't know for certain, but would it be possible for you to come down to the station, at your convenience, to talk to us about her?'

'Yes, yes ... of course,'

My appointment was made, and it was all very civilised, as if it was any meeting, at any time, between a respectable taxpayer and a customer-focused local authority.

I called Richard, who was on voicemail, so I had none of the satisfaction of being the bearer of big news. All I could do was picture his reaction when I told him that Mairi's body had been recovered from the River Mole. Then I took refuge on the sofa, under the throw, trying to work out what I would say to the police when the moment came.

The problem was that I didn't know. But one thing was certain, taking my passport and doing a moonlight flit was not an option. It would be tantamount to an admission of guilt. However Mairi had landed in the river, I was not going to be blamed.

After a while, I dragged myself off the sofa and tried to eat some bread and cheese. The dough lodged in my throat. It wouldn't go down, so I spat it out into a piece of kitchen towel where it sat, like a gob of clay, before I binned it. How could I swallow, how could I keep anything down when Mairi had been in the river, dead, bloated, until she'd floated up with the arrival of spring, back again to ruin my life? I visualised her white decomposed body, I wondered what she'd been wearing, how long she'd been in the water, had she been eaten by fish? And then it got worse, that old elephant lumbered into the middle of my sitting room. You know the one: dusty, parasite-ridden, wrinkled, swinging its sodding trunk. The creature I sought to ignore. How had Mairi got into the river?

Richard's silence that evening spelt 'guilt' to me in neon flashing letters. I kept thinking of his cold blue eyes and his even colder description about acting out on dark revenge fantasies. He'd been oblique about how ill, or not ill, Mairi had been after I called from Florida. What if, after we'd spoken, he attempted to warn her off Greg and the stupid bloody woman had told him to back off or, worse, she had threatened to reignite her accusations about rape and going to the GMC? With his career on the line, I could easily see him deciding that she needed to be eliminated before she screwed up anybody else's life. He would do that without a moment's compunction, and it would certainly explain his behaviour, his disappearances and why he hadn't called back this evening. He knew about her, he'd slept with her. He would treat her like the surgeon that he is and hack her off like a sick and poisonous limb.

Was I imagining it? What about Richard deftly pointing the finger at Greg, saying there was something wrong with him?

Or maybe it was Greg? I held my head in my hands as if the action would contain my rattling, scrambling thoughts that were chasing each other, bouncing, clicking, like a mechanical pinball machine.

What was the "something" that had happened that Greg mentioned as he lurched off, drunk and useless in Bridge Street? What if Mairi wanted to go public about their affair and he wanted to stop her?

She wouldn't be the first mistress who had been silenced by a lover who wanted to squirrel away his indiscretion; it would certainly explain why he'd imploded into this miserable trace of his former self, this shambling suggestion of the man I used to know. How did upright, responsible Greg become a dribbling drunk? Guilt could do that to a man, and if anyone was likely to be affected by guilt, Greg would put his hand up and be that man.

By midnight, I was so tired that my head ached with exhaustion. I took myself off to bed, where I lay in the dark and looked at the ceiling. My mind bounced between Richard and Greg, and even the least disruptive possibility that miserable Mairi might have killed herself, and I was scrambling my brain for no reason at all. The one option I wasn't prepared to entertain was that Emms was responsible. But how could I possibly avoid the towering thought that Emms' so-called dream of pushing Mairi into the river was based on fact? No matter how much I wanted to ignore that elephant, I knew that when I met with Emms the next day to talk, I would have to try to find out the truth, and act on it.

thirty-two

Next day, I phoned in and told the troops I was working from home. With black shadows under my eyes that my specs did nothing to camouflage, I could hardly affect my persona of leaderene, so I stayed in bed and didn't answer the phone. Emms and I had arranged to meet by text and I was not prepared to talk to anyone else until I'd seen her. My head throbbed, I felt sick and I didn't know how much of that was the wine I had necked or the fear that overwhelmed me.

We met at the Prince of Wales, which was a short walk from Emms' house. I didn't want to give her any excuse not to be there and neither, of course, did I want to meet her at hers, not when the last time I'd seen Greg, I'd accused him of adultery, among other things. By the time I got to the pub, I was even more of a wreck.

By contrast, Emms glided through the door of the pub, looking as if she'd spent the past month in a health spa. She was radiant, lush, confident, and for the first time I can ever remember, she wasn't wearing black and white. Above a pair of patterned trousers, she had a cerise shirt that made her skin seem translucent and her eyes sparkled. She was also a couple of pounds heavier, so less angular around the face, which made her look softer, and her hair had grown. Her face was clear, lit up and even allowing for the fact that I hadn't seen her for a while, she looked five years younger.

What a relief. She certainly didn't look like someone who had committed murder and was guiltily expecting the denizens of the law to be feeling up her collar. Psychologist or not, I know Emms and she wouldn't have looked so relaxed if she was guilty. What's more, if I thought for one moment that I was being guided by an intoxicating cocktail of hope and sentiment, I only had to look back at Tony's accident, when Emms had been gibbering and wriggling and lying her head off. For the first time since I'd heard the news about Mairi, my shoulders lowered and I realised just how scared I'd been that Emms did have something to do with the bloody woman's death. Fuck Mairi. I meant it. She'd been a constant source of anxiety since we'd met and even dead she was still stirring up the shit pot.

Emms and I air-kissed and I smelt Eau Dynamisante on her soft skin.

'You look fantastic,' I said. 'What have you been doing with yourself? Clothes, hair, hey, Mrs Makeover.' It was like old times. What's more, no one would believe in a million years that we were there to talk about the death of someone we knew. 'How's everybody, Tessa, Robbie, Greg?'

'Kids are fine, Tessa is ninety per cent better, she still has a slight cough which I'm keeping an eye on, but she's a robust little thing. Robbie is really doing well since I've been able to spend more time with them both – thanks to you.' She met my eyes with warmth. 'I know you've taken on more than your share with the business and I don't quite know how I'm going to do it, but somehow, I promise, I'll make it up to you.'

'What about Greg?'

'Don't ask.' Emms went up to the bar and came back to our dark oak table with a bottle of wine, two glasses and two packets of crisps. 'Let's live a little,' she said, as she placed the tray between us.

'Crisps? You?'

'Crisps. Me.' She poured the wine into two glasses and the straw coloured Pinot plopped and splashed. 'I can't tell you how pleased I am that you called last night; your voice was the sound of sanity after Greg's rants.'

'Why? What's going on?' I took a mouthful of wine. It went down well, just like the countless bottles of wine, cups of cappuccino and glasses of Baileys that we'd shared in the past. The "us" of us was back. It felt as if I'd used a key into our very own time warp lock, because we were true friends. Once you've been really close to a friend, even if you drift apart for a while, it's easy to slot the key into the lock and connect.

'Things are really rough at home, total rubbish,' Emms frowned and the rest came out in a rush. 'He's pissed half the time, even in the morning, and when he's not pissed he's whining about something or other. Before Mairi reappeared - as it were - it was all about the money and being conned and looking like an arse to his father. Now he's banging on about feeling guilty for misjudging Mairi through all her pain, suffering, yada yada yada. Meanwhile, do you think he's looking after the kids? Do you remember him saying way back in the autumn how he wanted to spend more time with them? Enjoy their early years. Do you think any of that has actually happened? The pizza delivery is on speed dial, and he can't even get out of bed in the morning.' Emms took a large mouthful of wine and as she raised her head to swallow, I noticed her neck.

No amulet. Even though Emms looked pretty down about Greg, my spirits lifted further, because she was obviously out the other side of her anxiety rituals. Tears of relief welled up and I blinked them away to concentrate on the problem in hand. Greg.

'I really don't know what to do,' Emms said.

'This is very hard for me to ask Emms but do you think Greg might know more about Mairi's disappearance than he's actually saying?'

'Like what?'

'I don't know,' How the hell could I say that Greg had more or less admitted that there'd been something going on with Mairi, even if it stopped short of shagging. 'I don't know,' I repeated. 'What happened when the police came round?'

My feel good moment of relief dissolved like mist on a summer morning as I started to consider the full implications of Greg being responsible in any way for Mairi's death. At best, Mairi might have topped herself because he rejected her and at worst ... I forced myself to think through 'at worst'. What if Mairi had pushed it too far with Greg, threatened to expose whatever had gone on between them and somehow ended up in the river? The "somehow" was secondary. If Greg was connected, it was a total disaster.

'The police were fine,' Emms brushed the hair off her forehead. 'Very polite and sympathetic. Greg wasn't there and I didn't want them to talk about Mairi in front of the kids, so we have to go to the police station tomorrow. I told the police that we felt a little responsible because Mairi was, well, you know, how she was. I don't suppose there's any chance of you staying at the house whilst I go with Greg to the police interview?'

'Sure. My interview's tomorrow afternoon, but anything I can do. You know that. Just ask.'

Emms sighed, 'If you put it like that, do you happen to know how you're supposed to talk to children about death?'

'As a matter of fact I do. One of my essays in Year 2. Do you want me to tell the kids about Mairi?

Emms nodded. 'Would you? I'd really appreciate it. Ever since Christmas, they've been asking where Mairi is and they've only just stopped. Seems like a suitable task for a godmother.'

I drank a little more but left the rest for Emms. She seemed not to want to talk about the whole sorry mess, and who could blame her? So we caught up about the business, the staff, her new rainbow look and the amulet. I tapped away at the base of my neck.

'No more magic?' I said.

'I don't need it now that the wicked witch is dead, do I? Remember when Tony died, we talked about not pretending that he was a nice guy. That's what you said. That it was rubbish to pretend that he was a good person just because he was dead. Same goes for Mairi. She deserved to die.'

'Do you really think she deserved to die?'

'Don't you?' Emms was smiling a secret smile.

'Were you the executioner, Emms?'

'Wouldn't you like to know?'

'That's not funny, Emms; if you did something then you have to tell me. I need to know.'

'Why? That would only make you complicit, an accessory, and would that be fair after all you've done for me?'

My heart started racing, it was my nightmare, the thing I was trying not to think about at any cost, the truth, that I'd dug and dug and dug down and deep to bury in the sand to avoid hearing, but it was what I knew, had known all along, ever since Tony's inquest. I'd known what Emms was capable of doing, I'd known how her logic and temper would combine and I had also known the stress she was under.

'What are you saying?' I rasped out. 'Did you ... Emms, did you do something to Mairi?'

'Are you trying to ask me if I murdered her?' Emms smiled happily. There was a thrumming in my ear as the blood in my head raced, pulsed and I felt dizzy. Across the oak table, Emms laughed and drank some more wine. I had the most terrible sense that I was sitting opposite a stranger who was in her body, a demon who had taken her over and was mocking me. This woman across the table looked like Emms, even sounded like her, but she was not my friend. She was some other thing.

'Oh lighten up, Liz,' Emms put her glass down. 'Of course, I didn't murder Mairi and before you ask, neither did Greg. Think about it, can you seriously see Greg hurting anybody, even someone who was trying to hurt him? And as for me – yes, we all know about my vicious temper, but that's really not enough to make me do whatever was done to Mairi and dump her in the river. I'm rather insulted that you should think that.'

'What about the dream, the fantasy,' I said. 'Remember what you told me in the hospital?' Did I really sound pathetic, did I sound like someone who had been beaten and would accept any explanation, would believe a husband when he said that he wouldn't beat me again; was I back in that world? No, I wasn't. I grasped the life raft to reality and kicked hard. There was no way I was going to be sucked down. Across the table, Emms was quiet for a few moments, 'That was weird, wasn't it?' 'But I did dream it, or something like it.'

'Dreams are either wants or fears. In other words, you either wanted to kill Mairi or you were scared that you might.'

'What about the river?' Emms said.

'Coincidence,' I said. My confidence was back. 'Mairi talked about the river, didn't she? Remember, when she turned up at yours on her birthday. Your river dream didn't come from nowhere; it's a vestigial memory of that conversation that was in your subconscious.'

'What do you think happened to Mairi?' Emms said.

'Dunno. I don't know what to think. How about you?'

Emms refilled my glass, 'I don't like it, because I don't want to feel guilty, no matter how much of a bitch she was, but my guess would be she committed suicide.'

'Why do we have to feel guilty?'

Emms shrugged. 'Because she's a human being. Anyway, how about this for a great idea, if you're going to be kind enough to look after the kids tomorrow morning, when I take Greg to the police station for his interview, then why not sleep over? You can leave your car here, walk back to ours, and the sofa bed downstairs in the front room is all yours. I'll even find you a new toothbrush and a pair of clean knickers. How's that for an offer?'

My answer was to drink the glass of wine and kick back. We stayed in the pub till chucking out time and Emms elaborated on her chocolate truffle business idea. I let her ramble on. What was the point of raising the issue that she'd fought to take over Tony's company and now wanted to become a chocolatier? As Marcus might say, 'Go figure'. Once she'd exhausted that subject she went off on another riff about meteors and metaphysics. I will spare you the details. We staggered back arm in arm to the cottage and fell through the door, but even our clattering didn't wake Greg, who was lying on one of the kitchen armchairs with his head to one side, mouth wide open and snoring the snores of the drunk. Oh, what a happy house.

After drinking a pint of water and taking a berocca to aid the inevitable hangover, Emms and I hugged, she to go upstairs and me to lie on the sofa bed and worry the night away because, whatever spin I'd managed to fix on events while at the pub, there were two police interviews the next day. Mairi was back in the room again. Even in death, she was controlling our lives. I managed to pass out for an hour and then I was wired awake as if there were electrodes taped to my head sending impulses all the way round my brain. There was no choice but to get up off the sofa bed and find my way into the kitchen. Outside the sitting room, the considerate hostess had left a nightlight burning so I could find my way to the loo; the light threw up shadow shapes and turned the narrow hallway into a cave of dark threat and ominous gloom. My heart pounded as I padded to the safety of the kitchen where I made myself a hot drink, sat at the pine refectory table and listened to the big old clock tick away the night. In that house of parents and children that had always seemed bursting with love and laughter, I felt sadder than I've ever felt in my life.

By the time I'd finished my camomile tea, I was no further on than when I started, the same questions rattling in my head. Was I mad, was Emma mad, was everybody fucking mad? And what was I supposed to do about it? Because I struggled to believe that Mairi had committed suicide - not on the basis of my last conversation with her. Was it possible that during the two weeks after I'd seen her she'd gone into a massive mental tailspin and ended her life? Or was there another explanation?

thirty-three

The following morning Emms was sparkling in a teal tee shirt and black jeans. Her hair shone and she looked as if she had enjoyed the sleep of the just. In contrast, poor old Greg was her polar opposite. Not only did he look as if he should be pushing all his belongings in a supermarket trolley, but before he went off with Emms, I caught him taking a nip from his flask.

'I hope that's vodka,' I said, trying to be supportive and act as if everybody starts the day with a refreshing hit of forty per cent proof alcohol.

'I've got mints,' Greg said. He'd shaved but had cut himself, so there were a couple of bits of toilet tissue stuck to his chin, like confetti. The extra weight he'd recently put on sat flabbily above his jeans, he was wearing odd socks and his Tintin hair looked thin and greasy. From outside the cottage, I heard a little toot from Emms, already in the car, and Greg took another gulp from his flask before shuffling out to join her. As he stood on the doorstep, he turned back, a picture of desolation, 'Look after my kids,' he said and closed the door behind him.

In the kitchen, Tessa and Robbie sat at the pine table, colouring in. This was an after-breakfast treat because Aunty Liz was there for the morning. Of course, they knew something was up.

'Where have Mummy and Daddy gone?' Tessa said.

'They've gone to talk to some people about Mairi.'

Robbie's head popped up at the mention of his heroine and he held his green pen in the air. 'Is she coming, will she be there?' he asked excitedly.

'No,' I said. 'She's dead.' I gave him a hug and kissed the down on his cheeks. The book said reassurance and physical contact should be part of the process of talking to children about death, and it was no hardship to hold Robbie close.

'What does that mean?' Tessa said.

'It means there was an accident and now her body doesn't work.' This was all textbook psychology. They were too young to understand the concept of heaven but they would understand that things are broken and disappear.

'Where is she?' Robbie said.

'She's in a place where dead people are.'

'Like the hospital?' Robbie frowned and I could see him struggling to grasp the idea.

'Not quite, but she won't be coming back. Come and sit close to me, Tessa, feel my heart,' I put Tessa's tiny hand on my chest. 'You feel that? It's my heart and when that stops working, I'll be dead and I won't work any more.' Tessa's face started to crumple and I hugged her close. Robbie was still trying to grasp the idea, or maybe he was in shock. I may be a psychologist, but let me stress that training customer service teams is several million miles away from paediatric bereavement counselling. In other words, I was screwing it up and worse, I knew it. 'Come on, Robbie, come and give me a great big hug and then let's all go outside and see if we can find some flowers to put in a vase for Mummy and Daddy?'

'Can we find some for Mairi?' Robbie said.

'We can get some flowers to remember Mairi, but you won't be able to give them to her, because she's dead.'

I had my arms round both children, holding them close, trying to make them feel safe in what was, and is, an unsafe world. After a while, I stood up, took them by the hands and led them into the garden.

By the time we'd been out into the early spring garden and found a few daffodils forcing their way up, the kids seemed more settled. Only an hour later, Emms came back with an ashen-faced Greg who looked, if anything, worse than he'd appeared earlier on. He muttered something about needing to see someone and left Emma and me in the kitchen with the kids.

'Pub,' she said. 'He sits there with a newspaper and a pint. If he does the crossword, he doesn't feel so bad about drinking at 11 o'clock in the morning.'

The children were still outside pulling up weeds and they scrambled around, bouncing and absorbed with the task. Why should they have to go through all this; wasn't it our responsibility to look after them?

'How did it go?' I said.

Emms just shook her head and massaged her brow before pushing her hair back. 'The interview went okay, but ... '

'But what?'

The children were running towards the open door, clutching their flowers.

'I just can't believe it. We were early, I parked and we sat in the car for a few minutes,' Emms shut her eyes and the anguish was evident in her expression. 'Greg's told me everything. Everything.' Her voice broke. 'I've been so stupid and now we just have to get through this somehow.'

Triumphant Tessa was the first to reach the door and thrust her mangled daffodil at Emms. Robbie was right behind, face on the brink of crumpling because his sister had beaten him to the finishing line.

'Look at this,' Emms said pinning on her happy face and welcoming the children back to her arms.

'What happened?' I hissed before they reached her.

Emms scooped up Tessa in her arms and then knelt and kissed Robbie so they became a swirling mass of chubby toddlers and mother, enwrapped in one hug.

From the ground she looked up at me, 'I'll come by tonight after they're settled. You. Will. Not. Believe it. Meanwhile, Greg's insisting on us organising her funeral and having the wake here because she had no family.'

'Blimey.'

'Oh, it gets better. I said we should get it catered to save the hassle and he says he wants to do it, he wants to do it for Mairi,' Emms rolled her eyes just as Robbie piped up, 'Is Mairi coming?'

'No, darling,' I said. 'Mairi can't come because she's dead.'

'And she's in the place with the dead people,' Tessa said.

'That's exactly right, Tessa, That's very clever of you to remember,' Emms looked up at me from the floor, she nodded and mouthed, 'thank you' over the kids, heads. There was nothing else for it, so I slumped down and joined them on the floor and Robbie sat in my arms for a hug. 'We're going to make a little party to remember Mairi,' I said. 'Maybe we'll make some biscuits for the party. Would you like that? We can make them together. How about that?'

'Yes,' Emms said. 'Isn't that a terrific idea? I could make those special chocolate truffles that you all liked,'

The children spoke together: 'Yeah!'

Once the drama had been averted with hugs and speculation about what sort of biscuits and sandwiches we would make for the party, Emms and I untangled ourselves and stood up. 'Thanks again,' she said, 'I really do seem to spend too much of my time thanking you. You really are my best friend.'

She hugged me, her whisper tickled my ear, 'I'll come by later and fill you in when there are no flapping ears.'

thirty-four

I stumbled out of the cottage into a keenly blustery spring day. It was the type of day that made you feel that it was blowing the dust of despair and cobwebs of doubt all away. But it did nothing for me. What exactly was "everything"? If Greg had indeed told Emms everything, that would certainly include my accusation that he'd shagged Mairi.

I sighed and heard my own loud exhalation. The wind outside buffeted my car as I drove out of the village, past the swan's nest, and the newly erected sign warning drivers not to run over the big white birds. 'Fuck it,' I said aloud.

Traffic was heavy on the way to the office and I didn't push and wriggle or race off at the lights to get ahead of the queues. I was content to meander past the long drives, the high walls concealing houses and other people's dirty secrets. Of course, the real problem was that I wasn't the best friend that Emms thought I was. Guilt. That's what it was. She believed in me and that she could trust me. In return, I hadn't trusted her with what I'd been told so that she could draw her own conclusions. I'd made a judgement that she was too fragile to make her own decisions. At best, I'd been patronising in the guise of being protective. At worst, I hadn't been truthful with her because it was easier not to be.

I pulled into my allocated spot in the car park and rubbed the leather of the steering wheel, feeling the give of the hide. Exactly how bad was "everything"?

I had an hour at the office, during which I ate a sandwich that I didn't taste, gulped down a coffee and dashed off half a dozen holding emails on everything that was urgent. Then I drove to the police station for my interview.

The interview room at the police station was oddly quiet. After I had sat down on a wobbly plastic chair, I was offered something to drink by a young P.C. with bad skin. It was so quiet in the room that I noticed the diet cola fizz as I poured it into the plastic cup. The thought occurred to me that the room must be soundproofed. In the corner of the ceiling I saw a small camera, and even though I had done nothing wrong, my heart started racing and I felt shaky. Was the camera already on? No doubt they had concealed microphones in case suspects talked to each other. How would anyone know? This was all a million miles away from the beat officers who hovered around the high street. I tried to do some deep breathing, slowly in and out. Gradually my heart rate slowed. All I had to do was stick to what I knew for fact. I sipped at the drink, and after only a few moments, a tall, gentle-faced cop came into the room accompanied by what seemed to be his boss. The tall cop carried six inches of files and the other one, who smelt strongly of cigarettes, was studying his mobile phone.

'Hi' the smaller of the plain clothes cops said. 'I'm D.C. Lapham and this is D.C. Andrew Errity and you are, Ms..' he hesitated.

'Elizabeth Verrall' Errity said.

'Of course you are, I knew that. You're going to have to bear with me; I'm a slow reader. May I call you Elizabeth?

'I'm known as Liz.'

Lapham twinkled at me. He was mid-forties, clean-shaven with curly hair and overweight. But he looked as if life wasn't something to be taken too seriously. Immediately, I was on my guard.

'I see someone got you a drink,' Lapham continued. 'Andy, save my life and find me a cup of coffee, please.'

Errity looked as if this wasn't the first time that he had been coffee boy, but accepted it. 'Would you like anything else?' Errity asked. I heard Birmingham in his accent.

Lapham chipped, 'Some biscuits would be great, I happen to know there's a box of homemade chocolate chip biscuits in the squad room. A grateful homeowner and fan of our community policing,' he needlessly explained.

The airless, badly lit room was making me feel claustrophobic and my heart started pounding again. Quietly, I tried to take deep breaths, tried to stop my muscles tightening up and ignore the trickles running from my armpits. I willed my hand not to tremble and took a sip of coke and smiled at the pair of them.

As soon as Errity left the room, Lapham opened the buff file and started to read the contents. He paused and fished out some gold reading glasses from the pocket of his battered leather jacket. He smiled at me, as if he wanted to share, 'Old age, coming on fast.' Then he looked down. 'Now, let's see what we've got here.'

As Lapham read, flicking the sheets back and forth, licking a finger as he turned a sheet back to check on something, I concentrated on my body language, I needed to appear composed, but sad. That would be the right impression for the situation. Somewhere in the back of my mind, the phrase "right impression" echoed. I shook it away. This was no time to be fanciful, I had to concentrate.

'Right,' Lapham said, finally closing the file. 'I understand that you went with Mrs Harens to Ms Sondergaard's house on 7th January. She wasn't there but you left her a note.'

'That's right, I did.' I'd forgotten about that.

'When was the last time you saw her?'

'Before I went on holiday at Christmas, we all went to a kids' Christmas concert and then out for a pizza.'

'How was she then?'

Suddenly I saw Mairi, in the cocktail bar, claiming that she was a hair's breath away from snagging Greg and blathering on about how it was her turn. I felt the heat rise from my chest and my ears burn.

'She enjoyed the concert, and was apparently, looking forward to the New Year.'

'I'm sorry if this is distressing for you but did she ever talk or write about ending her life?' Lapham said.

'No, but she was volatile.' And that wasn't a lie.

'Were you aware that she'd been prescribed anti-psychotics and anti-anxiety drugs?'

'She didn't talk about it.'

I shuddered. I wanted to tell Lapham. I'd feel better if I told him. 'She once said that no one would miss her if she died. I'm not surprised to hear that she was on medication. Apparently her sister died when she was young and it really affected her. I don't think she had family. I really don't know what I could have done for her.'

Lapham looked sympathetic. 'I'm sure you did your best. Were you aware that she walked by the river?'

'Yes, I remember her talking about walking by the river on her birthday.'

Lapham closed the file, 'I have the forensic report here which we will be passing on to the coroner's office for the inquest. Thank you for coming in.'

By the end of the day, I was hit by wave after wave of weariness, and with that came more self-loathing and despondency. And even worse, fear. No matter how much knowledge I've accumulated during my pitiful working life about how the brain works and how chemicals affect perception, it makes not an ounce of difference when faced with the distorted reality of mood swings. All this is a long way of saying that I was dreading seeing Emms. Back at the flat, I had a hot shower followed by a text exchange with Richard. I told him that I'd done the police interview. He wanted to come round but I steered him away. This had nothing to do with him. It was between Emms and me, and if he was here, he'd take over.

I got dressed again and stood by the French windows looking at the darkening sky and the river. Until now, the river had seemed a pleasing vista and a place for boating parties, sculling rowers, swans and fishermen. Not a place of death. Fortunately, my buzzer rang and disturbed that particular train of thought. Emms came in with a bottle of Bailey's and thrust it at me.

'Oh no. Not after last night, please,'

'Okay, I'll take it away with me.' She looked strained but fundamentally well. 'How did your interview go?'

'Good enough. They don't seem fussed, and I managed not to say that Mairi was a conniving bitch, so I suppose that's a result.'

Maybe the Baileys wasn't a bad idea, as it would give me a chance to get through my starter before we got to the meat and potatoes of exactly what Greg's "everything" implied. Emms followed me into the kitchen, where I took down a couple of small, mismatched, crystal glasses that I'd bought in the antiques emporium in Hampton Court.

'It's not cold,' Emms said.

I found a bag of ice and clinked in a cube per glass before pouring the putty-coloured drink. Then I took Emms' hand and led her to my glass dining table by the window.

'Me first,' I said. 'You need to know a couple of things. Most importantly, Richard tried to warn me about Mairi after our nightmare double date, but I was so angry with him, I chose to believe that he was exaggerating. He said that Mairi stalked him, left crazy messages on his car, eventually told his wife and did the whole boiled bunny routine favoured by discarded mistresses and, indeed wives: scare the bastard.'

Emms opened her mouth to speak and I silenced her with my hand. 'Don't stop me, Emms, otherwise I won't be able to go on. There's a lot of stuff about me that you don't know because we never talked about it back in the day, but I felt sorry for Mairi. Because of what my husband did to me, I felt sorry for what Richard had done to her. And I also – this is the difficult part ... I didn't think you were robust enough to have all that dumped on your plate. I thought it would go away. I'm sorry, I'm not the friend you thought I was.'

Emms took my hand. Her own felt dry and hot. Her nails were neat, softly glazed with varnish. 'You are. I've never had as good a friend as you, and I would have done exactly the same.'

'Really?'

'Of course, I felt sorry for her. Remember that birthday business when she wept and wailed about being all alone in the world and no one caring if she died. I felt bad for her, and when she started to put the moves on Greg, he said I was over-reacting. I thought that being jealous was my insecurity because of Dad going off with Aunty Jane.'

'Did Greg tell you I accused him?'

'Yes.' Emms poured herself out another Bailey's, this time dispensing with the ice. 'He still maintains that they didn't shag but he did say she jumped him and he pushed her away. I think I believe him.'

I shrugged. It was her decision and I wasn't going to comment. Emms took a sip of her drink, 'The thing is, it doesn't actually matter whether Greg shagged her or not: her poison still got into him.'

'Poison?'

'Figure of speech. I have to hand it to Greg, he certainly chose the worst possible moment to tell me. Can you believe it?' Emms shook her head. 'He said she came on to him on Christmas Cake Making Day. Apparently she came round with a celebratory bottle of fizz while the kids were at nursery, and insisted that they drink a toast to the nursery.'

'So she planned it,' I said, remembering the expression on Mairi's face. 'That's appalling. I thought he looked uncomfortable. What happened?'

'It seems they had a glass of fizz and then she tried to jump him. According to Greg, he told her that nothing was ever going to happen between them and they could only ever be friends and business partners. And it seemed to Greg as if that was enough, and that she'd got the message. Did I tell you she wrote him this long rambling letter that he showed me, all about her miserable childhood? Anyway, it really doesn't matter. My poor naïve husband thinks that because they've talked about it everything's okay and they're friends. So when she gets ill, we both take soup round to hers in a good neighbourly way. And then ... he says, she came on to him again. It was the day after the big storm. He took her to the cashpoint and she begged him to take her for a walk by the river so she could gather some kindling from all the broken bits of wood that came down in the storm.'

'Oh fuck. Did she come on to him again?'

Emms nodded and swallowed. 'So she tells him some shit about it being destiny or whatever, tries to grab and hug him, he pushes her off, she stumbles back and ... When he was telling me this bit, Greg was sobbing. Apparently, the riverbank crumbles because of heavy rain, she falls in, and Greg stands there like an idiot not knowing what to do. There's nobody around, it's getting dark, the river's fast, she's washed away ... and ... He leaves her.'

My hand was on my open mouth. 'He left her?'

'Yep, he left her.'

I could see it. I could understand it. It could have been me.

'He panicked, didn't he? Christ, Emms, why didn't he go to the police then?'

'He says he doesn't know. But if you ask me, I think he was ashamed and he didn't want to admit that he'd left her. And then he was terrified that he'd be arrested on a murder charge and jailed.'

'What about him saying that she'd gone off with the money?'

'All make-believe.' Emms finished her glass of Bailey's, I went to pour some more but she covered the glass with her hand. Then she brushed the hair back off her forehead. 'You won't appreciate this because it's so stupid, given the rest of everything that's going on, but the worst thing is that he told me just as we were sitting outside the police station waiting for them to ask questions about the last time we'd seen her. At first I thought he was joking, in bad taste, but then I realised ... '

'Wow ... poor you. How awful.'

'I didn't know what to do. I had to decide whether or not to tell them the truth, and I still don't know if I did the right thing. That's what I want to talk to you about. You see we didn't actually lie. We said we'd seen her the day before and there was evidence on her phone that Greg had called, but we explained, quite truthfully, that Mairi and Greg texted and talked several times, every day, because they were in business together with the nursery opening. They knew all about that because of the money in her account. They'd also been to the house, seen that she was on anti-anxiety and anti-psychotic drugs and asked if we thought that she might have ended her life. Believe it or not, they have quite a few floaters every winter. So we just said yes and that we felt guilty that we weren't there for her, and then Greg asked if we could organise the funeral because she had no friends and apparently that's it. Unless something else comes up, they'll close the file.'

I folded my arms, 'Bish bash bosh? And Greg?'

'Not good,' Emms stood up and paced. 'Not good at all. On the one hand, now that I know, I can understand why he can't get out of bed in the morning and why he's been trying to drink himself to death. On the other, now I'm frightened about what he might do. Liz, he's talking like a crazy man.'

'What, you think he might ...'

'I think he's depressed. At the moment he's focusing on the funeral and is planning an expensive event. I suppose it's guilt. I think the problem is going to be after the funeral, I don't know what he might do then.'

I felt slightly sick, and I didn't know if it was the Bailey's on an empty stomach or, more likely, the conversation. Beyond the load around my heart, in my head there was a pleasing sense of satisfaction, like when you finish a word puzzle. Finally, it all made sense. Greg's a nice guy, he's a good guy, but hey, in a crisis, I could see him panicking, especially if he was already feeling guilty about Mairi and whatever stupid crap she'd said to him. That moment of self-satisfaction passed when Emms stood up. She was close to tears.

'I'd better get back. I have to support him through this, and I don't quite know how. It's not just my responsibility, for better, for worse and all that stuff. It's my fault, Liz. All of it.'

I opened my arms and squeezed her tight. 'Hey, come on, it's not your fault. We'll get through this, I promise you. Everything will be okay. We just have to get through the funeral.'

thirty-five

After Emms had gone home, I responded to Richard's texts. He was insistent about coming round, and I toyed with the idea of telling him that he'd been right about Greg tipping over the edge and right about Mairi being a threat. During the half hour that I waited and cleaned up the kitchen, washing up the Bailey's glasses and wiping the surfaces, the notion of letting Richard, who suffers from a surfeit of rightness at the best of times, know that he had two strong scores was more than I was prepared to deal with. I'm not saying that he's a pompous prat - well I suppose I am, really. More importantly, I could just see him insisting that Greg needed to go to the police, and whilst I wasn't ruling that out as an option, there were practical considerations. If Greg had to experience an overnight in a police cell, in his fragile state of mind, I wouldn't put any money on his safety, either by others' hands, or indeed his own.

This meant that when Richard arrived, I only sketched in what Emms had told me, it was the acceptable version and reaffirmed his diagnosis, giving him a sense of his own superiority and getting him off my case.

'So you see, you were right,' I said. 'Greg needs help but whether he needs a stint in rehab or a therapist or what - I don't really know; this isn't exactly change management psychology. What do you think, Richard?'

We were lying on the sofa, he was stretched out underneath me and I was lying on top of him, comfortably, enjoying his faint, end-of-day smell and end-of-day beard growth.

'It's not my field, as you know, but I'll look into it. There are a couple of people at the hospital I can talk to. First thing is probably to get him to his GP: do you know if he's been yet?'

'No, I'll talk to Emms tomorrow.'

It was only a week until the funeral and I decided to trust Emms that Greg would be fine until then. What else could I do? I'd been repeatedly wrong; now was the time to trust her, and by trusting her, I was also protecting her.

We raced towards the funeral, the days gathering speed, and I found myself constantly checking my watch to gauge how much time I had during the course of any day to do what needed to be done. Why? Because Emms was understandably still absent from the office. Needless to say, I had a few irritable moments when I had to deal single-handedly with various crises but, before I got too pissed off, the question I asked myself was, would I want to swap places with Emma? What was better?

A seriously disturbed husband or endless work hassles? Short answer on that one.

Emms managed to keep me up to speed on the funeral developments with a stream of emails and texts, and there were times when I wondered if she was exaggerating, most notably when she told me that Greg had booked a horse-drawn hearse. Apparently, the black plumes on the horses' heads were extra.

'You are joking, aren't you: please tell me it's a joke,' I said over the phone.

'I wish I could,' but she sounded okay.

'How is he?'

'Okay ... sort of. He's out at the moment, so I can speak. He's busy, focused on the funeral, he's actually gone to see some people who knew her, because he's writing an obituary for the local paper.'

'An obituary? That'll be interesting. As far as I was aware, Mairi didn't do anything except fuck people up,' I said. 'Sorry, Emms, but some sort of hagiography for Mairi is a little ridiculous,'

'The whole funeral is ridiculous, but isn't that the point? It's as if Greg has flipped a switch and his responses are all inappropriate. For one thing, there's no logic in spending shedloads of money on her funeral and then not having caterers do the hard work. He's trying to make all the food himself because "she would have wanted me to".' I could hear the inverted commas in Emms' tone. She sounded understandably, pissed off.

'On the plus side, he's drinking less, but that's only because he's driving round doing all this organising and he doesn't want to get nicked. And before I forget, you know why he's getting an obituary in the Elmbridge Gazette? Because he's also paid for a quarter page ad, so who knows how many people are going to turn up.'

I heard banging in the background and men's voices. 'What's that noise?'

'The marquee going up. At least he's hired the tables and some chairs.'

'I am not going to ask you how much this is costing. I'd find the answer too distressing. How is he with you and the kids?'

She exhaled as if exasperated. 'With the kids, he's okay, overly sentimental and he keeps slobbering over them, but with me he's aggressive and hostile. He walks out of the room when I come in and turns his back on me if we're in the same space. Then, as soon as the kids are down for the night, he goes to the Prince of Wales and doesn't come back till chucking-out time, so I really don't know how he thinks he's going to cater for this bloody circus. I have to tell you, Liz, it's upsetting, because I'm trying to help him.'

'I know you are. Listen, Richard's given me some names of psychiatrists, why don't we try and get Greg in to see someone before the funeral, or at least go to the doctor and get a referral?'

'At the moment, he won't listen to a word I say, he hates me, won't even talk to me, unless the children or other people are around. After the funeral will be the time. Gotta go. He's at the door.'

I had a few fearful moments wondering just how dangerous Greg's growing paranoia might be, I even discussed it with Richard, who said that if Greg had a commitment to making the funeral the greatest show on earth it was unlikely he would do anything until afterwards.

About four o'clock on the afternoon before the funeral I got a text from Emms.

Melt down over catering. Can you come over - please? Xx

The timing was rubbish, because I had a scheduled conference call, so it took me a good hour to get to their place and then I stood on the doorstep for five minutes waiting for someone to let me in. Emms opened the door; she had bath foam in her hair.

'Thank you,' she mouthed. 'See what you can do.' And she went upstairs.

Feeling ever so slightly as if I was going into the lion's den, I trudged into the kitchen and hovered in the doorway, waiting for Greg to turn round. It was noisy. He was standing over the food processor, pulsing up a rusty orange mush. The machine juddered and he held it still while he dribbled oil down the funnel. His phone rang and he stopped the machine.

'Yes, it's at two o'clock, Kingston Crematorium, no flowers, just donations to the NSPCC.' He saw me and waved a welcome as he continued the call. He looked haggard, but that was to be expected. As he talked, the scent of hot suds and hot children drifted down the stairs and I caught snatches of Emms' voice. She was singing the songs that she'd made up for each child when they were born. It was an echo of the past that seemed to have dissolved like the memory of summer during dank winter. Greg finished his call and smiled at me. 'It's really kind of you to offer to help, come in, come in. How about a drink to get you started? I've got a nice Rioja and a Viognier for tomorrow.'

'No thanks, maybe when we've finished laying the tables.'

'Go on, try it, can't serve up foul wine when everything else is first rate. I'm just making taramousalata - from scratch.'

He sounded wired, but he was at least present. 'Greg, forgive me for saying this but haven't you got enough to do just arranging the funeral, never mind doing the food?'

'I want to do it.' He looked mulish.

'I'm not saying that it isn't a nice thought, but do you have the time?' At that the phone rang again and Greg snatched it up, 'Hello, yes that's right, 2 o'clock, Bonner Hill Road. Yes, there's plenty of parking.'

Greg ended the call and put the handset back in the cradle, then massaged his aching shoulder and looked at me ruefully.

'Look at yourself, Greg,' I said. 'You're run ragged, why are you doing this?'

He looked down, away, anywhere but back at me, but at least he spoke, 'I don't know, Liz. I really don't know anything any more.'

There was silence between us for a few moments, only the sound of Emms' voice, upstairs, singing to the children, then I picked up my car keys and said, 'Right, get your coat, we're going to the supermarket, we'll get a few quiches, some crisps, then Bob's your uncle, Fanny's your aunt and we'll get through this bloody funeral.'

I led him to my car, drove him up the road and marched him towards the supermarket entrance. His back was bent against the wind, and in the dark he looked frail, older and uncertain. His mouth kept opening and shutting as if he was trying to say something.

'What is it, Greg?' I took his arm to support him. He stopped walking and turned to me.

'Liz, I'm so scared. I'm not just scared for myself, I'm scared for Emms and what might happen to the kids.'

Poor Greg. Anxiety and paranoia were leaking out of him and it was evident that he was struggling to function. I could feel his anxiety, not as an observation, nor even as an echo of my own mad mind-set when I was in the world of John, but as a tangible experience that was viral. It was as if I was inhaling and absorbing his fear, making it my own and making it bigger, more jagged, darker and more despairing. I could almost visualise it splitting and multiplying, so that by the time we'd laid out the quiches and crisps, piled up the paper plates and plastic forks and covered it all with cling film, I was shaking.

I drove home, grasping on to the steering wheel as if it could save me, and I spent the entire night squirming at shadows, agonising about what would happen if Greg decided that his pain was so great that he had to kill himself that night. Maybe we shouldn't have waited till after the funeral to get him in to see a professional. What if he didn't make it through the night?

thirty-six

Grey day dawned through my curtains and there'd been no night-time phone call announcing a disaster. That was one thing to be thankful for. After a scalding shower, coffee and compulsive checking of my mobile, I took a slow drive to the crematorium. Since Mairi had no family, we were to be the notional head mourners, and instead of sitting at the back or even better, sitting in another county, I had to trudge past the other mourners all the way to the front of the chapel to perch in the second row of pews next to Emms. For today's occasion, Emms had resuscitated one of her many black outfits, a simple suit with velvet collar and cuffs that made her look sleek and well groomed, like a lucky black cat. By her side, Greg wore a shambolic grey suit that only emphasised his pallor and red eyes. We all air-kissed and then Greg beetled off to talk to the ushers and mourners who were still arriving outside the chapel.

'He looks likes shit,' I said.

Emms opened her hands and shrugged, 'I just don't know what to do; all I can hope is that after this, he'll have some sense that he's done the right thing by her. Anyways, for the moment, we've just got to get through this performance.'

From the bottom of her bag, Emms pulled out a snap lock plastic container and holding her hands low, so that no one behind us could see what she was doing, she opened it. Inside, were four chocolate truffles in individual pleated cases.

I frowned, not sure what to say. I don't know what I was expecting her to reveal to me in the plastic box, but it certainly wasn't a funeral snack. Once again, I had the sense that I wasn't seeing the world around me the same as everybody else did, particularly as Emms was oblivious to my reaction and the appropriateness of funeral picnics. What was she going to do next, bring out a flask?

'I made them this morning, I thought it was rather symbolic and my contribution to the circus. Mairi liked her chocolate,' Emms said.

'She certainly did.' I thought back to Christmas Cake Making Day and Mairi's grubby fingers, thrusting a chocolate-coated strawberry at me, saying that she could make herself sick from eating them. 'She would have loved these.'

'I made some for her at Christmas. Very special ones. Not the same as this batch. Why don't you try one, Liz? They're really good.'

What was Emms rambling on about? Maybe obsessing about chocolate was her way of coping with the propsect of the day ahead. Emms held out the box to me, 'Try one. Enjoy the moment.'

We each took a truffle and the cocoa dusted my fingers brown, then Emms tucked the box away and I slipped the sweet into my mouth. Emms was right. They were good – no, they were wonderful. Inside the chocolate shell there was a liquid salted caramel centre, and I immediately felt the chocolate hit. Maybe Emms had the right idea; maybe having got over the OCD she was enjoying the moment and dealing with what she could do, when she could do it. There was certainly something to be said for that.

I was just running my tongue over my back teeth when Greg came back and seated himself at the pew in front of us next to a fresh-faced woman with magnificent tits.

'Who she?' I whispered to Emms

'One of Mairi's co-workers at the hospital. She's doing the reading,' Emms pointed at the order of service and showed me the heading. The reading was called "Do Not Stand at My Grave and Weep".

'What do you think Mairi would have made of this show?' Emms said.

'I think she would have loved it, all the attention, so at least in that respect, Greg has done her proud. Too bad about the rest of it.' I whispered. 'This ... this all seems so ironic given where she thought she was going to be. I bet she was probably planning a church wedding.'

'For God's sake, Liz. Not here.'

Emms looked over her shoulder and then stiffened.

'What?' I said.

'I might be wrong but I think I recognise the policeman who did the interviews, D.C. Lapham or whatever his name was. Take a look, they're at seven o'clock about nine rows back,'

I waited a few seconds and then casually turned my head as if I was checking the other mourners. Emms was right. By the pillar, I could see the fair greying hair of a besuited Lapham, but he wasn't with Errity. His head was down and he was talking to a woman.

'You're right.' I said. My heart started beating and I could feel the chocolate in my chest.

'Don't you think that's peculiar?' Emms gripped my arm. It hurt.

'I don't know. Really I don't. Maybe it's some community thing and if they have some sort of visible presence then we all feel we're on the same side and don't complain about the council tax.'

There was no point saying that maybe the police lied to Emms when they said that the investigation into Mairi's death was closed. It would accomplish nothing. Her previous cheery relaxed demeanour had shifted. Her hand was still gripping my arm; I gently lifted it away and tried to sound calm.

'Listen, didn't you say Greg put an ad in the paper? Maybe they just wanted a free feed. I don't see it as being threatening, if that's what you mean.'

'What if they come back to the house? What if they get Greg on his own and he tells them what really happened? We can't let that happen, Liz.

We've got to keep Greg away from them. Who knows what he's likely to say if we're not careful.'

Before I could respond, an ascetic looking bearded priest came into the chapel and began the proceedings. I only listened with half an ear because my mind kept going back to the police turning up at the funeral. Whatever I may have blathered to Emms about community support and council tax, I wasn't remotely convinced that a police presence was without sub-text. After all, who goes to funerals for fun? Maybe it would have been better if Greg 'fessed up and was done with living a lie. Chances are it was all going to come out anyway, because as soon as we got him to see a shrink, if they thought that Greg was a danger to himself or others, the police would have to be involved, so maybe we were making another big mistake.

I looked up and realised that the reading was over and had been met with an appreciative hush and mutter. Mairi's workmate had stepped down from the lectern and, head down, was making her way back to the pew. The priest stepped forward and spoke.

'We will now hear a few words about Mairi from her friend and colleague, Greg Harens,' I felt Emms' body stiffen. Greg stood up and shuffled towards the lectern as if it was the guillotine. If he was going to go into meltdown, the funeral address would probably be the place to do it. I squeezed Emms' arm as Greg's hesitant voice trembled into the church.

'I first met Mairi when she looked after my children at the hospital crèche. She was joyful and vibrant, and she quickly became close to the children who loved her as much as she loved them. Mairi was a free spirit with a generous nature and a way of communicating with children that was both instinctive and inspirational. It was based on boundless love and self-sacrifice as well as hope that she might give the children she worked with a better early life than the one she'd known herself.'

The eulogy continued in this somewhat sickening style. Glancing to my side, I saw that Emms had her head down and was studiously pushing back her cuticles. It was another one of those times when I had to hand it to her. If it had been me sitting in the pew listening to my husband getting poetic about a would-be home wrecker, I'm not sure I'd have been so forgiving, whether or not Greg was on the brink of a breakdown. There was no doubt that we had to get him to see someone before the inquest, because if he was called as a witness there's no knowing what he might say. You only had to look at him, standing at the lectern, swaying back and forth, seeming as if, at any moment, he would topple right over. He could crack up at any moment. At that moment, Greg's voice went up a heart-stopping pitch and broke with emotion whilst his expression spoke of deep despair.

'Mairi held out the hand of friendship and perhaps, perhaps ... I think ... we all let her down by not holding out a hand to help her.'

If ever evidence was needed for Greg's disturbed state, this barely veiled reference to Mairi drowning was it. A trembling Greg stepped down from the lectern and shuffled back to his seat, and the service resumed. At long last, the coffin disappeared behind a curtain to the strains of "Circle of Life", that, according to the order of service, came from the Lion King. Afterwards, there was an announcement inviting people back to the house, and we were able to get out of there fast. There was no doubt in my mind that if Greg were left alone with the police for five minutes, he would find himself in custody before teatime.

thirty-seven

The traffic was thicker than day-old porridge and I soon lost sight of Emms' and Greg's white Golf as we snarled along the A3. Frustrated, I banged around into my car's radio, clicking between BBC Surrey and Radio Jackie to see if there was some major accident up ahead, but all I found was cheery, foot-tapping music and a magazine programme about nonagenarian achievements. As far as I could see, cars were crawling at twenty miles an hour, and we were so slow that other drivers were able to exchange exasperated looks, window to window.

Trying to be clever, I took a right turn to see if I could wriggle up Robin Hood corner through Kingston. I had to get to the house to keep Greg away from the police. I'd be completely failing Emms and, indeed, Greg if I left him with the police for anything more than thirty seconds. Greg was a grenade primed to go off.

In spite of my casual reflection to Emms that attending the funeral was part of happy Surrey community policing, the really bad feeling about their appearance at the chapel was like a mushroom cloud. It was growing, spreading and poisoning any attempt at keeping a clear head. As I saw it, there was only one possible reason why the police were at the funeral. It had to be because they had unanswered questions. In other words, Mairi's body may have been released for burial, but the file was not closed.

With one hand I pulled at the collar on my shirt, I could feel the label scratching at my skin and I tried to tear it away. How much longer was this bottleneck going to go on for? Impotent, I thudded my hand at the steering wheel, and then reached into my bag for my phone to try to text Emms. Then the traffic moved again, just fast enough to make texting impossible.

This extra delay was my entire fault for taking a right turn and trying to be clever. Now, I had no possible hope of getting back to the house in time to drag Greg away so that he didn't confess to God only knew what. My only hope was that the police either didn't go back to the house or were stuck in the same traffic. Fat chance.

Up ahead, I could see the obstruction: road works and a man in an orange jacket controlling portable traffic lights whilst talking to the man on the truck with the cones. He was completely oblivious to the queue, more interested in whatever his chum was saying. My hand hovered over the car horn. I stroked the plastic and ached to press down and give orange jacket a blast so he could turn to green.

I looked at my watch. They'd be back by now, they'd be back at the house and I'd totally screwed up. Terrific.

It wasn't simply about being late and trying to stop Greg from confessing to what I supposed was technically manslaughter; the issue was accepting that Greg was mentally ill and what the long-term repercussions might be.

He'd told Emms he'd let Mairi drown. In anybody's book, that's hardly the same as pushing her into the water and holding her under until she died. Maybe there was an argument for 'fessing up and telling the police. Greg can't have been the first person who had had a total mind melt moment and let someone die. At every single accident site, not to mention hospital, there are people who have been in the wrong place at the wrong time and made the wrong decision. Was it really too late to admit to that?

Yes. It was.

I was past orange jacket and his portable lights and at long last the traffic thinned out enough for me to put my foot down and swing up to 30 mph. The road curved out of Kingston and over the bridge where I glimpsed the river. It was green, grey and choppy. How could I not help but think of Mairi, her hair floating in the green water, leaves catching, fish eating her? The sight of the river made my stomach roll.

After another twenty minutes, I pulled up two hundred yards away from the cottage. There were cars all around the cottage, banked up round the green, down side turnings. It seemed that the ad in the paper and the obituary had done the trick. It was a sell-out funeral. How ironic. For a moment I remembered Mairi, sitting at Emms and Greg's kitchen table, weeping on her birthday. Mairi, whose self-pitying wail was that nobody would miss her, was in death, hosting a packed house of well-wishers.

Richard had refused to come, at first citing work commitments, and then admitting that it would be hypocritical to sit in celebration of Mairi's life when his feelings towards her were, at best, ambivalent. And finally saying, that he didn't want to be publicly associated with her.

'Oh, come on,' I said. 'It's not often I ask you to do something.'

'No,' he looked tight-lipped and immovable, 'She may be dead but I have unresolved issues about her behaviour, besides which I really do not want to be railroaded into taking part in this tawdry event,'

To emphasise the offending tawdriness, Richard had waved the local newspaper that contained Mairi's obituary and included a rather attractive head and shoulders shot. Her head was to one side, twinkling tendrils tumbled to her shoulder and she had a sparkly smile for the photographer. I'd read the piece and Richard had a point. The main thrust of the obit, authored, of course, by Greg, was that Mairi had been snatched away from our now diminished community when she was on the brink of making a great contribution to society, at first with her nursery and then by doing who knows what else.

'I take your point. I on the other hand, have no option and I would be pathetically grateful for a supportive hand on my elbow.'

That didn't work. The bastard refused, so it was all down to me, Liz No-Mates, trying to stop Greg gibbering to the police.

As I walked across the green, dodging dog-walkers and Canada geese, I felt drained of energy. My neck muscles ached, and each step closer to the cottage made me want to simply turn around and head in the other direction. But of course, that wasn't the option of a true friend. I pasted on what I hoped was a suitable expression for the occasion, straightencd up and prepared to do my best for Greg and Emms.

The first person I recognised when I squeezed through the front door into the mass of people was Greg's mother. Daphne was holding a tray of glasses between her arthritic hands and was in danger of being mobbed. I pushed my way towards her.

'Here, let me take that.' I held it above my head.

'Oh, hello, dear, who'd have thought Mairi was this popular. I'm sure I won't get anything like this sort of turn out when I pop off.'

'I am sure we won't have to deal with that any time soon.' I guided her through the mass of people who all seemed to be talking at the top of their voices and trying to go in different directions. I pushed a path through them with Daphne in tow and reached the marquee, where there was certainly more space and you could at least hear. As soon as I'd parked the tray, I gave a glass of wine to Daphne, took one for myself and cut to the chase:

'Have you seen Greg?'

Her mouth tightened, the little lines in relief. 'He's in the kitchen.'

'Is he alright?' How much did she know? Her expression said, "worry", but I didn't have time to explore her concerns, whatever they might be, and then pour soothing words onto them. I took a gamble that she was solely concerned about her son's boozing and general ill health. If she knew the full story, she wouldn't be making witty asides about her own funeral.

Just as Daphne said, I found Greg in the kitchen, his back against the units, necking what looked like a long vodka and tonic, light on the tonic. Emms clung to his arm and when she clocked me, she flashed an unmistakable, "Thank God you're here" smile that made my heart thud. To add to the heart thumping, my ears rang when I recognised one of the cops from the chapel. So they had come back to the house.

D.C. Lapham stood next to a sandy-haired, pleasantly frumpy looking woman I thought I recognised from some supermarket, bank, shop or other local location. Lapham had put aside his leather jacket and was in a suit that was functional if not smart, no doubt his go to court, go to funeral outfit. From where I was standing, I could see him smiling and listening, head to one side, when Emms spoke, but his eyes darted around, clocked any subtext and when Emms had smiled at me, he'd read her face, followed her gaze and met my eyes. He winked at me. Arse. Definitely a man one should approach with extreme caution.

By Emms' side, Greg shifted from foot to foot, arms crossed around his body as if he was trying to hold in his internal organs. His gaze was vacant. I didn't know whether his empty eyes were due to an excess of booze and emotion or whether he was having some sort of catatonic episode. I marched into the fray.

'Sorry, sorry, total screw-up on the A3, I shouldn't have gone through Kingston but by the time I realised it was too late.' I looked at Lapham politely, smiled and waited to be introduced to his sidekick. Emms did the honours.

'Liz, you already know D.C. Lapham, this is his colleague, D.C. Graham.' She nodded to me. She looked friendly. We all shook hands and I noted that Lapham's hand was warm, dry and firm.

'Great turn out, Greg,' I said. 'You've done Mairi proud.' Greg nodded, head bobbing, and he avoided my eyes.

'Can I drag Greg away to talk to some of Mairi's colleagues?' Emms said.

'Only if you leave Ms Verrall behind,' Lapham said with grin that did nothing to make me feel relaxed. But at least problem 'A' was solved. Emms took Greg's arm and he barely registered a response. This was worrying, but at least Emms was getting Greg away to safety. Before Lapham could say a word, I launched into some innocuous chat, asking where he lived and attempting to talk pubs, since he had the air of a man who might stand at the bar in a low ceiling hostelry and discuss the relative merits of whatever ale there was on tap.

'Somehow I can't see you taking the minutes at the local CAMRA meeting,' he said. 'You look like more of a fancy cocktail kind of woman.'

'Not me, though you're right, I don't like those beers that taste as if a rat died in the cask.'

'Lager then? White wine?' he narrowed his eyes and, once again, I wondered if he was flirting. There were twinkly creases at the corner of his eyes and he knew how to use them. 'You can tell a lot about people from what they drink, like your friend, Emma. I'd put her down as a Black Velvet or Campari sophisticated kind of woman.' He <u>was</u> flirting. I laughed.

'You're not very good at this. Try again.'

'Alcopops.'

'Warm. She's a Bailey's girl.'

'How about Mairi?' he slipped in.

It was an innocuous question; after all, what difference did it make what she drank? I answered without thinking, 'I don't think I ever saw her drink anything stronger than coffee.' I thought back to all the times I'd seen her and tried to remember. 'No, I don't think she drank.'

'Do you think that was significant?'

I was starting to feel uncomfortable, as if the conversation was like a train on tracks and it was going somewhere, but it was a mystery train because I had no idea where it was going.

'Lots of people don't drink, for all sorts of reasons,' I glanced down at the urine-coloured apple juice in his own plastic cup. 'Some people don't like the taste,'

'But most people have a passion,' he said. 'Something that drives them, some goal, some vision of how their life might be, some hunger that they feed. It can be completely innocuous, like the guy who is a tightwad and hungers for security.'

'You sound like a psychologist.'

'I'm police.' The mystery train speeded up, the landscape rushed past and any minute there was going to be a major pile-up.

'And what's your passion?' I said, turning the attack on to Lapham. Before I finished the sentence, I realised what an unbelievably stupid question that was. Of course, I knew what the answer was, and with sickeningly predictability it came back at me.

'Finding out the truth,' Lapham said.

'And there was I thinking you just might say something a little less TV cop show,' I smiled sweetly.

'I'm just police.' Our eyes met again. Whether the case was closed or not was secondary: he was someone who didn't give up.

D.C. Graham had been watching quietly, not contributing and she excused herself to get more juice, leaving me alone with Lapham. My heart rate ramped up in anticipation of what he was going to say next. And he didn't disappoint.

'I didn't realise that you were in a relationship with Richard Annley,' he said. How the hell did he know? 'There was some gossip about him and the deceased; did you know anything about it?'

A simple question and I felt the heat from my neck go all the way up to my ears. I shrugged, 'So what? They both worked at the hospital, whatever Richard did before we got together is nothing to do with me. We all have baggage, don't you?'

'Oh, yes ...' he looked at me with appraising eyes, and I wondered how much of a check he'd done on me and if he knew who I really was.

'Well, I suppose I should see if there's anything I can do in the kitchen.' I said. 'And you must have the call of "the job" - that is what you call it, isn't it?'

'Yes, and that's what I'm doing, my job,' he was smiling. 'Weren't we talking about Mairi and what her passion might have been? I'd say married men, wouldn't you?'

'What of it?'

'Why don't you ask your doctor boyfriend, next time you see him?'

I eye-balled Lapham, 'Thanks for the tip, it's been lovely chatting to you.'

Without waiting for a response, I turned and marched out of the kitchen, manoeuvred my way through the hall, around two men, deep in conversation, and out of the front door. And I kept walking, across the road, onto the green until I found a bench by the pond, where my legs gave out.

What was that all about? What if Richard hadn't come to the funeral because he was scared that he might bump into Lapham? But what did Richard have to be scared about? He didn't know about Greg's moment of panic by the riverside unless there was some other big fat lie that was throbbing in the background ready to burst open if any pressure was applied. I felt breathless, no doubt because I'd been holding my breath, but I tried with every ounce of mental strength to concentrate on the willow overhanging the pond, its branches draped like a waterfall, budding, fresh and green. Don't ruminate, focus on what needs to be done, keep going. Focus. Keep going. Focus. Keep going.

I was swaying a little on the wooden bench as I mouthed the words like a crazy street woman trying to hold on to a magic spell to ward off the darkness. Maybe that's what prayer is. The same magic spell. After a few minutes, I'm not sure how long, I was aware of the sun warming my back. I stretched out my neck and began to breath normally. Of course, Richard had said that he had dark fantasies, but did that mean that he put them into practice? Yes, Richard had pointed at Greg and said that he was in meltdown, but so bloody what?

Let's imagine for five fanciful minutes that Richard had gone to Greg, warned him that Mairi was an unhinged, home-wrecking, minx and persuaded Greg to take Mairi down to the river and shove her in. And afterwards, Greg couldn't live with the guilt, but decided to protect Richard and take the rap. Absolutely ridiculous. I shook my head and exhaled. That really was the silliest idea. It was far more likely that Richard, with his customary patrician superiority, had pissed off Lapham at the interview and Lapham wanted to mix it when he suggested in his louring tone that I ask my boyfriend.

From where I was sitting I could see Emms' and Greg's chocolate box cottage, with its pinpricks of pink from the roses around the front door. The door itself was open and people were emerging, drifting off towards their cars, engines started and the funeral circus began to ease out of the village. Up ahead, I saw the two men that I'd wriggled round in the hallway. They were still jabbering, but now they took out mobile phones and were probably exchanging numbers. With the lack of sobriety, the event could have been simply a jolly party, and I wondered how many people even knew Mairi. Lapham and D.C. Graham skirted the men, turned left and walked at a clip towards their car. They were deep in conversation and didn't look my way: so much for the eagle eye of the law.

It was completely absurd to suggest that Richard had anything to do with Mairi's death, and the police knew it. If they had anything on him, or anyone, they wouldn't have closed the file; they would have stopped the funeral and arrested him. That's their damn job. Lapham was winding me up: whether it was a perverse way of flirting or a power trip was irrelevant.

I took off my specs and polished the lenses against my scarf. Over the sound of cars starting, I heard the chirruping of spring birds and the lazy hum of an airplane overhead. Even though I had totally discounted Lapham's wind-up, there was something else about the conversation that was bothering me, an unconnected link at the back of my mind, lodged there like the smallest silver weight that unbalances the scales. But I couldn't put my finger on it and I wasn't going to waste any more energy in that direction. And I certainly wasn't going to ask my boyfriend anything. Bugger Lapham. I was staying on message, helping Emms to get Greg sorted out and not letting the police muddy the waters for their own vainglorious "it's the job" motivation. I went back to the cottage.

thirty-eight

Inside the cottage, I found post-party carnage and I discovered Emms in the marquee with a black plastic bag that she was methodically filling with the paper plates. Daphne was in the kitchen stacking the dishwasher, and Greg himself was nowhere to be seen.

'What can I do?' I asked Emms

'Help Daphne, if you want. Or help me, or go and get yourself a drink, or get me one. We're getting through this mess and it's not too bad thanks to you doing the Waitrose run,' Emms looked around to make sure there was no-one within earshot and lowered her voice, 'Thanks for taking the heat off Greg. If you hadn't stepped in, I wouldn't have been able to drag him away. You arrived just in time; Lapham was getting ever so slightly pushy. How was he with you?'

'An arse: he went on about Richard and Mairi and suggested I talk to "my boyfriend." If you ask me, that man's seen too many cop shows.'

'What else did he say?'

'Some shit about what did Mairi drink and how her poison was chocolate and married men, I can't -'

Emms dropped the paper plate of curled-up sandwiches and fairy cakes she was carrying towards the plastic bag. The uneaten food went all over the lawn, speckling the trampled green with pink icing and small squares of bread. Emms' face was white with strain. It looked as if the day had suddenly caught up with her.

'Come on, let me do that,' I said. 'You go and have a drink and I'll bag up the rubbish. You're exhausted. I bet you didn't eat anything apart from the chocolate, your blood sugar's probably somewhere round your ankles.' I held out my hand for the bin bag.

'No, no.' Emms sounded shaky, confirming my theory. 'You've done more than any friend would or possibly could. Did Lapham say anything about Greg?'

'Not a word. I'm telling you, it was a wind-up, it's probably what he does for fun and the reason he hasn't got any friends and has to go to funerals to find someone to talk to. Where is Greg by the way?'

'Gone to the swings with Theo and the kids. Daphne told me that she and Theo are worried sick about Greg: the terrible thing is that she thinks it's just a drink problem, she's got no idea about the rest of it. Apparently, Theo had some uncle who drank himself to death,' Emms picked up a squashed sandwich from the lawn and put it into a separate food recycling bag. 'As much as anything else, I don't want to let Daphne and Theo down. They've always been so kind to me, from the moment I met them:

the least I can do is be a good daughter-in-law and get Greg out of this mess.'

'I don't suppose you've had the chance to suggest he sees someone?' I said. Emms shook her head, 'No, he won't talk to me. I told you, every time I come into a room, he walks out of it, and if we are in the same space he turns away so he has his back to me. It's quite mad. I don't know how he got through today without spitting at me. Apart from anything else, it's incredibly hurtful,'

'Listen, he's not well, you need to understand that and not take it personally. This isn't about you, it's about what's going on in his mind and the personal hell that he's in. How about if I go to the swings, chat about restaurants and get you and Greg lined up for a dinner date?'

Emms face lit up, 'Do you really think you might be able to persuade him? I'm sure if we were across the table, away from the kids, just for one, single evening, I could reach him. I don't blame him for what happened, really I don't, it only happened because he's a nice guy and I want him to realise that I don't blame him for anything.'

I walked to the playground with an easier step. The sky seemed to have cleared, and I had a sense that with Mairi both dead and cremated, and having ring-fenced my anxieties about the police, we were on the home run. There was only the formality of the inquest and persuading Greg to get professional help. These were hardly insurmountable problems. Having said that, I must admit that when I spotted

Greg I thought otherwise. He was sitting hunched on the picnic seat in the playground, back curved, apparently absorbed in the empty picnic table. God knows what he was thinking about, but he certainly wasn't present. By the swings, Theo, with an echoing hunch of age, was pushing both children on the swings and they whooped and squealed as he pushed them higher and higher. Meanwhile, Greg was motionless, and then I saw his shoulder jerk. Christ, I hope he isn't crying. I waved to Theo and the kids, who waved back, and then slipped onto the picnic seat next to Greg.

'Hey.' Greg nodded and looked away but there was enough time for me to glimpse his face. Red-rimmed eyes and greasy white skin: Greg reeked of bitter sorrow. It seemed to seep from his pores and it made me shudder. 'Greg, I know things haven't been great lately,'

'Fucking understatement,' he grunted.

I sat in silence for a few moments, 'You have every reason to feel upset and angry, and perhaps it would help if you try to talk things through with Emms.'

'Don't you think I have, don't you think I've talked to her till I'm blue in the face? I've been trying to talk things through for months, so it's a bit late now, much too late, it's all over, I'm finished.'

I caught a whiff of sour alcohol on his breath and forced myself to touch him, to take his hand between my own. He was close to meltdown; maybe he was even past the point where she might be able to pull him back.

'Listen to me, Greg, you trust me, don't you? You know I would never do anything to hurt you or Emms or the children. You are like family to me,'

'Of course I do, that's why we made you the children's godmother.' His voice softened, and for a moment, I had a glimpse of the old Greg. He was in there somewhere, he was inside that wretched body, if we could just reach him, pull him back from that dark place of misery, throw him the line to haul himself out of the hole. I squeezed his hand; I wanted him to feel some human warmth.

'We've all got to move on, Greg. Even if it doesn't feel like it now, things will change and you will feel differently about what's happened. Okay?'

He nodded. I don't know if I was getting through. It was like standing in front of a tunnel, calling into the darkness, but I was resolute. I went on, 'So let's all try and behave as if we are feeling differently. What if you went out for dinner with Emms, just like the old days, somewhere nice, somewhere relaxing?'

'I can't leave the kids, I can't leave them, if I leave them, something bad will happen, they'll get sick, something bad will happen.'

'Come on, it's only one evening, Greg. You said you trusted me, didn't you? One evening and I'll babysit, with Richard, who's a doctor, so if anything happens, anything at all, the kids will be safe. What do you say?'

thirty-nine

The night of Emms' dinner with Greg was cold. After a brief, teasing taste of spring's sparkling air, the weather had returned to wintery gloom and the grey damp was like being trapped and entangled in a dirty, wet blanket. My mind kept drifting back to the Florida Keys, the clear light, aqua sea and shushing waves on the beach. It had only been three months since I'd been there and it seemed like three hundred years or, indeed, that it had never actually happened at all.

Richard and I were due to be at Emms' and Greg's for babysitting duties at 6.30. By then, the children were supposed to have already had their tea, been bathed and be in their pyjamas, ready for their story. My allotted job was story time, Richard would do the takeaway run, and poor Emms had the bitter task of convincing her husband that he was out of his mind and needed urgent medical attention.

Needless to say, there was no doubt in my mind that story time was far and away the best option. Poor Emms. No one wants to give a loved one bad health news and "you're mentally ill" was an unlikely prelude to a cheery date night dinner. That's why

Emms and I prepped the content of the evening. Part of the agreed preparation was that Emms was going to make an effort to glam up for Greg, to show that she cared about him. And yes, I am fully aware that this smacked of 1950s, "don't let your husband see you in your curlers" lore, but by dressing carefully for their night out, Emms would be sending a subliminal message to Greg that she valued their relationship and what she was going to tell him was said out of love.

Emms was going to drive because it was hard to know exactly how much Greg had drunk on any given day; he had become so secretive about it. They were going to start the evening enjoying the view from Newlands Corner. Standing at the top of the ridge of the Downs with the country tumbling beneath their feet, she would try to engage with their past and what they shared together, which was, of course, their love for their children. Then it would be on to Carlo's, where Emms would make the pitch that Greg was naturally distressed about Mairi and would have nothing to lose by seeing someone.

'No blame, no recriminations, no finger-pointing,' I said. And Emms repeated it like a mantra.

'No blame, no recriminations, no finger-pointing, I've got it, I will sit on my bloody hands, if I even think I'm heading that way,'

'Or, failing that, hold his hand,' I said. 'Physical contact is a great way of connecting, and if you can touch him and consciously think kindly of him, the yet to be proven theory is that you will engage his alpha waves. Either way, it can't hurt.'

'I'll try anything,' Emms said. 'Greg is the love of my life, I am not going to give up on him.'

Her face was close to crumpling into pain, so I changed the subject.

Once Greg had agreed to see someone, it would be down to the doctor. Richard had assured me that not only was his man primed and available, he was one of the top five in his field.

'It'll be okay,' I said. 'Trust me, this is just a bad time and it will pass, I promise you. When have I ever lied to you?'

'Just tell me when it's okay to cry.'

Every single night after the funeral, I ruminated over the cop's lines, 'Ask your boyfriend,' and every single morning, I loathed myself anew for being too scared to ask Richard outright, too stupid to work out what Lapham was hinting at and too neurotic to forget about it.

Richard picked me up at 5.30 to drive me over to the cottage. Tapping away on his steering wheel at the traffic lights, he sounded strained.

'I want you to know that this is an absurd situation. In my medical opinion, Greg needs urgent attention, and I mean urgent. Are you aware that if Emma can't persuade Greg to see my man, we may have to get him sectioned? From what you've told me, he may be a danger to himself, and that's not a responsibility I am happy about shouldering,'

Was he actually expecting me to have a conversation about this now, when we were on the way to the cottage? I tried to sound reasonable.

'Let's just see how the evening pans out. Emms and I have talked it through, and while I may not have your or your medical friend's superior knowledge, I do have some skills. And don't forget, Emms loves Greg. Even if he is unhinged, he must know that she loves him.'

'Not necessarily.' Richard was tight-lipped.

Greg opened the door and gave me a weak but welcoming smile. He and Richard shook hands in a way that did nothing to make me relax. Meanwhile, Emms was at the top of the narrow stairs, and I was pleased to see that she had eschewed her crazy rainbow colours and was wearing black, a lace top over evening trousers. As she stepped down, I saw black patent court shoes. Party shoes. They looked new.

'Like the outfit,'

'Sexy shoes,' Greg said in a voice that sounded miles away. He was jiggling on the spot, rubbing his hand against his hip in a way that made me momentarily wonder whether the core problem was physical and not mental.

'Thanks for babysitting,' Greg said. 'We really appreciate it, don't we, Emma? Hey, Liz, why don't you come up and see the children? They're already in bed and they've promised to be extra good.'

'Greg, love,' Emms said. 'Why don't you offer Richard and Liz a drink first? I'm sure the kids will make their way down in their own good time,'

'No, I want to take Liz upstairs to see them in bed. Can't I do that? Do I have to do everything you say, when you say it, all the time?' He glared at Emms and waves of hostility beamed out of him like radio signals from an antenna. Hats off to Emms, she smiled warmly back at Greg, as if he hadn't snapped at her, as if everything was fine and sunny in the house of love.

'Of course, you don't, I'm sorry, Greg. I'll get Richard that drink, whilst you take Liz upstairs to see the kids.'

Greg jiggled and turned his back away so that he wasn't looking at her. Boy, they were going to have one hell of an evening if he was as disturbed as he now seemed to be. Maybe, once again, I was screwing up by not listening to Richard. I followed Greg upstairs; he was talking non-stop, and when he turned to me outside the kids' bedroom, I smelt the alcohol on his breath.

'If they're hungry,' he said in a stagey, loud voice, 'there's oatcakes and banana downstairs and some milk, but they know they have to clean their teeth afterwards, that's the trade-off for a snack.'

The moment before we went into the room he pulled a crumpled white envelope out of his pocket and shoved it towards me. He looked me in the eyes, his own filling with tears, 'I'm so sorry, Liz, so so sorry.'

'What is it?' I held the envelope.

He hissed back at me, 'Don't open it till after we go, promise me.' He was gripping my hand, tightly. It hurt. 'Promise me,'

'Okay,' I whispered.

'Thank you, thank you.'

He loosened his grip, sniffed and we sidled into the bedroom to find the children sitting up in their bunk beds.

'Ready for the big story tonight, are you?' I said.

'Yeah!'

'See you in ten minutes, okay, and for tonight, for one night only, we've got my friend Richard who will be the scary monster,'

Through the fabric of my jeans I could feel the crackle of the envelope and was both anxious to read it and, I'm sorry to say, a little resentful. Why now, and why did Greg have to entrust this document to me? I was bone-achingly tired. But Greg's creased face and his shaky voice were enough to silence my mean "poor me" attitude - the man was in torment and his emotional pain was like an unstoppable tsunami, pouring out of him, smashing up and dragging all reason in its wake. Of course, the contents of the letter would be a tirade of psychotic fantasies and I would have to tell Emma, and that would be bound to upset her even more than she was already. But it couldn't be helped. Next of kin and all that.

At least we were doing something, and the letter would be further evidence of Greg's mental condition and perhaps aid diagnosis, so, if Emms didn't manage to persuade Greg that he was mentally ill, we would have to follow the necessary but distressing route and get him sectioned. Either way, the chances were that Greg would be seeing someone who could help him within the next twenty-four hours. Thank God for that.

Unless.

What if the letter was a suicide note?

'Come on, Greg.' I heard Emms from downstairs. 'We'll be late for our table if we don't get going.' Greg stood at the side of the bed and hugged Robbie, clutching him as if he was never going to see him again. That didn't look good. Then he did the same to little Tessa, who squealed with delight.

'Greg.' came Emms' voice. He tore himself away from his daughter, pushed past me and clattered down the stairs.

I had to stop them for five minutes so I could read the letter, 'Emms, you forgot your scarf, didn't you say you wanted to wear a scarf tonight? It'll be cold at Newlands Corner.'

Of course, we hadn't discussed scarves and I sounded like my grandmother but it was the only excuse I could think of at short notice. Emms paused. Had she got it? We always used to be able to understand each other's sub-textual messages. How many times had we finished each other's sentences, exchanged glances, used unrelated words and still knew what the other meant? She had to understand what I really meant.

'Oh, thanks Liz,' Emms sounded puzzled. 'I'll button up my coat. Promise. See you later, won't be late,' And I heard the door close behind them.

'Shit.' I said. I was standing on the landing looking down at the front door.

'Aunty Liz,' I heard from the kids' bedroom, 'That's a bad word.'

'Yes, it is, and I'm very sorry,' I said on autopilot. I ripped open the envelope and pulled out the sheets of paper, it was handwritten, in a tiny scrawl that was almost illegible and certainly couldn't be read in the gloom of the landing. I opened my mouth to swear again and caught it just in time. Should I just be done with it and call Emms? My hand went to my mobile and hovered for a second over the keypad. No, there was no point in phoning her with a half-baked story about a letter that I hadn't actually read. I had to read the damn thing first. I went into her bedroom, sat on her side of the bed and read what it was that Greg had to say.

forty

I'm frightened. No, I'm not frightened, I'm fucking terrified. I can't believe that I'm writing this, I think she's trying to kill me and I don't know what I can do to protect myself or the children. Or Emms.

I read the words and heard my own heavy sigh, like air from an already deflated balloon. Poor Greg, he sounded desperate; well at least, help was on the way. And at least it wasn't the suicide note that I'd been dreading. Everything I knew about self-harm and suicide directed me to believe that Greg was unlikely to commit suicide on an evening out with Emms but I was happy that it had been confirmed.

In spite of Greg's transparent anguish, I felt a little easier as I read on, struggling to decipher his lousy handwriting, not good at the best of times but now exacerbated by his mental state.

This is fucking madness. Maybe I AM imagining it and I have some terrible psychotic illness. But I'm not mad, this is really happening. Oh fuck. What am I going to do? I've got to do something to protect the children. If she kills me, what will happen to them?

I should have gone to the police when I found out about the poison but I didn't believe her. Or did I?'

Poison? I reread the sentence.

I heard Richard's steps on the stairs, 'Isn't it supposed to be story time?' he said. 'Aren't you weaving magic tales about fairies and teddy bears delivering customer service training programmes while I go off and get a takeaway?' I shoved the letter under my jumper and came out of Emms' and Greg's bedroom. The hairs on the back of my neck were standing up and I needed to read the rest of the letter quietly, calmly, without my heart thudding so hard against my ribcage that I couldn't swallow. Richard loomed over me. In the small space of the tiny upstairs landing, I felt claustrophobic.

'Is there something wrong?' Richard said.

'No, no, everything's fine, everything's absolutely fine. I'll tell you what,' I said raising my voice to include the kids. 'As it's a special Saturday night, Richard will start off the story, and I'll nip downstairs and order the takeaway. I'll be back in ten minutes.'

I handed Richard the storybook and ignored his "I don't do young children" look. Downstairs I opened and shut the table in the hall and made a show of looking for the restaurant phone number, then locked myself in the downstairs loo to continue reading.

Sitting on the wooden loo seat, my hand shaking, I re-read the last sentence:

'I should have gone to the police when I found out about the poison.'

Poison? What was Greg talking about? If this was a significant psychotic delusion, why hadn't Emms mentioned it?

Maybe I pretended I didn't believe her because I couldn't bear the thought of what was happening. Our family being split, our lovely, lovely life being over. And then she disappeared. That's when I should have gone to the police, when she disappeared.'

She? My hand went to my mouth my heart rate had gone from thudding to hammering hard. Heart attack hard. Greg wasn't talking about a delusion, he was talking about a confession, just like Emms' confession to me in the hospital. I went back to the beginning of the letter; he said that he didn't believe her. Who was he talking about? Mairi or Emms? Was it possible that Emms had actually poisoned Mairi? Was that the crust of logic I couldn't swallow?

For a couple of seconds I was too frightened to read on and concentrated on trying to slow down my heart rate. 'Don't think, don't think,' I muttered. I exhaled slowly, then stood up and ran cold water; the chill on my wrists and random splashes over my face helped. I was just about to sit down and continue reading when there was a knock at the door.

'Sorry to disturb you but the natives are rather insistent that you join them for story time. Shall I go and pick up the food?'

'Yes ... yes ... Just give me a minute.' Let him go, let me gather myself and find out for certain this time.

'I put the order in at the Indian in Sunbury,' I said. 'Not the one on the corner, the one on the main road.' It would take Richard at least fifteen minutes to get there, which would give me enough time to phone them and place the order. That would give me plenty of time to read the rest of the letter, put the kids down, then do what I was dreading - look for evidence. Look in the places that only a friend would know, because only a true friend recognises how you think and just what you might be capable of.

As soon as Richard was on his way, I phoned the restaurant, gave the kids some hot chocolate and, while they brushed their teeth, read the rest of the letter. The next section seemed to have been written at another time and was even less coherent. Maybe he was pissed: he was certainly emotional or clumsy as there were smudges through the black ink that could have been tears or some other liquid. There was a lot of rambling about how much he loved the kids and Emms and I was starting to wonder if, I had got it wrong, and it was all psychotic fantasy until I reached the direct appeal to me.

Liz, I tried to tell you when we were in the car park at Waitrose buying the food for the funeral. She doesn't trust me to say the right thing at the inquest so she's going to kill me because I know why Mairi was sick. Emms gave her poisoned chocolate truffles. Mairi got sick but then guessed why, and said she was going to get them analysed. Mairi accused Emms and there was a row by the side of the river. I don't know what happened. I don't blame Emms, but I can't trust myself. And I can't get away either. It's my fault; Emms says it's my fault for bringing Mairi into the house. I accept that. Please, look after the children, please protect them and tell them how much I love them and will love them for eternity. Speak of me kindly.

I had to have proof. Either Emms had poisoned Mairi and then murdered her, or Greg was tormented by psychotic fantasies and was going to be hospitalised for some considerable time. I heard my shaky breath as I exhaled.

Unthinkable as it was, I had to look for clues to support or discount Greg's disturbed inventions. I knew Emms of old; she plans and ponders, she examines and compares. If she were going to kill Greg or, indeed, anyone, she would have written down the pros and cons and then weighted the various elements. That's how she'd do it; she'd probably even draw a chart with functions, formulae and outcomes. What was I thinking? This was crazy. Just reading Greg's letter had sent me off the edge; it was nonsense, the babble of his unhinged brain. Poor Greg.

'Okay ... everybody back to bed!' I said in rousing tones. 'Rinse and spit, rinse and spit and then everybody back to bed. And the last one in bed is a ...'

'Lemon!' they yelled in unison. I chased them into their room, Robbie scrambled up to the top bunk and they hunkered under the duvet.

'What are we reading?' I said.

'This one! It's new. Mummy bought it for us.' Tessa handed me a brightly coloured picture book. I started to read, all the while thinking about the letter and how quickly I could tuck up the kids and go through Emms' attic office. And then my attention was drawn back to the book I was reading aloud. The idea of the book seemed to be that it was fine to only have one parent. My muscles stiffened and I shuddered.

Of course, this is how she'd do it, I know Emms. Everything would be thought through, checked, double-checked, organised, itemised, ticked and deleted. And Emms would prepare the children for being in a single-parent family. Or maybe she was just preparing them for Greg being hospitalised for a long time. I had to find out. I turned to the end page, read the last three words, and left the children with the night light on.

There was only one place to look, Emma's study at the top of the house. It was the converted attic and the ceiling sloped. The Velux window looked out on to the back garden and I could hear light rain gently tapping on the glass. Emms' beech desk was immaculate, everything in order, little piles of files in different colours. What was I looking for? I didn't know. I tapped the keyboard and woke up her computer, only to be asked for a password. I didn't bother trying to guess what the password might have been because there'd be nothing on the computer. I knew that for certain: if Emms was planning to do something, or had done something, there's no way that she would have kept information on her computer. It would be on paper that she could cut up and destroy.

Suddenly I saw it. Suddenly I remembered, coming back from holiday and finding her in the office with her torn up bits of paper that she'd made into little hills. I groaned. She'd said it, she'd told me. 'It's my new thing, I tear up the bits of paper into smaller and smaller pieces and my problems get smaller and smaller.'

I started to go through her files, looking for handwritten notes. I scrabbled through the files, sifting the paper, searching in her drawers, not knowing what I was looking for and finding nothing. There were lots of spreadsheets but the only handwritten notes were in her black-bound shopping list books that she always carries and dates. They were in a drawer in chronological order.

If something had happened, it had started when I was away. I leafed through the latest one, which ran through to February, it contained Emms' Christmas list and that was long, running to three pages in her spidery writing, with all her food preparations, presents and cooking. I found a list dated the Saturday before I'd flown to Florida, the day after Christmas Cake Day.

Dis gloves; chocolate; moulds; plant; knife; board; rubbish bags; cash.

There was something there. I scratched my head. "Dis gloves" must be disposable gloves. That was reasonable if Emms was making something messy, like chocolate truffles. I stared at the list, mouthing the words to myself, like a chant. Trying to see the shape and form of the list and how it demonstrated Emms thought process. Like a plane coming through cloud, and catching glimpses of land, way, way below, there was something fading in and out of my understanding.

Then I broke through and saw land. It was the juxtaposition of the items on the list. Was it possible? Could the plant have been some sort of poison that Emms cooked into Mairi's chocolate truffles?

I took the book and shoved it into my pocket. It was something, maybe nothing. I felt my mobile vibrate and it was Richard, he was outside the front door but didn't want to ring the bell and wake the children. I was ready to tell him now. Let him be the judge of my suspicions. And let's see if he already knew.

I texted back, 'coming down now,' and pressed send. But I didn't stand up from Emms office chair immediately. I needed a moment to process the last thirty minutes and at least attempt to order my thoughts. My stomach was rolling and there was a sour taste in my mouth. Legs like lead, I pushed the chair away from the desk, stood up, and on remote tidied up Emms' files. It was the least I could do. In an attempt to drag out precious moments before I had to tell Richard what I feared, my eyes lingered on Emms' chocolate truffle business plan spreadsheet. The title said ChocEmms but the column headings didn't make sense. Weight, Mass, Velocity, Force.

Bile rose up in my throat and I had to choke it back because I knew. With terrible clarity, I knew exactly what she was going to do. And what's more, she was going to do it tonight.

I dashed down the attic stairs, ran across the landing and almost fell down the last flight to the front door. Hauling the door open, I pulled Richard and the plastic bag he was holding through to the kitchen and shut the door. He looked startled, probably because I was wild eyed. To his credit, he shut up and waited for me to speak. I took a deep breath, and although my voice was shaking, it was controlled, 'There is a distinct possibility that Emms is going to stage a car crash tonight and attempt to kill Greg.'

The moment I finished speaking I was certain, for the first time, that my fears about Richard were groundless. His expression was blank, confused: in other words, appropriate. 'What makes you think that?'

'Just before they went out, Greg passed me a letter in which he rambles but seems convinced that Emms is going to kill him. I thought it might be part of his psychosis but he talked about poison. I looked in Emms' office and I found a shopping list that may or may not indicate that she poisoned Mairi, using chocolate.'

'Mairi had norovirus, I was certain it was norovirus. She said it was the chocolates and she wanted me to do a blood test on her and send the chocolates away for analysis. I thought she was being manipulative and hysterical -' He trailed off.

'And, Richard, I found this,' I gave him the spreadsheet and he looked at me and shrugged. 'What am I looking at?'

'I think it shows the necessary velocity and impact force for a controlled car crash.'

'Why would Emma do that? What evidence have you got beyond this piece paper, which could refer to anything. Maybe they were looking to change their car and she was comparing safety in different models.'

I closed my eyes and allowed myself one second of guilt. 'Because she's done it before,' I said. 'Tony's crash wasn't an accident. I think she planned it and got away with it, and she's going to do it again.'

Richard's voice broke through my self-absorption with cold precision. It was the slap on the face I needed.

'Right, let's phone the restaurant. And if they're there, we'll say there's an emergency with the kids.'

Richard dialled from his mobile and I shrugged on my jacket and nervously picked at a poppadum that was poking out of the top of the brown bag. He put the call on speaker and I heard the clatter and chatter of the Saturday night trattoria.

'I believe you had a reservation in the name of Harens. I'm a doctor attending the children and there's been an emergency.'

I heard the flurry at the other end as the restaurant staff went off to find Emms and Greg. 'Not strictly true,' Richard said. 'But true enough and it gets a reaction.'

The phone crackled into life. 'Haren? Sorry. We have no reservation.'

'Thank you.' Richard ended the call. He looked at me. 'I'm calling the police, don't argue Liz, we have to call the police.'

'No we don't. No police, by the time you explain, it'll be too late. You stay here with the kids. I know where she is.'

forty-one

It wasn't until a few weeks later that I found out the full story of date night. On a sunny afternoon, Emms and I were sitting by the lake at the private psychiatric clinic. Beyond the wire fence, a fish slinked in the shallows mottled with floating pollen. Apparently, part of Emms' recovery was recalling the events and challenging her beliefs at the time of "the episode", and who was I, who had got almost everything wrong, to argue?

'I had it all planned,' Emms said. 'Right down to the last detail, including making the restaurant reservation in your name.'

Emms looked tired and drawn, and her hair was greasy and could have done with a cut. But in spite of that, for the first time in months, I had a sense that she was back.

Emms tucked her overlong fringe behind her ear. 'I can't believe it, but I was convinced that if I didn't kill Greg, and kill him before the inquest, he'd be at the police station unburdening himself to Lapham about what I'd done to Mairi. And I was angry with Greg as well. Really angry. He didn't understand that everything I'd done, right from the very beginning, I'd done for us. For the family.'

Emms shook her head, remembering. Behind her, over the lake, a dragonfly hovered over the water. In spite of how bizarre the conversation was, it felt like we were us again, talking and sharing moments, trying to work out lives and relationships in the way that we always had done.

'I understand that you were angry with Greg,' I said. 'But your solution?'

'It seemed entirely logical. The way I saw it was that once Greg turned me in to the police, I'd be arrested for attempted murder - because of the chocolates. And the chocolates weren't meant to kill her, just make her ill enough so that she couldn't open the nursery. You see, I thought if she didn't have the nursery excuse to keep in contact with Greg, she might buzz off somewhere else.'

'Why didn't you tell me?' I asked.

'Because I knew what you'd say. You'd have talked me out of it. Remember Christmas Cake Making Day? That's when I decided to do it. Remember Mairi saying that she could make herself ill eating chocolate?'

'Yes.' I also recalled how triumphant Mairi looked and how she'd deliberately wound up Emms by licking the spoon and sticking it back in the cake mix.

'You're right,' I said. 'I would have talked you out of it.'

'And you wouldn't have understood my logic about Greg,' Emms said.

'Logic? Come on, Emms, there was no logic in where you were.'

'That's not how it felt at the time. When the river bank collapsed and Mairi got washed away, it was logical not to call for help, because I <u>was</u> angry with her. She was talking about her right to have the kids and Greg. I <u>did</u> push her shoulder, and she <u>did</u> take a step back - but she tripped, Liz. I promise you, she tripped and the bank fell away. It was getting dark, there was no one around, so it was logical that I just went home.'

'So all that stuff about Mairi running off with the investment was completely made up?' I said.

'Yes. And when I told Greg, he couldn't cope. He just started drinking. And I reasoned, that even if I'd got a reduced sentence, the stigma of a conviction would've really damaged the kids. How could I let that happen? You know yourself, Liz, Robbie is more than a little sensitive compared to most kids his age, and as for Tessa, anyone can see that she's just the kind of kid who could go completely off the rails when she hits her teens. So I weighed it up, did pros and cons and came to the conclusion that Robbie and Tessa would struggle without a strong father figure in their lives, but they'd be no different from many of the kids in the village, where every other house is a single parent family. And how many of those fathers aren't around when they hook up with new girlfriends and start new families? And you know I'd never had done that; I'd have been there for them.'

God help me, but hearing Emms' justification did seem kind of logical. Emms was right. Greg would have gone to the police. Emms would have been banged up and the kids would have suffered. And I hadn't forgotten that the last time I saw Mairi, after the Christmas show, I'd have happily beaten the crap out of her. I reached out and held Emms' hand. It was hot and dry, and she squeezed mine before letting go. 'I have to tell you the rest.'

Emms stood up from the wooden bench where we were sitting and walked to the lake. She cleared her throat and went on. 'So Greg drank most of a bottle of red on top of the vodka and two double brandies. He was well-oiled. It was all quite amicable, Liz, and I remember wondering if he knew and was even relieved that we were getting to the end of our marriage.'

I remembered poor Greg's desperate letter.

'Maybe he did know,' was all I said.

'When we left the restaurant. I took Greg's arm and hoped that people at the tables by the windows saw us. It was dark on the road, Liz. Greg's head slumped on his chest and I knew he was drifting off. Then he suddenly perked up and said, "I feel so bad about Mairi. I didn't mean for this to happen".'

Emms' had her back to me and her arms were stiff by her side. I could see that she was clenching and unclenching her hands. She was silent for a few seconds, obviously trying to compose herself. After a few moments, she sighed and continued. She sounded matter of fact: 'So I headed off towards Gomshall. I saw some lights in the rear-view mirror so I sped up, but the lights kept up with me, and the same thing happened when I slowed down. And I started to imagine that it was Mairi.'

Of course, those lights were me.

Emms continued her side of the story. 'I remember a smell. A smell that was both sweet and musky. Her smell. Mairi. And I thought, what if she isn't dead? What if she's in the car following me? What if the whole funeral was a charade to trick me? What if that was why the police came to the funeral and they knew everything, because Mairi was alive and was coming to rescue Greg. And now I had to kill both of them. I switched off my headlights and took a left into the lane. Then I slowed down. It was pitch black and I'd lost the car behind me. Step 1 Greg, I thought. Step 2 Mairi. Did you know that oak tree is exactly .87 of a mile from the main road? I knew I had to approach it at 32 miles an hour, so I set the cruise control. You see, thirty is the minimum necessary to engage the airbag on my side of the car. And then ... and then ... I closed my eyes, took my hands off the wheel and braced myself for the crash. It was a real déjà vu moment.'

Emms walked back to the wooden bench and sat down. She didn't make eye contact, just sat hunched, her back a soft 'c' shape, staring at the ground as if she was completely alone. I suppose in a way she was.

'Go on,' I said. 'If you want to.'

She nodded still focused on the ground, 'No surprises, but the crash woke up Greg. I remember seeing the whites of his eyes shining. The windscreen had shattered and there was blood trickling down his face, but Greg hadn't gone through the windscreen like Tony, because he was wearing his seatbelt.

'"You sit tight, Greg," I said. "I'm coming round to get you out." Then I wriggled around the airbag and opened the boot where I'd put the petrol can. It was so quiet out there, Liz. So still and dark. I remembering hearing a night bird, the far-away hum of the road and poor Greg groaning. And then I heard the car coming up the lane. Mairi's car.'

A half choke half sob escaped Emms, 'Liz, I can't go on. The shrink said I should tell you what happened because you are my best, best of friends, but I feel so bad about what I did to you all. I can't believe it was me. It's as if I'm looking at another person. I feel ashamed.'

'So forget it, then,' I said. 'You don't have to tell me, we don't have to talk about it, it doesn't matter.'

'No, no, you see I must tell you, that's what the shrink says because you are my friend, and then I will learn to live with it.'

'Okay.' I certainly wasn't going to agitate Emms by not allowing her to confess. I watched as she inhaled deeply before she went on, her voice now ragged, 'So I take the petrol can and find that I've done it up too tight. But I manage to get the bloody lid off and I splash the stinking stuff round the car all the while thinking I've got to hurry because Mairi will be here any second. And then I heard her ... coming, her footstep, the torch shining in my eyes, her voice calling me to stop.'

'It was me, Emms: you know that, don't you? I found you.'

Emms turned. There were tears streaming down her face and her voice broke.

'Thank you,' she said.

forty-two

Emms still wasn't driving and wouldn't be driving again for a year, so Richard and I had picked them up on a dull September day to take them to a pub by the river. Everybody was supposed to arrive early for a surprise lunch to mark Theo and Daphne's fortieth wedding anniversary. Even the children didn't know about the lunch. They were with Theo and Daphne on what was no doubt a challenging morning outing to the animal farm.

The sky was overcast and a few specks of rain spattered the windscreen. This meant we'd be sitting inside, around the long narrow table and not basking in autumnal sunshine on the terrace overlooking the river. But, you know what, rain or cloud, I thought, who cares? The most important thing was that we were together.

Emms sat in the back of the car. She looked heavier than her previously slinky self and was uncomfortably squeezed into jeans that were a size too small. Apparently, after telling me what had happened, her doctor - the one we'd lined up for Greg - now advised moving forward one step at a time. Emms was on a programme of gentle exercise, meditation for stress relief and so much medication that not only was her short-term memory shot, but her hair was coming out in clumps. But, like I said, who cares: she was back and we were together.

We were all looking after Emms and we managed to get through it. And I do mean, "we". In the ambulance on the way to A&E, Greg's first thought was of Emms, and he begged me not to dob her in it. Of course, I did have a dark night or ten wondering if I'd done the right thing and whether Emms really was safe to be around and, also, whether the shadow of her madness would ever come back again. I'll never know for sure, but it's on me; I made the decision and I live with that fear every single day. It's always there, like a label on a tee shirt. No one else can see it, but every so often it scratches the back of my neck to tell me that it could happen, she could go wrong again, given the right set of circumstances.

No surprises, Richard went ballistic when I said I wasn't turning Emms in to the police. Mr Cool and brainy banged on at considerable and somewhat tedious length about the rule of law, condoning murder and Emms' potential recidivism, but eventually he came round. After all, he couldn't deny that he might have been wrongfully arrested himself because Lapham had an attitude problem. Richard finally conceded and even agreed that it would serve no useful purpose if Emms was convicted for manslaughter and banged up in a penal system that was creaking, to put it kindly. As he put it, there are plenty of other people wandering round among us who have done much worse.

So, during the inevitable police interviews, we learned that if we anticipated the questions and stuck rigidly to the agreed story, then there really was absolutely nothing that the police could do. It wasn't unlike customer service training, where I teach people to repeat their apologies in various different ways. And since Greg wasn't pressing charges, the best the police could do was disqualify Emms for drink driving because she was one point over the limit.

'I know that there's more to this,' D.C. Lapham had said, looking at me over the top of his gold reading glasses as I sat on what I now knew to be the deliberately wobbly chair in that sweaty, sound-proofed, interview room.

I smiled, 'I appreciate your need to look into everything, but in this case, the accident was the result of an unfortunate sequence of events. In other words, Detective Constable, it could have happened to anyone.'

And I meant what I said. What happened to Emms could have happened to anyone. Given the right set of circumstances, the stress, her problem-solving nature and her type A personality, she was dealing with her recovery bravely. I admired her for the way she was handling herself.

'The worst thing is,' Emms said, 'that I don't know if my latest dreams are part of the illness or a side-effect of the medication - in other words the cure.'

We were at traffic lights and Richard was fiddling with the satnav. I nudged him for a response.

'The doctors probably don't know either, do they, Richard?'

'It's a question of finding the appropriate medication for the individual patient. There's no cure-all for everybody; there are too many variables.'

'Medical cop-out.' I said.

True to his nature, Greg was the most understanding of everybody who knew what had happened. I never saw him look at Emms in any other way than with love. Not once. But, of course, it must have been hardest for Emms. God knows what she goes through when she wakes up in the cold hours before dawn and remembers. I suppose that's why they're keeping her drugged up to the eyeballs.

On the plus side, Greg's fortnight in hospital had done wonders for his overall health. Forced to dry out, he'd completely stopped drinking and was now tanned from landscaping what had become a pre-school and after-school drop-off centre. Only the scar on his right brow showed how close he'd got to be being blinded or killed. By his wife.

I turned back to the front of the car, but not before I saw Greg squeeze Emms' hand. We arrived at the pub and parked a few feet from the river, piling out, preparing to dodge the rain cloud. Emms and I lingered for a few moments, waiting for Greg to get out of the car and Richard to lock up.

The river was grey and choppy. On the other side of the bank, a cyclist trundled along the towpath, with a dog running at the wheels of the bike.

'It'll get easier,' I said.

'I know. It's already easier than it was. And a lot easier with a friend like you by my side to protect me through the dark valley of my madness.'

Emms took my hand and squeezed, I was wearing the ring with the pink crystal quartz and felt the pressure of the metal against my flesh. Emms met my eyes, and her own were shining. 'We've got one thing to be grateful for' she said, 'At least Mairi's not coming back.'

I pulled away from Emms, 'What do you mean?' I said. 'How can you say that?'

'Just ignore me, I really didn't mean to say that, it's the medication talking.'

I shivered. It wasn't the cold.

'Are you okay? You look chilled.' Emms said. She put her arm round my shoulders, and we turned away from the river to walk up towards the men and the pub.

READ MORE BY MERLE NYGATE

SNAP – short story
A workaholic drug dealer has to stop his crime business erupting into the idyll of Darkbridge.

SHORT SEASON – short story
A single father shuns his friendly neighbours. What sinister secret is he hiding?

MOTHER CARE – short story
A daughter will do anything to keep her mother safe. Even murder.

AND COMING SOON:

THE HUNDRED RULE – novel
A cynical TV producer working on a crime reality show must conceal a murder and find the killer because the show must go on.

Book Club Questions

Question 1: Discuss Liz and Emma's friendship.

Question 2: Discuss the ending of the novel. What do you think might happen next?

Question 3: Do you sympathise with Liz and Emma? Given the circumstances were their actions reasonable?

Question 4: What does Be My Friend say about mental illness?

Question 5: What other writers would you compare Merle Nygate to?

ACKNOWLEDGMENTS

If you've reached the end of this book and connected with the characters, their lives and problems, thank you. The whole point of a novel is the one-to-one with the reader and thank you for listening to my story.

Getting to this point has taken a while, and a lot of drafts. One of the attractions of self-publishing is that all the mistakes are my own. In other words, if any of this stinks, it's entirely my responsibility.

I've had a lot of help on the way, from my friends, starting with Isabelle Grey, writer of both novels and TV, who has been a rock solid supporter and editor from the inception of the original idea, all the way through. My dear and lovely friend, author Harriet Castor, who gave me amazing and perceptive notes on the finished draft. Tricia May, my ideal reader, who held my hand through the great prologue debate, which was like the hokey-cokey (you put the prologue in, you take the prologue out, in out, in out, shake it all about). Tricia read and re-read and re-read. Lovely Laura Biggar, a talented new writer, who effortlessly solved the prologue problem. Theresa Boden, good friend, good laugh, skilled script editor and screenwriter who did the final read before I pressed the scary publish button. Gavin Collinson, novelist and TV producer, who read, gave terrific notes and shared writerly rants. Denise Moore, dearest friend who has always encouraged me to keep writing. Iain Meadows, producer, writer, director and friend who did the radio interview that makes me sound cleverer than I am. Rob MacGillivray, writer, producer, director, artist, - sick-making I know - whose wonderful film, now on YouTube, makes me look more charming than I am. Lester Baldwin, long time supporter and social commentator, whose talent makes me look blonder than I am. My darling James, who hates writers, but loves me. My darling mother, Doreen Nygate who loves me - whatever I do. Sally Scott, surrogate sister who is fearless and who I am proud to know. And Tika best, best, dearest friend and the sister I never had who made me think about the madness in all of us.

And lastly, Wooster, Charlotte, Rudi and Oberon – without you this book would have been written faster but with less joy.

Thank you all for being my friend.

M

ABOUT THE AUTHOR

Merle Nygate was born in London and now lives in Surrey with her husband and dogs.

For more about Merle and the world of Darkbridge, go to: www.darkbridge.net

Printed in Great Britain
by Amazon